MURDER
ON THE PRAIRIE

Julie Short

LEGAL INFORMATION

Synopsis

In June, 1943, confirmed bachelor, loner, State Department agent, Carson Grey, no sooner returns from an assignment in Europe, when he is given another at a newly constructed ammunitions plant in an expanding rural community in southern Wisconsin. The body of Peter Franke was found on the property of the plant. Franke, a colleague/rival of Carson's, was sent to work at the plant undercover as a Land Negotiator. His job was to acquire land from area farmers for the plant to be built, but along the way he also acquired dozens of enemies from his heavy handed methods of removing farmers and other abuses of power.

Local Sheriff, Ben Lyman, a widowed, single dad, tries to help Carson, but his burgeoning community, lack of resources, and family obligations tie up most of his time. Ben's suggestion to Carson to begin the investigation at the plant brings Carson an unexpected surprise. SHE is also working there. SHE is Laura Bradshaw, the love of his life who left him for Peter and has a secret no one can know. Her abrupt departure from work on the day Peter's body was discovered, and unwillingness to say why she left work only heightens her profile as a prime suspect.

Carson has to come to terms with his conflicting feeling about Laura and her possible involvement with Peter's death. When attempts to derail Carson from finding out the truth start happening, he is more motivated to find answers and reasons for Peter's death. Carson's biggest puzzle is trying to find out the identity of the person who stays in the shadows and is always one step ahead of him and the law. The stranger's arrival to the community is suspect, especially since he seems to know recent local events. He doesn't allow anyone to clearly see his face and he goes out of his way to imitate Carson's life. Who is he? What does he have against Carson? Why is Laura so resistant to cooperate with the investigation? What is she hiding? Or, did the farmers hate Peter enough to kill him?

Unless Carson is able to peel away the many layers of subterfuge, Peter's killer may very well get away with murder.

DEDICATION

I'd like to dedicate this to the communities of Sauk City, Prairie du Sac and Baraboo and all of the families whose lives were forever changed by the Badger Ordnance Works.

CONTENTS

JULIE SHORT

Chapter One

At first it was just a faint odor he recognized but couldn't place. The farther he walked into the woods, the stronger the smell became: sweet, rancid, revolting. Then he saw it.

Half hidden under a rotted, decayed oak tree limb lay a body. Or what was left of a body. Exposed bones showed where the skin, muscle, entrails and ligaments had been pulled apart by wild animals and bugs.

Last fall's discarded tree leaves attempted to bury the remains from sight, but they couldn't hide the smell. In turn, the smell invited other predators. Like a small dark stationary fog, the flies hovered over the body. They jealously guarded the spoils of death from larger prey and intruders.

Stevie Maier spent his whole life, all twelve years, on a farm. He'd seen many dead things in that time. Initially, he thought it to be the remains of a deer.

But now, this close, he knew it wasn't a deer or anything else that belonged in the woods. Before him were the remains of a human. He shuddered.

The curious bravado started to vanish. A dead body lay not more than eight feet from him. He needed to tell someone, but who and how?

How could he explain that while trespassing in fenced-off government land, looking for blueberries, he'd found a body?

It may be government land now, but it still belonged to his father as far as Stevie and his dad were concerned. It was still Maier land. Stevie had wanted to punch the government agent who'd come to tell his dad that their family, along with dozens of others, to clear out.

Stevie knew the layout of the land well. Many times before he'd come to pick mushrooms and blueberries with his sister. But today was different. Now he must do the right thing and tell someone, not only about where he'd been for the afternoon, but what he found. He swallowed down the feeling of panic that started to enter into his head. He yelled out for help, but it only sent the birds a flight. The woods he knew so well suddenly became a silent stranger.

Whether the heat of the day or the reality of his situation was kicking in, he could feel his whole body become flaccid. Taking deep breaths only made him dizzy. Slowly, he started to back away.

Why was this person even here? Stevie read about people who rode the rail going from place to place. Maybe this was a hobo. Maybe a hobo got off a train and wandered here and died. Or, maybe a hobo murdered someone from the area: someone Stevie knew.

With his every step backward, his heart beat faster and the clammy cold feeling of dread pulsed harder in his veins.

Thinking clearly became difficult. He stepped on an old dry twig. It snapped under his weight. He swirled around sure he saw someone hidden in the shadows. He turned and started to run for home. Blueberries spilled all over the ground along with the basket that contained them.

The smell. It was following him. No matter how fast he ran, the smell stayed with him. The desperate feeling to get out of the woods became overwhelming. He tried to run faster. The smell followed.

Blotches of sunlight that speckled the ground through the new spring leaves made everything suddenly look different. All of the plants, trees, wild flowers and bird sounds, once familiar and comforting to him, became foreign and threatening. He couldn't run fast enough. Underbrush and exposed tree roots turned into octopus tentacles. They reached out and grabbed at his pant legs and arms as he tried to get out of this tunnel of death. Panic accelerated his need to get out of this tangled patch of woods and into a clearing where he could breathe and think.

Up ahead, he could just make out what looked like a clearing. From there, only a fifty yards to the hidden hole under the newly installed fence. As he got closer, he could see it.

He wasn't sure if the pounding sound he heard came from his heart or his feet hitting the ground. Wherever it came from, it beat in unison with the throbbing at his temple. Quickly he covered the distance between the woods and the fence in the open land. He dove toward the hole; momentum propelled him through. His new shirt snagged on a rough edged strand of wire as he shimmied under it. Fear overwhelmed him. Tugging to get away from the wire trap, he ripped his shirt open the whole length, but now at least, he was free of the monster's claw. Afraid to look back, he continued to run frantically home. Had they been looking, the guards in the towers surrounding the perimeter of the government land would have seen a boy bolt from the woods as if his very life depended on it.

Somehow he remembered his dad would be milking soon. The cows were already making their daily trek on the well traveled path from the field to the barn yard. He skirted around the back of the herd and darted toward the gate, scattering several cows away from the fence. He launched himself at the rickety, five slat wooden fence, grabbing a hold of the top slat and quickly scrambled over the top, falling on him face.

"Steven!" An angry voice rang out.

Stevie rolled over, tears in his eyes.

"Dad," he said swallowing a sob.

"Where have you been? Look at you. You ruined your shirt. Your mother is going to be furious with you."

"Dad," Stevie repeated his voice hardly above a whisper.

"What? What's wrong?" Harold said now sensing something serious scared the boy.

"Dad, I saw a dead body in the woods," Stevie said looking in to Harold's steel blue eyes.

"What?"

Just being with his father helped Stevie gain a little control of his emotions.

"I went to the woods, our woods, to pick some wild blueberries for Mom to make a pie, and I saw a dead body in the leaves."

"Are you sure?"

****

The sun was setting faster than Sheriff Ben Lyman would have liked. Even the June daylight hours were never enough. He felt like he spent his day racing from one problem to another. The rural scenery blurred by his car window as he tried to focus on the conversation he would be having in a few minutes. The population in his jurisdiction seemed to be growing faster that he could protect. He was stretched to the limit with little man power and government rations making a hard job even harder. This was the last thing he needed; a dead body on federal land.

He slowed the car down just enough to make a left turn onto the county road that took him to Harold Maier's farm. When he drove into the driveway he noticed how long the building's shadows cast across the field surrounding them. The last time he visited the family a large collie greeted him. Not today. He briefly wondered what happened to the dog.

A screen door slammed behind him. He turned around to see Harold standing on the front porch.

"We're in the kitchen, Ben."

Ben walked around the car and up the steps and shook Harold's hand in greeting. He noticed the tension in Harold's eyes and a tight smile.

"Marie's pretty protective of the boy and he's been unusually quiet and closed off since he told me about the body." Harold said in a quite voice.

"I see." Ben took his cap off. "I'll try not to be too long with him."

"I appreciate that."

They walked into the house, down the long hallway that led into the brightly lit kitchen. Sitting at the table were Harold's wife, Marie, Stevie and a young teenage girl, who stole a quick peek at Ben before returning her eyes to her lap. They occupied three of the four sided, wooden table. He observed plates of mostly untouched food in front of them.

"Hello Ben," said Marie, greeting flat.

Ben nodded an acknowledgement to Marie and the young girl, who now made eye contact.

"Stevie," Harold said in a soft voice, "this is Sheriff Lyman. He is going to ask you a few questions about what you saw earlier today."

Stevie never moved a muscle. Ben thought maybe he didn't hear his father speak to him. Inwardly his sighed. This was going to be a long night.

"Is this going to take long?" asked Marie. "He's pretty shaken. Can you do this tomorrow?"

Ben shook his head. "I'm sorry, Marie. I'm afraid not. I need to do this while things are still fresh in Stevie's mind."

He saw Maire's mouth tighten. She got up and walked over to the stove.

"Then can I get you a cup of coffee, Sheriff?"

"No thanks, Marie."

His attention went back to Stevie who still had his head down and hands on his lap. He looked like he had turned to stone. Ben kneeled on one knee next to Stevie. He put his hand on Stevie's shoulder. There was no response. Then he put his other hand under Stevie's chin and gently tilted Stevie's head up. Large moist eyes filled with fear looked back at him.

"Stevie, I'm going to ask you some questions. Is that Ok with you?" Ben asked softly.

Stevie's expression remained unaltered. Finally, Ben saw the slightest nod, almost imperceptible. The fear in Stevie's eyes still raw. Seeing this tugged at Ben's own emotions. Outwardly he had to remain unaffected, but the dad side of him ached. He could only imagine how his own eight year old would handle such a situation.

"Did you see anyone else in the woods today?" No response. Ben continued. "Do you remember hearing anything unusual?" Still no answer. "Did you see any kind of weapon anywhere?"

Stevie finally blinked. His shiny eyes moved from Harold to Marie pleading for an end to the questions. The level of stress and fear he had sustained all afternoon left him exhausted. His shoulders slumped and his eyes rolled back into his head. Marie scurried over to Stevie wrapping her arms around him.

"I'm sorry, Sheriff, but this will have to wait until tomorrow. He's still too upset to be of any use to you. Maybe with a good nights sleep, he'll be better tomorrow.

Harold grabbed Stevie by the hand and pulled him to his feet. "Sue, take your brother upstairs and help him into bed," he instructed. "You're more than welcome to ask your questions tomorrow, Sheriff.

"My concern is that he won't sleep at all and he'll be even less able to answer my questions. His imagination will have that much longer to mix fact with fiction." Said Ben, frustration laced his reply.

"I'll take care of that." Marie walked over to a cupboard and started to take items down from a shelf. "I'll make him a toddy to help him sleep." She turned around with a knowing smile in her eyes. "It always worked on me as a child."

Ben smiled at Marie's resourcefulness. "I better get back out there and finish securing the area for the federal boys."

"Federal boys. What do they have to do with any of this?" Harold asked.

Quietly Marie set two cups of steaming coffee on the table in front of the men, who sat down, claiming a cup.

"Harold, there's a dead body on federal land. That makes it their business. I've contacted the guy in charge of Badger. He'll call the War Department. He asked me to secure the area, and have the body taken to the closest morgue. I'll have a report ready for their man who's doing the formal investigation."

Harold groaned in disgust, shaking his head.

"That's all we need, more federal people around here."

Ben sipped his coffee. He realized Marie had left the room.

Harold sighed a weary, tired, defeated sigh. "So, do ya know who it is?"

Ben drained his cup, setting it down on the table as he stood up. "I think so."

"Well, who is it?"

Ben hesitated.

Harold stood up. "I swear Ben sometimes it's easier removing a stump than it is getting information from you."

"The body is badly decomposed," began Ben. "From the few personal effects we found on the ground, it looks like it's that land negotiator you didn't get along with. If that turns out to be true, I'm going to have to take you in as the prime suspect."

Harold's knees buckled and he dropped hard back into the chair.

Chapter Two

All Carson Grey wanted to do was consume the sole content of his refrigerator – a bottle of beer – take a long shower and sleep for days. Although airplanes now made transatlantic travel much faster than boats ever did, at least he could sleep on a boat. The trip to Algiers with Churchill had been a success. So much so that he was able to leave a day early.

He sat in the cab, tired to the bone from the days of traveling, endless meetings, then more traveling. The cab stopped taking Carson out of his reverie. Some disturbance halted all traffic. He decided not to wait. He paid the cabbie, got out of the car and started to jog home.

Thankfully his sparse, third-floor apartment was only a few blocks away. His head still rang from the constant roar of airplane engines screaming in his ears. The beer would help numb the ringing.

It was just entering twilight, and the throngs of people who usually inhabited these sidewalks, shopping and dining a couple of hours ago, would now be home. He could almost feel the hot water of the shower cascading over his body, releasing the pent up tension he'd been living with for the past ten days. That thought alone inspired him up the last flight of stairs.

The lone, bare light bulb illuminated the obvious lack of furnishings in the room. It reminded him that he intended to get a shade for the light to mute the glare of the stark brightness.

He ran his hand through his short black hair, down to his neck and talked out loud to the dust that had collected over his absence, "A quick beer, an hour in the shower and thirty seconds to fall asleep." Once fully rested, he planned to write up his report on his trip to Algiers for FDR. William Denby would just have to wait to find out what happened.

The bottle of beer just touched his lips when the telephone rang echoing throughout the apartment.

"What?" he barked into the receiver.

"We have a situation in Wisconsin," shot back the baritone voice of William Denby.

"How did you know I was even here? And I don't give a damn about any situation in Wisconsin!"

He slammed down the receiver and chugged his beer. Seventeen hours later, Carson Grey ambled into the State Department building in Washington, DC. The five o'clock shadow from yesterday gone and his black eyes focused on the task ahead. As he walked past the typing pool, heads turned and longing looks from the typist followed him into Denby's office. He was used to the looks he got from women; he wasn't interested – not any more.

"Here's your report." He tossed it on the center of Denby's desk, directly on top of the ledger Denby was working on.

"Thanks," Denby replied indifferently without looking up from the ledger. "Heard things went well." He closed the ledger and slid it over to the left side of his desk.

"Well enough. So what's this situation?"

Denby played with the pencil, then put it next to the ledger. Carson sensed the stress and quiet uneasiness Denby always displayed when he became rattled and had no answers or solutions. Finally he looked up.

"Peter Franke is dead. His body was found in a wooded area within the property boundaries of the ammunition plant in Wisconsin."

"And you're telling me this why, so I can celebrate? Or maybe you have another recruit you want me to train." Carson replied sarcastically.

Several more seconds went by in silence. Finally Carson broke the stare down and walked to the window.

He assessed the man sitting at the desk. He saw a scary reminder of who he might become; a quiet, solitary man who rarely shared his thoughts or feelings. In a few years his job will become his wife, mistress and family. He'd have a great pension, but no one to share it with. In the years he'd known Denby, rarely did Denby let his guard down or talk about anything remotely personal.

"Can't they take care of things out there?" Carson asked. "Isn't that – the Midwest – Allen Clarke's area? Besides, that's the War Department's problem. Why is it any of our business?"

"Peter Franke is... was a State Department agent, and his body was found on government land. He was sent there for two reasons: to help the War Department with the land negotiations and see if there is any truth to the rumor that a small group of people are trying to sabotage all the plants in the Midwest. After the land had been procured, he assumed a pseudo management role at the plant. His assignment would have ended in three months, and now he's dead. I want to know how, who and why."

Carson left the window and sat in the chair across Denby's desk. Denby continued talking.

"I did send Allen to look into this as soon as I found out about Peter. That was three days ago. He hasn't checked in yet, and quite frankly, that's not like Allen. Something isn't right, so I'm sending you out there. Their local sheriff, a guy named Ben Lyman, hasn't seen or heard from Allen. He also has a suspect. I'd like you to question him."

"Who, the Sheriff or the suspect?"

Denby evenly stared at Carson for several seconds.

"The suspect. Evidently there was some bad blood between the suspect and Peter."

"I like the guy already."

"Come on, Carson. Regardless of what you thought about Peter Franke, he can't bother you any more."

"I still don't see how this affects me."

"I've loaned you to the War Department. They don't have the manpower to spare. In case you haven't noticed, the whole country is trying to do whatever we can to get through this madness. Since you worked for the War Department, before transferring here, I thought you'd be the best person for this job, especially since Allen is missing. So, I'm lending you to the War Department for this investigation, but you still report to me."

Carson got up and stood behind the chair he just left. In Denby's face he saw a look of desperation from a tired man.

"And," Denby went back to his ledger, "I want this wrapped up soon."

"Can't you send somebody else?"

"I can. I'm sending you. The background file of information is on your desk. I'll have a car pick you up and take you to the airport this afternoon." Denby looked up from his desk. His baritone voice steady, "One more thing. You can use Peter's car. He won't need it."

Carson knew continuing to argue was pointless. Denby wouldn't budge on this.

Carson went to his office, gathered up the file, and patted it against his hand. Instead of going immediately home, he headed back to Denby's office and stuck his head around the corner.

"This won't take long. We have a body and a suspect in custody. With any luck, the sheriff found a weapon. I'll wrap this up in a couple of days, and Peter Franke will be totally out of my life for good."

****

Sheriff Ben Lyman chauffeured Carson Grey to Sauk City in the Sauk City Police car. He used the pastoral scenery to introduce Carson to the area and referred to points of interest along Highway 12. He sensed that Carson was either annoyed with the situation or tired from the trip to Wisconsin. For a government man, Grey seemed much quieter than the rest he had met.

"Thanks for picking me up at the airport."

"My pleasure. Your boss, Mister Denby is it? He suggested it might be helpful."

"Now he wants to be helpful," Carson mumbled.

"He sounded like an all right sort of guy to me. Is there anything I should know about him?"

"Not really. He's a lifer at the department. Never married, no kids. Maybe that's why he sometimes treats his employees like kids."

"Well, for whatever reason, it gives us a chance to talk about the case in neutral settings without any interference."

The dilapidated, black briefcase at Carson's feet leaned against his leg as if begging for attention. Ben watched as the government agent reached down and pulled out a file full of notched pages.

"There was some bad blood between Peter Franke and this Harold Maier? What's the story there?"

Ben took a deep breath, "First off, I have to tell you that Harold Maier is no longer in custody."

"What! Why?"

The surprised irritation in Carson's voice made Ben choose his next words very carefully. "One of the benefits of being a long-time member of the community is knowing the people. Harold Maier is no risk to anyone. As for the bad blood, it goes back to the very existence of the plant being here."

"I read about that." Carson looked through the stack of papers in the file only to spill the contents onto the car floor. He tried to gather them up in his lap and put them in the same order. "No one else seemed to protest the plant with some much... persistence."

"Don't kid yourself. Everyone around here was plenty mad. You don't uproot eighty families overnight, some that have been farming here for five generations, without a lot of people being pretty upset. Harold only said out loud what everyone was thinking and feeling. If you want to get right down to it, if disagreeing with government-forced removal was a motive for your colleague's death, then anyone and everyone in and around the community could be a suspect. Maybe I shouldn't say this, but you don't know how hard it is to watch your friends being forced out of their homes, and there is nothing you could do for them. Also, there is another little problem, but I'll be looking into that for the time being. You have enough to do for now."

Carson never replied or questioned anything Ben said. He looked out the car window then decided to reread the file.

The silence gave Ben time to reflect. He'd been one of the few young men who'd left the area, when he came of age, looking for a better life after college and law school. The lure of a New York City law firm was too good to pass up. For six years, he'd moved up the ladder, making a lot of money and a good reputation for himself. Consorting with the city's political machine was a huge thrill for the small-town Midwest guy. Having Mayor LaGuardia call you at home for advice inspired a lot of self-confidence. For a while, there was talk of grooming him for political office, but some small voice in the back of his head always told him to decline the offer. Three years later he realized the reason for his reluctance.

It took the tragic death of both of his parents, killed while trying to subdue an out of control bull, to get him to come back home to Sauk City. He'd forgotten what "home" felt like. He missed the gentler way of life; the smell of newly cut hay and the genuine smiles on faces of people who were glad to see you. Not the smiles in New York that represented what people wanted from you.

Suddenly he realized that Carson had been talking to him.

"Do you know how Peter Franke died?" asked Carson.

"He was shot in the head."

"I see. Any ideas on where I should start this investigation?"

"Yep. The plant. I told them you'd be there tomorrow."

"Good. That should only take a few days, and then I want talk to this Harold Maier. I'd like to wrap this up within a week."

"Really. You can cover over 10,000 acres of land, interview 700 workers and Harold Maier, and wrap this up within a week? I guess the War Department does things differently. It would take me much longer." Ben replied irritated at Carson's flippant assessment.

"Sorry". Carson apologized. "I didn't know the plant area was that big. It just says sizable in the file. Seven hundred workers. Really?" He expelled a long, deep, breath, "Denby owes me."

****

At 7:30 a.m. the next morning, Peter Franke's silver 1941 Cadillac convertible coupe turned off Highway 12 into the main entrance of the Badger Ordnance Works. Carson saw the entrance long before he actually got to it. A small hut-like structure with a large billboard perched on top greeted all who came to Badger. The billboard declared Badger Ordnance had the best powder in the world. Carson stopped at the hut. A tall young man with a crew cut left the small hut and approached the car. He inspected the interior of the car, through the rolled down window, before turning his attention to the driver.

"Can I help you, sir?"

"Yes. My name is Carson Grey. I'm here from the State Department. I believe I'm expected."

The young man checked over the State Department

identification card that Carson held out. Seemingly satisfied with it, he gave it back with a forced smile.

"Here you are, sir."

The young man walked back to the hut. He grabbed a clipboard and scanned it. Then he picked up the phone. He turned his back to the car, as if trying to keep anyone from hearing the conversation. Since Carson sat in the car, and the guard seemed to be alone, the prospects of being overheard seemed slim. Perhaps seeing someone else in Peter Franke's car confused the guard. He suddenly turned and looked at Carson, while still talking on the phone. Then he stuck his head out of the hut telling the other person at the other end the tag number on the car. Finally he nodded his head in the affirmative. He returned to the car.

"Sir, you're to go to the Administration Office." Carson noted a large, long, white two-story building located in the direction of the guard's pointed finger. "Mr. Anderson will be waiting for you. He has your pass and will be your guide while you're here."

He lifted the rail barrier allowing Carson through.

The first impression that greeted Carson was the intense activity all around him and the over all size of the plant. A blitz of new construction surrounded him. Even though he'd read about all of this in Denby's report, seeing it made figures on white sheets of paper seem insignificant.

Carson pulled up to the Administration Office. A slight built, balding man in coveralls slid out the front door as Carson parked the car. The man checked his watch, then he walked over to greet Carson as he got out of the car.

"Mr. Anderson?" Carson extended his hand.

"Mr. Grey, good to see you again."

Carson couldn't remember ever meeting the man in front of him.

"I'm sorry you must have me mistaken for someone else. I just arrived here yesterday."

The little man chuckled at the confused look on Carson's face.

"Oh no, not here. In DC. Mr. Denby's office. I was a new hire accountant with the department helping Mr. Denby with his budget. You came in the office, and he introduced us. You wore a navy blue suit with a black tie. Your shoes needed to be polished. I had more hair."

The last two comments brought a pink shade to the man's face.

Nothing Anderson said came back as a memory to Carson. Why would anyone remember such an insignificant meeting with such detail?

"So, you're out here now."

"No, not really. Washington sent out a handful of us to help, until the place is up and running to their standards."

"I see."

"Oh," Anderson reached into the deep hidden pockets of his coveralls. He pulled out a three inch by four inch badge that clearly stated Carson's status – VISITOR. The words were written in big, scarlet red letters in the center of the badge. "You must wear this at all times," he explained. "And at least for today and tomorrow, you must stay close to me. After that, you'll have to come here and get a badge from my secretary. I'll find someone else to escort you. Any questions so far?"

Carson began to fasten the badge on his lapel, wondering if this was just a waste of his time. Surely he didn't need to check in like some school boy.

"And," continued Mr. Anderson. He reached into the pocket on the other side of his coveralls and pulled out another smaller badge, "this will allow you on the grounds tomorrow. Let's get started."

Carson suspected Anderson enjoyed acting a tour guide. He had an "I'm in charge attitude", yet a relaxed, calm almost proud demeanor. Anderson wasted no time jumping into a drab, olive colored jeep parked to the left of the building.

"Instead of calling me Mr. Anderson, call me Owen." He said over the clamor of the engine.

Owen talked non-stop as he drove, pointing out the hundreds of buildings in various stages of construction.

"We've got everything here from a 500-unit housing development, for the workers, we call The Village, a school, a library, grocery store, barber and beauty shop, rec center, a 24 hour child care and a hospital. You need it, we got it. That building to your right is an ether house for the production of the Smokeless Powder that will be used to make munitions."

Carson couldn't tell if Owen was bragging or complaining as he went through the litany of statistics that made up "Badger," as the locals referred to it.

"Although not fully completed, there is seventy-two acres worth of buildings. They spread over an area five miles by two miles. There is over 100 miles of road, nine miles worth of pipes for plumbing, eighty-eight miles of water lines..."

The list went on and on. After listening to endless statistics, Carson tuned Owen out and tried to focus on how he would go about his investigation. He noticed new cyclone fencing surrounded the whole compound, and a road was built next to the fence. Every so often, a motorcycled guard sped past them on a Harley Davidson. Light poles were placed every couple hundred feet. So far, he counted ten separate gate posts located at strategic spots with at least two men on watch at each gate house.

Owen's voice droned on. "We might have been further along with all the building and making more powder by now. But, the powers that be change their minds every other day, and Mother Nature could have co-operated a bit more, too."

"Sheriff Lyman and my report mentioned there was some bad blood between the farmers and the land negotiators," Carson broke in. "I can understand why. From our tour, this looks like a waste." He pointed at the rows of buildings they passed. "There's got to be more than 500 feet between each of these rows of buildings."

"Seven hundred." Owen stopped the jeep.

"Seven hundred! Why?"

19

"Ever since that explosion at the Kenvil, New Jersey plant in '40, the Corps of Engineers made some changes in plant designs."

"I see. About those explosion you just mentioned, there have been several at every new ammunitions plant. Some people think there's a core anti-government group of individuals setting off these explosions as a way to protest the use of good farm land" said Carson.

"I've heard that, too. I don't believe a word of it."

"Why not?"

"Well, here at least, you've got to remember that the work-force is made up of housewives, farmers and anyone else not in the armed forces. None of the folks working here have ever worked around nitroglycerin before. Unfortunately, mistakes happen: mistakes that take lives and limbs. As for the sabotage theory, everyone here is behind our boys."

"Everyone?"

"Everyone!"

Six hours after they started, Owen stopped the jeep next to Peter Franke's Cadillac. Carson sat in the jeep for a few seconds trying to absorb everything he saw and heard.

"Well, there you have it in a nutshell, Mr. Grey. If there's any place you'd like a better look at, we can go back there tomorrow."

Still stiff from yesterday's travel and today's six hour jumbled ride, Carson crawled out of the jeep. Either he was getting old or out of shape. Maybe if he didn't spend so much sitting in meetings or on airplanes he could get back in shape. This never used to affect him.

As he crossed to his car, a young woman ran across the compound toward the jeep.

"I need to take care of this. You can give your badge to my secretary inside. I'll see you tomorrow." Owen rushed to the young woman.

Obviously dismissed, Carson walked to the Administration Office. He stopped dead in his tracks not more than five feet inside the building. He knew this investigation was going to be very interesting.

Chapter Three

She had her back to him when he walked in, so he could observe her freely. There was no mistake here. Even with her back to him, he'd know that form anywhere. Her hairstyle looked new, pulled off and away from her face. One stubborn little curl, behind her left ear, kept escaping its tight confines. The same curl that always found a way free, no matter how she wore her hair. With that single curl, he could identify her in a crowd of a million.

As she filed away folders behind her desk, he almost laughed. What would her precious family think if they saw her now? She had gained a little weight. It looked good on her. The environment definitely agreed with her. Maybe being so far away from Boston, and from her family, she let her guard down a bit and wasn't so consumed with her appearance or the impression she made.

He waited for her to finish filing. She must have thought he was Owen or a plant worker. None of the other clerks were at their desks or in the office. He cleared his throat and she turned around. Eyes wide and a soft shallow intake of air escaped. She tried to recover quickly from her initial shock and act nonchalant.

"Hello Carson," she said coolly. "Can I get you something? It may take a while to find whatever you need." She pointed to boxes on the floor next to her desk and a pile of posters waiting to be hung. The top poster said: *I Need Your Skills in a War Job.* "We just moved in here last month, and I'm still not sure where everything is."

Self-consciously she put her hand up to her renegade curl and placed it back behind her ear, then smoothed out an imaginary wrinkle in her dress.

"How long have you been here?"

She didn't answer his question.

"You came out here with Peter didn't you?"

"About the same time, yes."

Carson suspected she and Peter were together, but couldn't get anyone to confirm it. Her evasive reply gave him the answer to the question he'd been seeking for over a year. He knew she left her job several months before Peter, but hoped it was just a coincidence. Now he knew without a doubt, she and Peter left Washington together.

"I asked Margaret at the office where you were. She said you went to visit your parents. You never came back."

She closed the file drawer and returned to her desk, and threaded a sheet of paper in her Underwood.

"How's Denby?" She asked as she began typing.

He deduced by her cool manner that he should explain his presence in a straight forward manner and be as business like and professional as possible. He would let her words and actions tell him how to move next.

"Denby sent me out here to tie up some loose ends. I'm here to investigate Peter's death."

At the mention of Peter's name, she winced and a tiny pang of hurt washed over her face. It was cruel to bring up Peter that way, but he wanted a small measure of payback. The second he said it he was sorry, but it was too late. The hurt in her eyes cut him like a knife. While he meant to hurt her, he only succeeded in hurting himself.

"Why you?"

Why me indeed he thought. "You'd have to ask Denby that question. I'm just doing my job."

"Hmmm". She sounded suspicious of his answer.

"So, how well do you know this place?"

She continued typing looking only at the handwritten correspondence on her desk.

"As well as anyone, I guess. Better than some. I have clearance to go into a number of buildings. Most plant workers aren't allowed to go anywhere else but the building they work in and the recreation center." There was a pause before she spoke again. "How long are you going to be tying up *loose ends*?"

"As long as it takes!"

His answer interrupted her rhythm for only a second, but long enough for Carson to notice. He knew his presence made her uncomfortable. He just didn't know if that was a good sign or not.

"I can see you're busy. I'll let myself out," he said, then stared at her for a bit longer hoping for one more glimpse of eye contact with her. There wasn't any. He took the visitors badge off and placed it on her desk in front of her and walked out.

When Carson closed the door of the Administrative Office the tapping from the typewriter stopped. He smiled.

He saw that Owen was still with the young woman, in the parking lot, standing exactly in the same place. Owen grimly shook his head, while signing a piece of paper. When the young woman left Owen, Carson approached him from behind.

"Say Owen, about tomorrow…"

"Sorry Carson," Owen cut him off, "something has come up. I won't be able to escort you around tomorrow. We'll have to make it another day."

Carson feigned disappointment even though he was actually elated. He jumped at the unexpected opportunity.

"Oh, that's too bad," he sighed, hoping Owen believed him. As if a last second thought came to him, he asked, "Would your secretary be able to step in for you? I'd really like to question people about Peter Franke, and the sooner I do, the less likely they are to forget anything. Washington wants this investigation over as soon as possible."

"Yeah, okay. That'll be fine," Owen responded, watching the young lady, with the signed paper, walk away. "I'll tell her as soon as I get back."

"Thanks, Owen. I really appreciate this."

****

A less-than-thrilled expression from Laura greeted Carson upon his arrival the next morning. She waited for him in front of the Administration Office, just as Owen had done the day before. Carson knew he'd have to be on his best behavior.

"Good morning," he chimed rolling down the car window. "Do you have my badge or do I need to fill out paperwork in your office?"

Even in her coveralls and turban, with a small tuft of hair peaking out, she still managed to look like a fashion magazine cover.

She unfolded her crossed arms and presented the badge he wore the day before. The scowl on her face told him her mood was even darker than he thought.

"Are we going to walk or are you going to get in?"

"Depends. Where do you want to go first?" She stood planted in her spot not show any sign of relenting.

Carson had actually thought long and hard about this. Knowing he had the whole day to spend with her, his main concern was how he could maximize his time with her and still actually do his job. Should they start at the far corners of the plant and work their way to the Admin building? Should he break the facility down into quarters and try to spend several days with her? Or should they start right here at her office and work their way to the farthest corner of the grounds? Sensing her reluctance to be around him, he found his answer.

"How about starting here at the plant, or... what did Owen call it? The C-line. Then, depending on what I learn, I'll decide where else I'd like to go and who else I need to talk to."

She nodded noncommittally.

Absentmindedly, he added, "Denby wants this wrapped up as soon as possible." Her eyes showed pain at his off-handed reminder of Peter's death, but today she didn't physically flinch. Her show of strength softened Carson. "Are you sure you're up for this?"

Tears filled her eyes. She shook her head slightly. "I need to know what happened to Peter, who killed him."

"Can you tell me who he associated with?" He wanted to say "besides you" but thought better of it. He was, after all, spending the day with her, something he believed he would never be able to do again.

"Are you looking for people he worked with or people he socialized with?"

Carson hadn't even considered that Peter may have socialized with anyone except Laura. Her answer made him think that there may be more to Peter Franke than he gave him credit for.

"Both. Anyone he might have had contact with socially or professionally."

"I suppose you want to know how much time we spent together."

Her directness surprised him.

"Yes. And anyone else he spent time with – for the investigation," added Carson.

"Are you really investigating Peter's murder or are you just here for show? Do you even care who killed Peter? Everyone in DC knew how much you hated him," she spat.

"I'm here to find out who killed Peter. I'm going to treat you just like everyone else, but I need your cooperation, too."

"You want to know if I killed him, so just ask me and get it over with."

"I don't need to ask. Sheriff Lyman already checked. On the day Peter went missing, you were here at work. On the day the body was found, you left work early, and went home. Your landlady swears you never left until the next morning. Owen told me that the only suspicious thing he can remember is that you left work in a hurry, after receiving a phone call. I'd like to know why. Do you want to tell me what the phone call was about?"

"No. It's none of your business or Owen's. It's just a coincidence." Her voice and eyes hard, arms crossed her chest challenging him to push her on the issue.

Carson backed off. If he pushed her any more, she would end her participation today, and he wanted to spend as much time with her as possible. So he chose to let the subject drop, at least for today.

"Who do you suggest I talk to?"

"Well, Peter dealt a lot with Owen simply because Owen is in charge of all comings and goings within the plant. He talked a lot about some of the farmers."

Carson took a small note book out of his inside coat pocket ready to write down a list of names.

"You might want to talk to Charlie Ballard. Peter met with him at a bar sometimes, after Charlie's shift."

"Great. Where does Charlie work? We'll start with him."

"Over in the plant. We can walk. You'd better park the car next to the jeep."

Relieved he convinced her to stick it out for the day, he rolled up the window and pulled the car ahead and parked where she indicated. Maybe this Charlie Ballard would lead him to another person to talk to or give him more information about Peter's interaction with Harold Maier.

The day promised to be another hot one. Already the fog in the valley burnt off, and the humidity high. Carson took his hat and suit coat off and tossed them in the front seat, before he closed the door. As he walked back to Laura, Carson noticed buses dropping off people in street clothes, lining up for guards to inspect.

"Lead on," Carson instructed.

Laura started walking in a less-than-direct route to the plant.

"Before we can get into the C-Line building, you have to go over to the changing house and put on the proper clothes. Go through 'Clock Alley,'" she pointed to the men's changing house. "Be sure you have your badge fixed to the front pocket where they can see it, or you won't be allowed in the building."

Carson's gave her a questioning stare.

Laura ignored his expression. "It's a requirement. Everybody wears a badge, and you have to sign in and out of the building every time you enter or exit."

The changing house stood at the rear of the parking lot. After being issued his coveralls, Carson was surprised that the shoes he wore were not allowed in the plant, either. An attendant gives him "powder shoes." The confused look on his face provoked an explanation.

"The steel nails in your shoe's soles might ignite a spark, sir. That would be deadly for everyone in the vicinity."

As Laura told him, when he left the changing house, he walked through Clock Alley. A series of time clocks and time cards lined the wall. On another wall rows of badges hung, belonging to workers on other shifts. Seeing the badges, he checked his own badges visibility. Before being allowed to leave Clock Alley, he was approached again by a woman guard.

"Excuse me sir, I need to check your pockets."

"What for?"

"For any matches, cigarettes and the like."

To keep the stranger from physically checking him over, he reached into his coverall pockets himself and turned them inside out. She smiled at him and indicated that he could pass through.

If the seriousness of making powder wasn't obvious to Carson before entering the changing house, it certainly was now. He walked along the fence that divided his changing house from the other twenty-eight men's and women's changing houses. At the end of the fence, he met Laura tucking her hair under the turban all women were required to wear. They were stopped, again, to sign in on the register when they entered the C-Line building. He waited for Laura to sign in and find out where Charlie Ballard worked. Carson watched as two young women were singled out and reprimanded by one of the supervisors for letting wisps of hair frame their goggles and turbans. He supposed it was their way of showing femininity in this unisex environment. The stringent safety rules at every level reiterated to him how serious and dangerous this environment could be to the employees.

Laura automatically checked her hair and shoved the escaped curl behind her ear. After the supervisor finished with the young women, Laura led Carson over to meet Lloyd Moore, the building supervisor.

"Laura," the man said with a strained smile, then directed his gaze to Carson, "I see you've brought a visitor. Any reason I wasn't given notice?"

The forced smile did nothing to hide his hard, piercing stare. Before any more words were spoken, Laura stepped between the men, breaking Lloyd Moore's eye contact with Carson.

"Mr. Moore, this is Mr. Grey." She stepped back, allowing the men to shake hands. "He's here from Washington to investigate Peter Franke's murder. We agreed to cooperate fully with Washington."

Lloyd relaxed at the mention of Washington, but clearly not happy with the situation.

"He needs to talk with Charlie Ballard," Laura continued. "Charlie and Peter were friends. He might be able to remember something that will help Mr. Grey find Peter's killer. I'm to blame for not getting you any notice, there simply wasn't time."

In just the short time Laura and Carson were in the building, they were already disrupting work. Women slowed down to take a long look at Carson, and the men did the same with Laura. Putting his thick, hairy hands on his generous girth, Lloyd asked Carson directly, "What can I do for you, Mr. Grey?" He clearly emphasized the "I."

"I'd like to talk to Charlie Ballard, if it isn't too much trouble."

"Well, it is. He's upstairs. He's a Wringer." The supervisor paused and glared at Carson for another minute before grunting. "Washington, huh? Fine. Follow me but don't touch anything."

Charlie Ballard stood, at the outside, all of five feet three inches tall. His glasses looked so thick Carson wondered if he could see anything without them. Even the coveralls he wore hung on him like a tent. On his head, he wore something that looked like a bucket. His helmet had a flat top and a small window to see through. Besides the helmet, he wore acid-resistant boots and gloves and a bib that hung down his front and back. To Carson, he looked like a miniature baseball umpire from outer space with too much padding.

As Carson approached, Charlie took off his helmet and gave Carson a wry smile and a strong handshake. It was clear by his easy manner that he was an amiable guy.

Lloyd grabbed Charlie's gloves, body armor and helmet and took over Charlie's spot as a Wringer, but spent more time eyeing them. Carson saw that Charlie's eyes shot over his shoulder to Lloyd. Charlie shifted from on foot to the other unsure what to do with himself. Carson guessed Lloyd's stare bore a hole in the back of his head straight through to Charlie.

After quick introductions were made by Laura, Carson started in with the questions.

"Miss Bradshaw tells me that you and Mr. Franke occasionally met for drinks after your shift."

The smile immediately left Charlie's baby face, replaced by a look of worry and unease.

Charlie's reaction gave Carson a glimmer of hope. The instant change in personality made him think that maybe this guy might know something about Peter's death.

"Yes, that's right. Once or twice a week we'd go over to Goerk's tavern in Denzer, for a quick drink, and a game of euchre."

"What did you and Mr. Franke talk about?"

Sweat started to form on his forehead. His eyes went back to Lloyd. "Look, Mr. Grey, I'm more than happy to answer all of your questions, but not here or now. I'd like to get back to my job, while I still have one."

"Okay, Charlie. Where would you like to answer my questions?"

"How about at Goerks? You know where it is?"

Carson nodded his head. He didn't know, but would find out by the end of the day.

"I'll see you at six o'clock, then." A small bead of sweat dripped down Charlie's forehead. He smiled his gratitude and headed back to his job.

After talking to Charlie, Carson spoke with several more people Laura thought might have some insight, but he learned nothing new about Peter. Carson sensed Laura still felt uneasiness around him. So, he would give her space, for now. With no other excuse to stay at Badger, and be around Laura, Carson spent the rest of the day in Sauk City and Prairie du Sac getting acquainted with the people and places where Peter and Laura visited and called home.

Chapter Four

Goerks was a small bar a few miles away from the plant in a little cross-road settlement. Those who needed to return home immediately after work did so; those who didn't found themselves at one of several local establishments. The beer and food were the main reason people came, it was the homey feeling that kept them coming back. People could eat, drink and talk to any number of sympathetic ears. They could pick up a game of poker, darts or euchre if they still had their wits about them at the end of their shifts. Tonight was no exception. The place was packed and loud.

After looking over every inch of the bar, Carson deduced that Charlie wasn't there. With no place to sit, Carson decided to stick close to the door so he could observe who came and went. Twenty minutes later, a couple occupying a small table in the corner near the door got up to leave. Before they had a chance to push the chairs in, Carson claimed the table. He waved his arms, until he made eye contact with the bartender. Hastily he grabbed an empty bottle of beer off the table and held it up. Using his index finger he pointed to the bottle indicating he wanted a beer. He returned the bottle to the table and sat down.

Fifteen minutes passed and Charlie still wasn't there. Carson looked at his watch for the hundredth time when a shadow covered the light on the watch. He looked up, but to his surprise, Sheriff Ben Lyman looked down smiling at him.

"That chair taken?"

"Yes and no. Charlie Ballard is supposed to meet me here after his shift. I'm still waiting."

"Do you mind if I take the chair until he comes? There are a few things about Mr. Franke you need to know."

Carson nodded. Ben pulled the chair away from the wall to sit. He looked at the bar and held up two fingers, then sat down. Before he had a chance to settle in the chair, two beers appeared.

"How'd you do that?"

Ben laughed and placed a beer in front of Carson.

"Wearing a badge helps, even though I'm just off duty."

"Thanks." Carson held the beer up as a mock salute. "I have one coming though. Maybe it'll arrive before I leave."

A small roar erupted from the other side of the room. Applause accompanied the roar.

"Someone must have hit the bull's-eye."

"So, what's this information you have?" Carson leaned closer to Ben. The background noise erupted in waves.

"Seems your Mr. Franke led a bit of a double life. There are very few businesses around here that he doesn't owe money to. In fact, if you add it all up, it comes to over thirty thousand dollars."

"What!"

"Yep. Thirty thousand dollars. This is that other little problem I alluded to that day I drove you into town. I got wind of this some weeks ago. I've been loosely monitoring his expenses and habits. He didn't break any laws as far as I know, so I couldn't do anything about it. He usually used the, 'I'm from the State Department' line or 'I'm good for it.' That doesn't bother me other than the fact that good people around here are going to get screwed by the government – again – since they won't be getting their money back now. I planned to confront him about it. Now I can't. Now, it's another part of the puzzle for you to solve."

"I thought being an officer of the law you'd have to be impartial on the subject." Carson shouted to be heard.

Ben smiled at the comment then his face became serious again.

"I'll be honest with you. What concerns me the most is that the day after the body was found, some guy posing as Peter Franke went to the bank and withdrew all the money in his account."

"Didn't the bank know to freeze the account?"

Ben took a long swig from the bottle.

"We didn't release the news about Franke's death right away. The bank didn't know he was dead. Unfortunately, a new teller started work that day. There are so many new people coming to the area every day, thanks to Badger, she took this guy's word that he was who he said he was. He signed all the papers and you know what? The handwriting would have fooled me if I didn't know any better."

"He still needed to have Peter's account number."

"He did."

Just then, another loud roar came from the other end of the bar followed by total silence. Ben's head snapped up. He disappeared into the crowd before Carson could react. Chairs scraped across the floor. Everyone faced the other side of the room in complete silence. Eventually, the crowd began to part and Ben came through with a subdued huge man. As Ben got closer, Carson saw that the man with him was an Indian, and looked shaken. Ben whispered something in the man's ear. The man meekly responded with only a nod of his head.

Before Ben exited the bar, he stopped at Carson's table for a second. "We'll talk later."

Carson opened the door for the two men to leave.

The door no sooner closed behind Ben when it opened again and Charlie Ballard rushed through. Small beads of sweat dotted his hairline. The worried look left his face when his hurried visual sweep of the room landed on Carson.

"I'm sorry I'm late. I hoped you'd still be here. The second shift wringer's car broke down. I can't leave without someone being there to replace me."

Carson watched Charlie acknowledge silent hellos from fellow workers with a quick nervous nod. The atmosphere sobered up quickly from the earlier disturbance. People continued talking and playing darts, but the mood toned down dramatically.

"What happened here? I saw Sheriff Lyman putting Floyd Whitefeather in his car."

"What? Who's Floyd Whitefeather?"

"He's a snake charmer and farmer. I've never seen Floyd so low-keyed. He's usually pretty happy and easy going. I don't even know why he'd be here. He doesn't drink as far as I know. He rambled on about 'stopping him in time' and wondering where someone else was."

"Stop who?"

"I don't know."

Carson indicated Ben's recently vacated chair for Charlie to sit. Mentally Carson thought he'd have to find out a lot more about Floyd Whitefeather.

"Tell me about you and Peter Franke, but before you do that, tell me what a Wringer is?"

Carson noticed a soft smile escape Charlie and got a feeling there was an inside joke going around, but he was the only one who didn't understand the punch line.

"When I first started, I was a Dipperman for a few days. After the Dippermen or Dippettes, the women, are done with the nitration, we, the Wringers, wring out the extra acid from the nitrocellulose, and it gets sent back to the Weight House to be used again. It can be pretty dangerous."

Carson nodded, accepting the explanation but still not sure what Charlie meant.

"I met Peter, Mr. Franke, on the day I got the Wringer job."

"How'd you get the job?"

"Well, I came here specifically to work at Badger." Charlie pushed the thick glasses back to the bridge of his nose. "I was new to the area and didn't know exactly what a Dipperman was when I accepted. I surely learned fast why no one else wanted it. It's okay, though. At least I'm helping the cause in some way. I'm a little hard of hearing, and I usually ignore or just plain can't hear most of the surrounding noise. That makes it easier for me to pay attention to my job."

"So you met Peter the day you got your job at the plant. When did you start meeting after work for drinks?"

"We weren't as chummy as you make it seem. One night after work, I came here for a drink. I'm single, so I didn't have to hurry back to The Village. He was sitting here, drinking alone. We started talking, then playing darts. That's pretty much all there is to it."

"What'd you talk about?"

"Oh, you know, the displaced farmers, the history of the area, my job and the plant. That sort of stuff. Nothing too radical. We only came here a couple times a week after work to talk, play darts, and have a drink or two."

"Did he ever talk about anything personal?"

"No, and I thought that was odd. Everyone knew he was sweet on Owen's secretary, but he never mentioned her."

"What makes you think he was sweet on Mr. Anderson's secretary, especially if he never talked about her?"

Charlie looked out into the thinning crowd as if it had the answer.

Carson used the break to order two more beers. Maybe he'd get better service now that he'd been seen with Sheriff Lyman. Then again, maybe not.

Charlie finally said, "Just by the way he looked at her. How they acted whenever they were together in public - their smiles, the accidental touches – little things, ya just know. The women at the plant would be better at answering that question."

"Did he ever mention he had any animosity toward any of the farmers or anyone else in the area?"

A heavy middle-aged woman deposited the beers in front of Charlie as she passed their table, on her way to her table of friends.

"Thanks, Mable," Charlie murmured quietly to the woman. "No, not really." Charlie returned his attention to Carson. "He knew they all hated him. They took out their frustration about the whole situation on him. Not much of a surprise. He was a little heavy handed in his methods sometimes."

"How so?" Carson casually sipped from his second beer.

"He actually had some of the farmers physically removed, when they refused to leave their land."

"That seems a bit excessive. Did you see that side of Peter when you met?"

"No. He was only nice to me and interested in my job."

"What was it about your job that interested him?"

"Same as you. The name of it puzzled him at first. He wanted to know if the plant used some sort of formula or recipe to get the right mixture levels for the powder."

"Why do you think that interested him?"

"I don't know."

"Is there?"

"What?"

"A recipe or formula for the powder?"

"Absolutely. If there wasn't, I'm sure I would be sitting with the angels by now."

Talking with Charlie was interesting but not very useful as far as finding out anything new about Peter. So far, Carson still couldn't see any clear-cut motive for murder. Sheriff Lyman didn't have a chance to go into detail as to who Peter owed money to. That fact alone could swing the balance of the investigation. Glancing at his watch, he realized that it was much later than he thought. He reached for his billfold and pulled out a dollar and gave it to Charlie.

"Here, I have to go. This should cover my bill and buy you a couple more. Maybe we can continue this another time."

As Carson closed the door, he saw Charlie move to the bar. Three other guys surrounded him immediately and ushered him toward the back of the bar.

The drive back to the motel was a blur. The whole way there, he raced through the list of facts in his head. He had a body. Someone claiming to be Peter Franke cleaned out Peter's bank account the day after they found Peter's body. The handwriting from the impostor resembled Peter's. Peter owed money to everyone, and most people hated him. And a snake-charmer Indian farmer wanted to stop someone from doing something. On top of all that, why didn't Peter and Laura let people know openly about their relationship? They could have said they were married. Who would be the wiser?

All of that, especially the Laura connection, would have to be put on hold. As soon as he got back to his hotel room, he went to the phone. Now he needed to call Denby. It would be an hour later in Washington, but Carson knew Denby practically lived at the office. He wondered how Denby would react to the information about Peter's debts, especially since Peter practically guaranteed repayment via the State Department. Maybe he wouldn't divulge that specific bit of information just yet, since he didn't know exactly who Peter owed money to.

As the phone rang in Washington, Carson untied his shoes. By the fifth ring, Denby answered.

"Hello."

"I knew you would still be there."

"Carson. What have you found out?"

Denby's voice sounded rushed, yet strained. For a man in charge of a couple dozen people and seen his share of tough situations, it took a lot to rattle him.

"Yes, it's me. I'll be here longer than I planned on. I'll be running down some new leads I just found out about."

"What new leads?"

"I don't want to get into it until I have hard facts. Have you heard from Clarke yet?"

"In a way."

"What's he got to say for himself?"

"Not much. He's dead."

Chapter Five

"They found him in the basement of his brownstone. He'd been there for some time."

The silence between the lines told Carson everything.

Carson knew Denby took this news hard. Allen Clarke was literally the boy next door. In the little time Denby spent at his home, he'd measured the years by the boy's accomplishments: little league team pitcher, star athlete in high school and honor student at Notre Dame. Allen got accepted at Notre Dame, because Denby called in a few favors, from former associates, and helped with the financial aspects of Allen's education.

Allen excelled at everything he did. When he graduated from Notre Dame, Denby suggested to Allen's parents he might consider a career with the State Department. Denby personally saw to it that Allen worked under him. When Denby said things like, "Nice job son," or "Take a seat, my boy," Carson knew a part of Denby thought of Allen as far more than his employee.

Carson could imagine Denby pacing around his desk while on the phone, a habit of his when agitated.

"What happened?" Carson asked hesitantly, genuinely concerned, feeling out Denby's mood. He liked Allen and would miss his upbeat attitude, and youthful out look on life.

"It had to have happened the same day I gave him the assignment for Wisconsin. We found his suitcase half packed. The landlord said he was there at 2:30 p.m. to pay rent and left. We think he went to the basement to check out a noise."

"Why do you think that?"

"The landlord said he had problems with street kids breaking in and stealing things from the basement. We think Allen heard noises down there, after he paid his landlord."

"Did anyone else hear anything?"

"No. He was strangled from behind. The killer must have been interrupted or scared off, because they left the rope still around Allen's neck. What have you found out?" Denby's voice tried to stay even, but quivered under the strain.

"Nothing concrete."

Carson changed his mind and decided to tell Denby about the money Peter owed. He hoped it would get Denby's mind off Allen and on to something he could use his experience to contribute to. "Seems Peter owed everyone here a lot of money and made it sound like the State Department would be paying for all of his debts. I'll find out exactly who he owed money to and how much. That might lead us to the killer. You might find this interesting. The day after they found Peter's body a man walked into Peter's bank and cleaned out his account. The signature matched Peter's, and he knew the account number."

"Okay," was the only response from Denby, which made Carson wonder if Denby'd really heard a word he'd said.

It had already been a long day, and not wanting to go into any details with someone barely listening, Carson decided to cut the conversation short. This was not the time to grill Denby about Laura and Peter. He would hold off questioning his boss until a better time.

"I'll check in again, once I have something solid. Give my condolences to Allen's family."

****

Usually, restful sleep came to Carson the minute his head hit the pillow. Tonight was different. Too many unanswered questions made him uneasy and that kept sleep at bay. There were too many people with reasons for wanting to see Peter dead. Now, Allen Clarke, the agent originally appointed to this assignment, found dead. Was Allen's death connected to Peter's, or just a coincidence? Carson didn't believe in coincidences. Deep down, he knew Allen's death was connected to Peter's in some way. He sensed it would only be a matter of time before the connection revealed itself. In the meantime, would there be any more corpses? Would there be injuries to him, or others, before he unraveled all the clues?

He knew the answer and it tickled his memory. Somewhere, someone had already revealed the key information he needed to solve this case. Had he seen or heard the answer, and not recognized it? Was it something he heard or saw long ago or recently? He sat up on the lumpy motel mattress and stared out the lone window into the star-studded night. Clamping his eyes tight, he strained his memory for any significant tidbit of information. Did Laura inadvertently say something that didn't ring true?

Wide awake, he decided to use an old tried and true method: write down all of the different possible scenarios. He made a list of everyone who had a motive to Peter. Then he made a list of all the facts as he knew them to be. Between every farmer he had bodily removed from their land and everyone he owed money to, those people alone made for a long list of suspects. Where else did Peter abuse his authority? One fact became abundantly clear: this case was more involved than it appeared on the surface. Years of experience and listening to his gut told him that. That same gut feeling saved his life on more than one occasion. He ignored that gut feeling once, and it cost him the life of someone very dear to him. Finally, satisfied with his lists, and tired, he fell asleep.

He slowly follows the faint snap of broken twigs on a steep heavily wooded hillside. Small spots of sunlight filter through the leaves and dot the ground, like the reflections off a chandelier. A thick carpet of moss covers the ground and fallen trees. He is too anxious to appreciate the natural beauty of his surroundings. The tree-covered ridge prevents a clear sight of anything but more trees and boulders. He's holding a rifle and crouches down behind a huge boulder waiting for the sound of another snapped twig. No sound comes. Cautiously, he stands up. Still fiercely gripping the rifle, he begins to climb up the steep grade of the hillside. Then it happens. Another twig snaps somewhere behind him. Swiftly he turns around and raises his rifle to his shoulder, ready to fire. Out of nowhere, a blood curdling scream pierces the silence.

Carson shot up in bed, shaking and breathing hard. Perspiration covered his body: his heart racing. It took several moments for him to be cognizant of his surroundings. In very small degrees, his heart beat slowed down and he could breathe evenly. Another bad dream: the same bad dream he always had when he found himself surrounded by danger. If only he could bring himself to get past the scream. It was still only 4:00 a.m. Only ninety minutes after he'd finished his lists. Getting any restful sleep seemed out of the question.

He slipped out of his room, careful not to wake others in the boarding house. He walked around the corner to the parking area, and noticed a small white piece of paper slipped under his car's windshield wiper. He first thought Sheriff Lyman left the message during the night. No, he thought, the sheriff wouldn't just drop off information. The note could be picked off by anyone, or fall off the car with a gust of wind. Sheriff Lyman was more professional than that.

Curious, Carson walked over to his car and grabbed the carefully encased, hand-made, square envelope. Amused by someone's shyness, he pried open the flap, and pulled out the note. Neatly folded in half, the message was composed of words cut out of the newspaper and glued on the paper. Four words comprise the message: IS SHE WORTH IT?

The hair on the back of his neck stood up. Instincts told him something was about to happen. He looked around the parking lot for any moving shadows or sounds of footsteps on the gravel. Suddenly, the motel door slammed open, flooding the parking area with light. A burly figure filled the door. He swayed between the door jams, trying to maintain an upright position. The clumsy movements indicated this would-be attacker was too drunk to be a threat to anyone but himself. From the spill of light, Carson could see the young man wore an army uniform. The soldier inhaled a large dose of fresh air into his lungs, and then rushed to the nearest bushes where he freed his stomach of its contents. Eventually, he lifted his head away from the bushes and leaned against the nearest car for support.

Quietly, slowly, Carson walked up behind the drunk.

"You need any help?"

Hearing an unexpected voice the soldier spun around off balance and fell to the ground.

"Sorry if I startled you. You looked like you might need a little help."

"Tha... Thanks. I thought the fresh air would help."

"Must have been one hell of a party."

"The party's over all right. She married him anyway. Why didn't she wait for me?" the soldier said slurring his words. His body swayed as if he couldn't find any balance.

The soldier finally looked at Carson when he spoke, "Yeah, well, it's over and done now. I'd like to just be here by myself for a while, if you don't mind."

The soldier's statement resonated with Carson.

In his case, she hadn't married the other guy, as far as he knew. And now the other guy was dead.

As he recalled, Laura's attitude started to shift one rainy day on their way back to DC, from a Labor Day picnic. The car got a flat tire. Peter suddenly appeared out of no where and 'rescued' Laura, taking her back to DC in his car. That was the day when their relationship started to end and Laura and Peter's relationship started. It was then she learned Peter would inherit a fortune from his mother. That's all it would take to win daddy's approval for her choice of companion. Peter's family had government contracts all over the world and would surely have the right connections. His little girl would never want for anything. It couldn't hurt his business either. It was all about pleasing her family and living up to their expectations.

Carson almost felt sorry for Laura. She'd gambled with her future, her happiness, and lost. She had no Peter, no money, and he knew, especially having met her father, without a doubt, she was tainted in daddy's eyes. Why didn't she go back to Washington or Boston after Peter was murdered? Did her family even know she left Washington with Peter? If they knew, did she tell them she and Peter were married? No, she'd be honest. That was part of being a good girl. More than anything else, Laura loved the image of being a good girl. The whole absurd idea made him laugh out loud. Good girls don't leave family, friends, jobs and a pricey family apartment in Washington to move across the country with a man without being married.

In the distance, a car backfired. Carson noticed it was dawn and he was alone. The soldier had left. He looked down at the tightly gripped note in his hands. He knew the answer to the question in the note.

He sighed and looked at the red sunrise. *Red sky in morning, sailor take warning.* His mother always said that when she saw a red sunrise. Supposedly, it meant it was going to rain that day. At the moment, Carson cared more about eating than the local forecast. He turned around to go back into the boarding house and his eyes swept over to his car...the very same car that had literally driven Laura out of his life. He would have the last laugh. Peter could no longer interfere or take Laura anywhere. Now the car was his to use, to bring Laura back into his life.

After a good breakfast, the first thing on the agenda - getting the list of people Peter owed money to. He also wanted to see the bank teller who helped the stranger close out Peter's account. Maybe she recalled something. Since it was her first day on the job, someone would have been hovering close by, and together, they might remember something. Then he'd go and talk with Harold Maier. Sheriff Lyman was sure about Maier's innocence, but that alone wasn't enough to pacify himself or Denby. Denby would want proof. He got in Peter's car – his car, and drove to the police station.

A police car and several other cars were parked outside the police station when Carson pulled up. The Sauk City Police

Station was housed in a non-descript building. The sign on the brick, two-story building said U.S. Hotel. This was not only the home of the police department, but home of the Village Hall and Library. Carson speculated that either Sauk City had a very low crime rate, which didn't justify adding to the force, or they were slow in catching up with the ballooning population.

When he entered the station, he could see into Sheriff Lyman's office. The sheriff stood looking out a side window, drinking a cup of coffee. Small fans strategically placed throughout the office, circulated the increasingly oppressive summer air. More WW II posters adorned the walls. The poster outside Ben's office read *Keep the home fires burning* and *More Protection*. The only other person in the office, a secretary, came scurrying from a back room with the coffee pot in hand. She was a petite, gray-haired, woman, with glasses hanging from her neck on a chain. Her carriage exemplified expediency and professionalism. She may be the secretary to a small town police department, but she exhibited pride in her appearance and, no doubt, her abilities.

"Its okay, Libby," Sheriff Lyman called from his office, "he's here to see me." He waved for Carson to enter his office.

"I would offer you some coffee, but Libby has to make more. We have a small coffee pot, and I just drank the last of it. Poor Libby spends more time making me coffee than they do at Maxwell House."

Carson smiled at Ben's honest comment. Ben's spartan office gave Carson the impression that it could belong to anyone in the department. The only personal items that distinguished this office as Ben's were the two pictures on his desk and his name on the door. One picture showed Ben and a boy at a baseball field. The other had Ben standing behind a seated pretty strawberry blond woman and the same boy with his arms around their shoulders, like a protective shield.

"I'll only be here a minute," Carson confessed.

"You're here for the money list, right."

"Yeah, and the directions to Harold Maier's."

Ben opened the top right drawer of his desk and pulled out a sheet of paper with a long list of names on it. He called out, "Let me know when the coffee's ready, Libby." He turned his attention to Carson. "You might want to close the door."

Carson did as asked, and then sat in the only other chair in the room.

"I'll give you directions to Harold's, but you won't be able to talk to him for days, not if you intend to question everyone on the list first."

"How many people are on it?"

"If you want every person Peter Franke owed a dime to, it's well over fifty people. If you want just the ones that he owes three hundred or more, the list narrows to twenty seven."

"Jesus, Peter."

"He owed something to virtually every store in town, from shoes to groceries. Interesting, considering the ration on shoes went into effect last February seventh. How he got away with getting such credit everywhere is beyond me."

"What did he buy that brought up his debts to thirty thousand dollars?"

"Land."

"Land?"

"Yep, land. A lot of it along the Wisconsin River; he preferred wooded land. That way it would be of little use to the farmer, and they'd be more likely to sell it to him."

"What the hell was he going to do with so much land?"

"Don't know. Rudie Helweg, one of the farmers, said Peter told him he was going to build a big house there as a wedding present to his wife."

"His wife!"

"That's what Rudie said. And as far as I know, Peter Franke was single. He had two more farmers on the line for more land. Those transactions never got beyond the talk stage, but it would have been another fifty acres."

Carson shook his head in disbelief. "This is getting more bizarre every minute. One more thing."

"Name it."

"Did you suspect Owen Anderson's secretary, a Miss Laura Bradshaw? She came out here about the same time as Peter Franke."

"Not really. Didn't you read my report?"

"Yeah, I did. Can I have her home address, too?" Carson stood up and another thought came to him. "And, if you're done with Peter's place, I'd like to move in there, if that's possible."

"Address for Owen's secretary? Hmmm. Libby," he called loudly through the closed door, "Could you get me the address of Owen Anderson's secretary? Her name is Laura Bradshaw."

Libby scurried in with the asked for information before the men could fully resume their conversation. Just as quickly and quietly, she scurried out.

"Looks like you're taking over his life." Ben looked at the paper and then handed it to Carson. "First his car, now his house. What's next?"

Carson smiled.

"Just parts of his life."

The word "wife" had been enough to change Carson's priorities for the day. His first stop now - Laura's place. He knew she would be at work. He really just wanted to see where and how she lived.

He drove up the long, dusty driveway to the address Ben gave him. He checked the directions and address again. At the end of the driveway, surrounded by corn fields, stood a large, stately, three-story Victorian house. A covered porch surrounded two sides of the house. White lace curtains accented all the windows. On the right side of the house, a dozen kids, ranging in age from around three to twelve, played on the tire swing, hanging from one of the oak trees. None of the kids stopped their activities when he got out of the car. He walked to the front porch where a heavy, middle-aged woman, with a thick, brown braid crowning her head, sat rocking a baby in her lap. When Carson mounted the stairs to the porch, the baby's big blue eyes started to water. The baby pulled away trying to hide in the folds of the woman's arms.

"Say dere, no need for da tears. Wait until we find out his business," she said to the baby in a broken German accent. The baby responded to her voice, but still looked wary. She smiled and patted the baby's full head of blond hair.

"Excuse me," Carson said hesitantly, "I was told a Miss Laura Bradshaw lives here?"

"Ya, dats true," she answered, not taking her eyes off the scared baby.

"Do you know her?"

"Ya. I'm da landlady. Miss Laura rents a room here."

"Is she here now?"

The sound of the phone ringing denied Carson his answer.

"Trudy," she yelled to someone inside the house.

On the fourth ring she rocked herself up and handed Carson the baby as she passed, on her way into the house.

It had been well over twenty years since he'd last held a baby in his arms. This baby, clearly leery of him, started to squirm. Carson tried to remember what he did to settle his little brother down, all those years ago. Taking the woman's place in the rocking chair, Carson sat the baby down on his knees, so that they were facing each other. Using the balls of his feet, he bounced the baby up and down. Slowly the baby began to smile. It took Carson a minute to realize the woman was watching him play with the baby.

"You gut mit babies," she said.

"I basically raised my little brother so my mother could work," he replied with a growing unease.

"His daddy vas kilt in da var," she said nodding toward the baby.

Carson sensed this conversation could lead into an area of his life he tried so hard to keep private. He stood up and handed the baby back to the woman.

"I'm sorry if I interrupted anything here," he said as he indicated the kids in the yard. "Sheriff Lyman gave me Miss Bradshaw's address. I was hoping I could talk to her. I'll try again at a more convenient time."

He started to walk down the stairs.

"Sunday's are gut. Dese kids vill be home mit die Mutter und der Vaters. Is quiet here den. Dat Sheriff Lyman, now he's a gut man."

Out of courtesy, Carson stopped to listen.

"To raise dat boy like his own now dat his vife is dead... und do such a gut job. My own boy vould be a gut Vater, too if he vasn't kilt in the var, like this poor little boy's Vater."

Before today, he sensed Ben was someone of integrity, someone he could trust. Now, with this new insight, Carson felt both respect and envy.

After leaving Laura's landlady, the rest of the day went downhill. Every outstanding debt of Peter's was recently paid, in full. All were paid in cash. Only a handful of store owners remembered seeing that the postmark was from Sauk City. Those who never looked at the postmark didn't care. The bill was paid in full. How and by whom wasn't something they normally cared about.

Armed with the information Ben had told him about the land and outstanding debts, Carson decided to pay the court house a visit and look deeper into Peter's land deals. What he discovered left him feeling numb.

Carson planned to call Denby around 7:00 p.m., Washington time, confident Denby would be the only one there. With an empty office, Denby could answer sensitive questions without anyone listening in on their phone conversation. But the day's events had made Carson edgy, and he decided to call much earlier than he'd planned.

"State Department. Denby."

"Bill, its Carson."

"I wasn't expecting your call for hours. You got a problem out there?"

"Maybe."

"Maybe doesn't tell me anything. You got a problem, yes or no?"

"Maybe. It all depends on what you know about Peter's personal finances."

Denby remained silent. Carson could hear papers being shuffled in the background. Seconds later, he heard a door shut, then footsteps and finally Denby answered.

"Peter Franke was a rich man."

"How rich?"

"Let's just say he was no Rockefeller, but he could hold his own against J.P. Morgan."

"That's interesting."

"You'll love the whole story. Marianne Franke, Peter's mother, was Marianne Himmel. Before that, she was Marianne Szecsy, a farmer's daughter in Germany."

"She did well for herself."

"Very. Evidently, as a young girl, she always saw herself living a better life. At seventeen, she found herself pregnant by the local baker's nineteen year old son. They married, and she had twin boys. Fourteen months into the marriage they divorced. Her husband, Erich Himmel, kept one son, Josef, and she kept the other, Peter. She hocked everything she could get her hands on and went to Amsterdam, then London. From London, she came to New York. There, she worked as a house maid for an importer. She caught the eye of a client's son at some fancy function, and six months later, she becomes Marianne Franke. George Franke adopted Peter and raised him as his own. We don't know if Peter was ever told about his brother and real father."

"Did you find them?"

"Yes. Both are dead. Erich was murdered in his bakery. Some suspect he was murdered by Josef."

"Really, when?"

More paper shuffling in the background.

"Let's see. Ah, 1936. Seems Josef, the other son, was getting too involved with the Nazis for Erich's comfort. One day, Erich was found dead at the bakery. All of his money and his ruby ring were missing. Josef seemed to have disappeared, too. Nothing was ever proven."

"How do you know Josef is dead?"

"He resurfaced again a few years later, in Grafenwohr, a training ground in Germany. Interpol told us his charred corpse, along with ten other men, was found in a house a few miles away from Grafenwohr. They think the house was a meeting place or party place for Nazi officers. Josef's motorcycle was outside the house and one of the victims wore the ring that belonged to Erich Himmel."

"I knew Peter inherited money. When did he fully inherit this fortune?"

"A year ago, maybe two. After George Franke died, Marianne spent more and more time traveling and less time at home in Virginia. She died in London, February of '42. Being an only child, he inherited everything."

"Okay, okay. So he is, was, a rich man. Why did he have over thirty thousand dollars on credit here? Why did he tell everyone that the State Department would pick up the tab, when he could have easily paid for everything himself? And most importantly, who did pay off all of the creditors after he died?"

"I didn't know they were paid off. The Why's, we'll probably never know. The Who, is what you'll have to find out."

Carson knew deep down that money was the key to all of this.

"I've answered your question, answer mine. He owed thirty thousand for what?"

"Everything. Food, shoes, on up to over 500 acres of land - lots of riverfront property."

"There's your lead. The land deed is in whose name?"

For several seconds the line between the men fell silent. Finally Carson answered, "I went to the court house today."

"And."

"The principal signature on the land is Peter Franke's. The co-owner is Laura Bradshaw."

Chapter Six

The next morning it rained with such intensity it seemed like an endless wall of water cascading from the sky. The wind made the rain horizontal and ragged. It didn't matter what you wore or how you tried to fend off the wind, the fact was you were going to get wet.

At nine o'clock it was still dark enough that Carson needed to use headlights to find his way to Harold Maier's farm. Highway 78 North out of Sauk City would normally be as picturesque as any of the drives he took in New England, if only he dare take his eyes off the road.

The windshield wipers struggled to keep up with the deluge of water pouring on them. He concentrated even harder on the road. He drove past a graveyard on his right. Ben had mentioned a graveyard about five miles out of town. Harold lived seven miles out of town. At least he knew he was close, even if he could hardly see the road.

Red brake lights, from a car in front of him, disrupted his focused stare. He slammed his foot on the brakes, thankful for the distance between the two cars, hoping it was enough to stop without hitting the other car. *What the hell is anyone doing out in a day like this, if they don't have to be?* Then from the headlights of the front car, he saw the outline of what looked like a large tree limb across the road. The front car's driver side door opened, and a small woman, wrapped in a dark raincoat and galoshes, got out. With the car still running, she fought the wind and rain, as she scurried to the obstacle. Grabbing the limb, she tried to drag it off the road by herself. She couldn't budge it.

"Oh shit," Carson muttered.

The force of the wind almost yanked the car door out of his hand when he opened it. It took more energy to close the door than he thought it would. The exertion was like a pantomime act in hostile elements; not a sound was heard. Holding his head down in a futile attempt to keep the rain out of his eyes, Carson ran out to help the woman move the fallen limb.

As he got closer to her, he saw she was an older woman of about sixty. Her glasses were just as wet as his windshield. It was a wonder she could see anything, or stand upright for that matter. Carson grappled with the large end and she grabbed the smaller end of the branch Together, they dragged the massive limb to the side of the road. No pleasantries were exchanged when the task was over. Silently, they both ran to their cars and continued on their journeys.

He located the Maier farm within minutes; it seemed abandoned. No vehicles or animals could be seen anywhere. Carson quickly ran up the porch and knocked on the front door. His hat brim used to be turned up. Now it curved down, like an umbrella, letting the rain run off evenly over his shoulders.

He could see the wary look on Marie Maier, yet she answered the door sympathetic to a rain drenched man.

"Come in, come in," she said. "Come in out of the rain. I guess you're the government man. I heard in town you were here."

The offer was welcoming, but he knew he couldn't come into her warm, tidy home. His soaked clothes would leave a small pool wherever he stood.

"That's all right, ma'am. I wouldn't want to drip all over your floor. I'd like to talk to your husband. Is he home?"

"You'll find him there, I believe," she said wringing her hands in her apron. She stepped to the right side of the door and pointed diagonally across the driveway.

At her instruction, he turned around and looked at the shed she pointed to. He gave her a quick smile, readjusted his hat, then he trudged through the wind and rain to the shed.

He noticed a young boy dressed in a yellow slicker and knee high black boots creep in the side door of the shed. His arrival was about to be announced to Harold Maier.

Using the same side door as the boy, Carson found Harold Maier and the boy bent over the engine of an old, dark green, Ford pickup truck. The boy, he assumed, was the Maier boy who had found Peter's body. He looked dwarfed next to his father. Stevie looked up when Carson entered the building and immediately looked down avoiding any eye contact. A collie, lying on a bale of hay lifted its head when Carson entered the shed and decided to greet him. Carson petted the dogs' soft head before looking back at Stevie and Harold.

At his father's bidding, tools were handed back and forth like a surgeon and his assistant. It was the kind of experience Carson wished he could have had with his father. Carson cleared his throat as he approached the two.

"That's okay, Mr. Grey. We know you're here and why you're here," Harold said, not looking up from his delicate operation. "Stevie, pull over a couple of crates for Mr. Grey to sit on."

Carson stopped walking toward the truck as soon as Harold gave Stevie the instruction. He saw the cautious glances the boy gave his father. After Harold nodded toward the crates with a furrowed brow, the boy quickly lugged two large empty vegetable crates over by Carson. Stevie placed the crates one on top of the other a good distance from the truck. Once the crates were in place, he hurried back to his father's side and picked up a wrench.

"Thank you, Stevie," Carson replied sitting down on the crates. "Sheriff Lyman assures me you're no threat to the community, and that's why he let you go."

"That and the fact he had no evidence. Anyway, as I told Ben, if you need me, I'll be in my fields or around one of the buildings on the farm. I don't have anywhere to run, nor do I have any reason to run. I rarely leave the farm. Marie goes into town to shop and such."

Harold pointed to a screwdriver sitting on the air filter. Stevie snatched the screwdriver and handed it to his father.

"How do you think the body ended up on your old property?" Carson ventured with an even tone.

"Don't know."

"There were reports that you and Mr. Franke had words."

"Words." Harold smiled at the polite phrasing. He straightened up to his full height and wiped his hands over his grease-spotted, gray coveralls. "I think we both know it was a little more then 'words'."

"Did you know that Mr. Franke bought up a lot of land: riverfront property? And one parcel is adjacent to the land you used to own? Stevie found his body on that parcel, your former property, only a few hundred yards from one of his own parcels."

"Nope." Harold answered returning to work on the truck.

His quick jerky movements showed Carson he was annoyed, but trying to control his anger.

"Did he say anything or do anything to you or your family that made you..." Carson stopped for a second looking for a proper wording to use in front of the boy. "...made you express yourself so vocally to him?"

Harold quit working on the truck and faced Carson. The smile left his face, and his expression turned absolute. His body constricted, his breathing became slow and deep, like a volcano trying to control itself. With flinty eyes focused, he answered Carson's line of questions.

"Mr. Grey, for three generations before me, my family worked and nurtured that land. Our sweat and blood are part of that soil. Being forced off that land by an uncaring, smug, arrogant, Washington bureaucratic clown, who probably never got his hands dirty in his life, did not set well." Harold reached for a rag and angrily wiped his hands with hard jerky motions. "Just his being here was a threat to my family and every family in the community. I'm one of the lucky one's. My wife's father was willing to retire and sell me his farm, so I could continue farming." Harold motioned for the dog to return to the hay bale, which it quickly did. Then he leveled his eyes on Carson. "Thankfully, he lived very close to us. Most of my former neighbors were not so lucky. Some were able to stay in the county and continue farming. The rest are spread all over the state. That is, the rest who wanted to start all over again." He pointed to a different wrench. Stevie quickly handed it to his dad. Harold clinched the wrench holding it up like a weapon. "But, before you ask, I'll answer your next questions. No. No, I didn't kill your Mr. Franke. And no, I wasn't sorry to hear he was dead."

As Harold spoke his last sentence, a loud clap of thunder rang outside and shook the shed, as if to put an exclamation point on his statement. Carson wanted to believe Harold, but seeing how close to the surface his rage toward Peter clung, Carson knew he just witnessed a side of Harold Maier Ben had never seen. Just for the time being, Harold Maier was going to stay near the top of the suspect list. He wanted to ask more questions, but he knew it would be pointless, besides he had another appointment to make.

The rain and wind had all but stopped by the time Carson left Harold Maier's farm. Just before noon Carson drove up to a small white Cape Cod style house on First Street in Sauk City.

This house Peter Franke called home. The yard looked small, but well proportioned to the house. The lilac bushes, on the south side of the lot, had finished blooming for the year, and the apple tree would be the only source of shade. A tiny spot behind the house indicated where a garden had been. Weeds looked to be the only crop in the space now. Rose bushes flanked the gate inside the whitewashed picket fenced yard.

He saw two cars parked on Grand Avenue, which connected to First Street. The first car looked vaguely familiar to him. The other he recognized as Sheriff Lyman's. Ben told him he was through checking over the house. If that was true, what was he doing here? Carson reached up to knock on the front door. It opened with Ben on the other.

"Sheriff," Carson said. "Is there a problem?"

"No." Ben continued out the door to the front stoop. "I'd like to introduce you to…"

At that moment, a woman walked out from behind Ben into full view.

"You," said the woman who he'd helped move the tree limb. Her wet, short silver hair lay flat against her head.

"You've met?" Ben said surprised.

"Not formally." She extended her hand to Carson.

"As I was about to say, this is your new landlady, Mrs. Richard Neuman."

"Call me Esther. Everyone does."

"And Esther, this is Mr. Grey, your new tenant. Now, how do you know each other?"

"This is the man who helped me move that big tree limb off the road this morning."

"Excuse me." Confusion rang clearly in Carson's voice and showed on his face. "But I was told the owners of this house live in Madison. Why would you be on a road north of here at nine o'clock if you're from Madison? This house is five miles south of where the tree limb fell. Isn't Madison southeast of here?"

She covered a smile at his obvious confusion and winked at Ben.

"I am from Madison. After I left home this morning, I got to this side of Middleton when I realized I didn't have my keys for this house. I was already running late and didn't want to turn around and go home. My sister lives north of here. She has a set in case there's an emergency and I can't be reached. I was on my way to her house when you helped me."

"Okay," Carson said as he thought out loud, "Okay, then why is Sheriff Lyman here?"

"Esther came early to check things over before you got here. She noticed a broken window in the back porch. It looked like someone tried to break in recently. She went next door and called me to look into the matter. We'd just finished looking through the house when you arrived."

"And thankfully, nothing is missing," Esther chimed in. "Must have been just a prank, from one of the neighborhood boys, or it could have been an accident caused by the storm. Nothing is missing, that's the main thing."

"So, Mrs...." Carson caught himself, "Esther, when do you think I'll be able to move in?"

"Now. You're lucky Sheriff Lyman called when he did. Another man stopped by here just this morning, as I was about to go the neighbors and call the Sheriff. He asked me if he could rent it. He seemed to know all about its vacancy. I asked him if he was new here and planning on working at Badger. He laughed and said he wasn't new, exactly, and had no plans to work here. I thought that was odd."

"Esther, you never mentioned this to me earlier, when we went through the house."

"It must have slipped my mind."

"About what time did this happen?" Carson asked.

"Do you remember what he looked like or his name?" Concern evident in Ben's voice.

"Well, let's see. I couldn't really see his face. It was still raining hard, as you know. His hat was down over his eyes and his coat collar was up. Actually he has a hat and coat like yours, Mr. Grey. He was very polite and had sort of an English accent."

"Sort of an English accent?" Ben asked.

"Yes. It sounded British, but not quite. I know that doesn't make any sense, but that's how it sounded to me."

"His name, Esther." Something about this guy didn't set right with Carson. "Do you remember his name?"

"His name." She tapped her lips with her forefinger and looked to the overcast sky. "James, James, James somebody. Let's see... James Holler, no, James Holden. That's it, James Holden. He said he was here on holiday. That's the word the Brits use. We say vacation, they say holiday."

"Esther," Ben pushed, "how did he know you were here?"

"Oh, that's easy. He's here on holiday, and he knew Mr. Franke was..." her voice dropped to a whisper, "...murdered. He needed a place to stay. He was driving by and saw the lights on in the house. I had the lights on, because the storm made it so dark, you know. He stopped and asked if he could rent the house, while he was here. I explained to him it was already spoken for. I told him that I was waiting for the new tenant to arrive and about to call the Sheriff to come look into the broken window."

"What happened then?" Carson asked.

"He politely apologized for taking up my time and left."

Carson sensed he needed to direct her attention back on the house. He could nonchalantly continue asking questions as they looked through the house. "So, could you show me around the house now, Esther?"

Carson knew Ben would understand, play along and take the grand tour, again. Somehow the broken porch window didn't look or feel so innocent anymore. Taking a second serious look through the house might reveal something overlooked the first time through. They could use each other as distractions. Esther would be busy answering questions, she wouldn't suspect anything.

Esther took the lead and reentered the house, with the two men following. Left of the front door revealed a tiny living room. Immediately ahead of the front door was another door, which Carson assumed, went up to the attic. The kitchen, connected to the living room. The cupboards and appliances were on the left of the room with a hutch next to a table and chairs on the right. From the end of the living room, Carson could see a short hallway that led to two more rooms. Esther decided to start the tour in the kitchen.

"The house is pretty much like my in-laws left it. My husband and I are using it as a rental." She opened all of the cupboards for Carson's inspection. "It's fully furnished, as you can see."

The lights flickered and dimmed just for a second. Carson flashed Ben a doubtful look.

"That's the dam," Esther quickly explained.

"The dam?"

"Some people think the dam causes the lights to flicker or dim," Ben said.

"It does," Esther insisted.

"Around the noon hour, some folks believe more electricity is being used to make dinner and that puts a strain on the power. Also, when the dam water gets to a certain level, the spill gates open. With all of the rain we've had here and upriver, I'm sure the water levels fill up fast."

Carson really didn't want a detailed explanation for the flicker. He wanted more information on Holden.

"This Mr. Holden... can you remember anything else about him?" He pretended to look at the dishes and pans in the cupboard.

"He's about your height, medium build. I didn't see his eyes or hair because of his hat and coat."

In the living room, Carson listened to Esther as she pointed out when, where and how certain pieces of furniture were collected. He followed her as she walked down the hallway. The bathroom was on the right of the hall and the bedroom was on the left. Just as she opened the bedroom closet to show Carson, Ben reappeared.

"Say, Esther," he interrupted, "I want to show you how I plugged up that broken window on the porch."

Carson knew that Ben would keep her occupied long enough for him to do a semi-thorough sweep of the bed room. Esther excused herself and followed Ben out to the back porch.

Before Esther ever totally left his sight, Carson started to check the underside of the dresser drawer. He looked and felt behind the mirror. He slowly walked over each floor board, listening for any hollow sounds. He looked at and poked the corners of the closet. Everything looked, felt and sounded fine. Annoyed that he didn't find anything, Carson decided he would have more than ample time to go over everything, once he moved into the house.

He knew Peter Franke, and by extension, he knew Peter never trusted anyone. Peter knew his killer. That was one fact Carson felt sure about. If Peter had something on anyone, he would have kept it a secret and used it when the time was right. Carson couldn't get over the feeling that there was something in the house that would open up the investigation.

"Thanks for coming out on such a day, Esther. I'll take good care of the place," said Carson.

"Don't mention it. Always good to see the old place."

As Esther's car pulled away, Ben and Carson shared their findings – nothing.

"I guess I'll go back to the boarding house, gather up my clothes and move in," Carson said walking to his car.

"Hey, you like baseball?" Ben said from his car.

Carson stopped and laughed.

"Of course I like baseball."

"You know where the baseball field is?"

"Yeah."

"Meet me there in ten minutes."

The baseball field was only a few blocks away from Carson's new house. He'd driven past it the night before, while trying to get a feel for Peter's old neighborhood and stewed over the possibility that Laura might be Peter's killer and owner of a lot of property.

Carson pulled up to the ball park at the appointed time. A group of young boys were in the middle of a pick-up game. Carson got the feeling, just by the way the boys talked and acted, that these boys all knew each other and went through this ritual every day. A minute after Carson parked his car, Ben pulled up.

"Come on over and watch with me."

Carson accepted the offer, walked over to Ben's car and slid into the passenger side.

"That's my boy out there, on second base."

Carson understood he was being allowed into Ben's private life. He sensed Ben's love and pride for the boy. A fleeting tone of sadness briefly washed over him as he allowed himself to remember his own childhood.

Ben reached into the plain, brown, paper bag between them and offered Carson an apple.

"No, that's okay. I'm all right."

"No, take it. I packed an extra one."

"This is a nice field for the boys."

"It's been at this location for about ten years or so. Tommy and my brother love baseball. Fred fills Tommy's head with the stories of the old days of baseball here. Traveling teams used to come to Sauk City and play. In fact, some of the players involved in the 1918 Black Sox World Series scandal played here."

"Really?"

"Tommy lives for those stories. He sure takes after his mother. She was a good athlete. I'm too clumsy to be good at any sport."

The young boy standing on second base looked nothing like Ben. Carson ate in silence, letting Ben talk.

"He knows I'm here, but acts like it don't matter." Ben laughed. "As hard as it rained this morning, you'd think they'd have sense enough not to play in that mud."

A lumbering boy hit the ball far out into center field. Ben's son jumped up and down, trying to get the attention of the outfielder, to use him as the cutoff.

"But," Ben continued, "it could be a blizzard in July, and they'd still come out and play."

The previous hitter got to second base. A younger, scrawny boy came to bat. The pitcher pitched two strikes in a row. The young batter just stood there and watched as his teammates yelled encouraging comments to him from the sidelines. On the third pitch, he connected with the ball. He hit a pop fly to the short stop. Game over.

The sandy-haired, green-eyed second baseman trotted to Ben's car continually tossing the ball into his grimy glove. Ben got out of the car, taking the paper bag with him. He handed the boy the bag, then gave him a big bear hug, squashing the contents of the paper bag between them.

During this show of affection, Carson got out of the car and stood by the passenger side door.

"Who won today, Sport?" Ben asked as he escorted his son back to the car.

The boy shrugged his shoulders, peeling away the waxed paper covering of his smashed strawberry jam sandwich.

"Nobody wins. We just play until dinner time. Some of us come back later and play, too. The rain made us late today," he answered in between inhaling bites of his sandwich.

Then he noticed Carson standing by the car. He looked down, then at his dad, and then he turned around completely looking back at the muddy baseball field.

"Tommy, this is Mr. Grey." Ben physically turned Tommy to face Carson. "He's here from Washington, working on the Franke case. I thought he might enjoy watching you play."

Carson judged this to be a good time to leave. The boy seemed obviously uncomfortable with his presence, and Carson wanted to give them back their lunch time together. He wanted to do at least one more interrogation before he moved into the house.

"Thanks for letting me watch you play, Tommy. I wish we'd gotten here sooner. Maybe another time. Right now, I have to go. Thanks for the apple, Sheriff."

"Call me Ben."

As Carson walked back to his car, he knew Tommy watched him like he was on the FBI's most wanted list -Public Enemy Number One.

"Say," Ben called out to Carson, "get a phone hooked up at that new place of yours, and leave the number with Libby. I'll give you a call in a few days – see when ya can come over for dinner. I make a great spaghetti and meatball, right, Tommy?"

Carson got back in his car and watched Ben and Tom play catch as he drove away.

Chapter Seven

Laura's morning started just as unsettling as Carson's. The landlady's dog woke her up at 4:30 a.m. barking at shadows around her car. The wind and rain rattled the house and knocked tree branches against her bedroom windows all night. When she got in her car to go to work, she realized someone had actually been in it during the night. The mirrors were all rearranged. The glove compartment's contents littered the floor. In the back seat lay a rumpled unfamiliar blanket, left as a memento. As she lifted the blanket off the seat, shiny silver objects fell out and rolled under her car seat. Curious, she bent over to retrieve them. She caught her breath as soon as she opened her hand. There, settled in her palm, lay a pair of silver cufflinks; the ones she gave Peter to wear to his mother's funeral. She had her jewelers make them especially for Peter, and the occasion, as her way of letting him know she shared in his sorrow. After that day, she never saw the cufflinks again. She assumed the association with the funeral, made it too painful for Peter to wear them.

Numbly, she curled the cufflink in her palm, too afraid to admit that they were left there on purpose as a message of some sort.

"You forget something, Miss Bradshaw?"

Laura jumped at the voice coming from the house. She hadn't noticed her landlady, who came out onto the front porch, assessing her yard littered with twigs and limbs.

"No, Mrs. Schultz. I wish I wasn't already late for work or I'd help you clean the yard," Laura called back.

"Yeah, yeah. Dats okay. I make Trudy and da kids pick up."

Confident that she'd sufficiently masked her emotions from her landlady, Laura waved goodbye, closed the car door and drove down the long driveway to work.

The tension she'd felt at home followed her to work. She found herself surrounded by a confused secretary pool. Owen hadn't come to work yet. He usually arrived at work earlier than his staff and made his rounds on the Badger grounds before going to his office. Not today. His car wasn't there, and there were no phone calls regarding his whereabouts – very unlike Owen. Since Laura was his personal secretary, the other secretaries all looked to her for guidance.

She was just as confused as they were. The previous afternoon, Owen went his way to remind everyone of a mandatory meeting set for first thing in the morning. New policies, handed down from the top, needed to be discussed. So where was he?

It took all morning to focus on her job and not think about the cuff links. Getting the other secretaries to calm down and not worry about Owen took just as much effort.

Shortly before 1:30 p.m., Owen breezed into the office genuinely sorry for not being there to conduct the meeting.

"Oh my. I'm so sorry for being late. We'll have the meeting tomorrow. A car ran me off the road and I had to wait for the rain to let up, before I could go for help."

A logical explanation, except his clothes, the same clothes he wore the day before, were dry. Plus, today lipstick smudges on the collar.

"Understandable. We'll have the meeting tomorrow."

Whatever his story, she didn't care. She hadn't eaten all day. She was tired and hungry. "I'm taking lunch now, Owen," Laura said.

She opened the bottom drawer of her desk and grabbed her purse, took out a compact and checked her tired eyes. She readjusted the renegade curl, turning her head from side to side several times, before deciding she didn't care what anyone thought of her looks today. With a sigh, she snapped the compact shut, dropped it back in her purse and walked to the front door. She opened the door to leave, but Carson blocked the entrance.

He backed out, allowing her to exit the office. He grabbed her forearm, before the door completely shut.

"We have to talk," he said

"Yes, we do." She yanked her arm out of his hand. "Where I live is off limits to you. Understand!" she hissed under her breath.

"Listen," he shot back, "I'm here to find out who killed Peter. I've discovered some interesting facts that make you the number one suspect."

Her nonplussed attitude only seemed to agitate him. She refused to let him see her upset or disturbed.

"I'd rather we go to my car and talk, unless you want everyone to hear our conversation," he continued.

"Stop these games, Carson. You don't know anything. You're just looking for an excuse to come out here and pester me."

He crossed his arms across his chest. "Fine," he said his voice with a sharp edge. "If that's what you want to believe. Let's talk about you and Peter Franke."

Laura now understood Carson would embarrass her in public if she called his bluff. When she left Washington, part of her died at the thought she would never see him again. Now, to be around him again, in the shadow of Peter's death, she needed to keep him, at least for now, at arms length. She knew he still loved her, but she couldn't permit him to know her secret. She decided to change her tactics. Maybe she could pacify him with some answers, then he would leave her alone. Dropping her head, she hoped that it appeared she had surrendered to his request. Obediently, she walked to his car.

Neither spoke a word, until they got to Sauk City. The tension felt like a wall between them. She played with her watch band to avoid any conversation with him. Its sparkling jewels caught the afternoon sun. It was from Cartier, her favorite jewelry store in New York. Her father had given it to her for her twenty-first birthday.

Carson pulled up to The Dinette on Water Street: a little mom and pop place where the locals gathered and newcomers to the area adopted as an inexpensive place to eat.

The earlier rain and the time of day made for slow business. They found a booth in the corner, just what Laura hoped for. Three other patrons sat at the counter, talking to the waitress. The waitress pulled herself away from her other customers long enough to take Carson and Laura's order, and then went back to her friends.

Carson wasted no time assaulting Laura with questions.

"What's your opinion of James Holden?"

"Who?"

"James Holden. An Englishman."

She could see by the scowl on his face he didn't believe her.

"What were you and Peter going to do with all that land?"

"All what land?" she replied hesitantly wondering why Carson changed the subject. "Peter bought two acres somewhere around here. He said it would be a good place for a summer cottage."

"He bought five hundred acres and your name is on the deeds as co-owner."

She could feel the blood drain from her face. Suddenly it became hard to breathe and focus.

Before Laura could answer, the waitress came back to their booth with Laura's order of meat loaf, mashed potatoes, green beans and pie and Carson's order of pie and coffee. Slowly, she picked at the potatoes, but the fork fell away from her hand. She stared into Carson's face, searching to understand why he was saying such things.

"No," she whispered, "two acres."

"No. Five hundred. You own five hundred acres of mostly lake front property, Laura. Five hundred. The land was paid for the day after Peter's body was found. And all of his many other unpaid bills were mysteriously paid, in full, too. I suppose you know nothing about that, either."

She could only shake her head in denial, as Carson hammered away at her in a sharp, accusing voice.

"Another man, claiming to be Peter, went to the bank the day after Peter's body was found and withdrew Peter's whole account. Who was he? How did he know Peter's account number?"

The incriminating inflection in Carson's voice got increasingly venomous with every detail he uttered.

Lack of sleep from the storm, finding Peter's cufflink in her car, Owen's mystery car trouble, and now all of this information about land and money and strangers made her head spin. She felt numbed by all the questions. Her vision blurred, her heart raced and a chill blanketed her. Somewhere in the background she could still hear Carson talking.

"Laura, look at me," he said softly.

Several seconds went by before her brain processed what he had said. She complied with a vacuous look on her face.

"Laura, how do you get to work?"

"In my car," she muttered back in a quiet monotone.

"Where did you get the car?"

"Why do you care?" She answered sounding stronger than she felt. "That is none of your business."

"I'm doing my job. Just answer the question."

"Peter. He insisted that I take his old car when he bought the one that you're now driving."

"Tell me about the house Peter lived in. Were you ever in the house?"

"Yes, often. I tended the garden last year and the rose bushes."

Talk of the house relaxed her. She remembered there was food in front of her and how hungry she had felt. She picked up her fork and cut into her meatloaf.

"I suppose there won't be a garden this year. There's no one to tend to it."

"I'm living in the house now. If you want to put in another garden this year, feel free to come over whenever you like."

She stopped eating and looked at Carson. Could she trust that invitation to be as innocent as he made it sound? What was in it for him? Memories of the house with Peter started to surface. She had to shut them down before Carson could read her face.

"I don't have the time." She went back to the meatloaf.

"Why not?"

"I just don't."

How did he do it? One minute he accused her of killing Peter for land and the next he'd relaxed her enough she started telling him about her private life with Peter. He was getting too close. She needed to pay attention or he would find out. *Just answer enough to pacify him. Be honest but vague.*

"You knew Peter better than I did. Tell me about the Peter Franke you knew," asked Carson.

Thankfully, he sat back in the booth. The extra space between them helped her think and breathe. A sad smile crossed her face. How could she ever completely describe the Peter she knew to Carson?

"Peter was all the things you thought him incapable of being: warm, funny, smart, generous, caring and ambitious. At least half a dozen people, who now work at his father's business, were people he found living on the streets. He gave them back their self-respect.

"He loved children. He had a special connection with children. They trusted him more than other adults. Maybe it was because he was an only child and never had anyone to play with when he grew up. He said he learned to cook from the chef in his mother's house. He would go to the kitchen for companionship, and along the way, he learned a skill useful in life. Did you know this was going to be his last assignment with the State Department?"

Thankfully, he said nothing. He just sat back and let her talk without any snide side remarks about Peter.

"He planned on going back to Virginia to run his father's company. The Board of Directors have been running it since his father and mother passed away. I think he would have been good at it. He needed to get away from the agency. It was starting to make him very irritable and short tempered. Not like the Peter I loved." She looked out the window while talking. Her eyes and voice projected a heavy melancholy.

"When did you start to notice a difference in his behavior?" he asked calmly eating his pie.

"Oh, it was after a trip to Europe with his mother. He just seemed more preoccupied. I think that's when the doctors told him there was nothing more they could do for her."

"You said earlier he became short tempered. Short tempered, how?"

She picked at the green beans is if trying to remember.

"It became more pronounced, after his mother died. When he came back from her funeral, he really changed." She sighed and put her fork down. "He'd say one thing one day and the next deny it. He would get upset, throw things, and become loud when I corrected him on things he'd said to me earlier. The whole time you two were in London, last November, he never once called me. I needed him here with me." She heard the anxiety in her own voice as she answered afraid Carson could hear it too.

"Laura, did he ever hurt you, when he was behaving like that?" Carson asked softly.

She dropped her head to her chest, letting the long tresses curtain her face from Carson. She could feel heavy tears slowly inch down her cheek.

"He didn't mean it," she uttered through her hair. "It was just a couple of times, and he apologized to me for his behavior. He did love me." She looked up and saw Carson's ridged body and his furious expression. "Leave it alone, Carson. He can't do it anymore. He's dead."

The second she said that, she knew she slipped up. The rage she saw in Carson was palpable. Was he angry that Peter hit her or did he think this gave her motive to kill Peter? She could see the pulse in his temple throb. She had inadvertently given him even more reason to suspect and watch her.

"Laura, where did you go in such a rush on the day Peter's body was found?"

She dabbed her lips with her napkin. "I'm done with my lunch. Take me back to work now, please."

Chapter Eight

Laura's memory of Peter completely differed from Carson's. He'd always thought of Peter as a spoiled, rich boy, so the temper tantrums were believable.

But, her statement about London stood out. Peter never accompanied him to London, last November, or any time before or since.

He watched her search for a lacy handkerchief from her purse and dab at the tears in her eyes. Her resolve reappeared as quickly as the tears disappeared.

"I'm through with my lunch I said. I'm ready to go back to work."

"I can see that," Carson said. "You know I'm going to find out why you left work so fast the day they found Peter's body sooner or later. Just tell me."

"You know the answer," she lashed back.

"I know you got a phone call at work and immediately went home – or so you say. I know your landlady backs up the story.

What I don't know is who called you, and what was so important you had to leave work with no explanation to anyone. All of this happened on the day they found Peter's body. A man you just admitted hit you."

The tears returned. This time, she made no attempt to wipe them away.

"Leave it alone Carson. My leaving work had nothing to do with Peter's murder."

As before, nothing but silence filled the car on their way back to Badger. When he pulled up to the administration building, she opened her car door and looked back at Carson with utter contempt before exiting the car. He watched her walk away with a determined gate he hadn't seen in a long time.

Until he knew why she left work so abruptly, and what the phone call was about, she would have to remain on the suspect list. What was she hiding or afraid to share? He would continue keeping tabs on her and hope she would slip up somewhere. Why did he give her so much leeway? Were his feelings for her blinding him from the truth?

Checking out of the boarding house was quick and easy. The only possessions he'd brought with him easily fit into his well-traveled, battered old suitcase. Since the rental house was already furnished and clean, all he had to do was drop off his clothes. Tomorrow, after he finished his talk with Floyd Whitefeather, he hoped to buy a few groceries.

The house looked the same as he left it earlier. From the kitchen windows, he could watch the traffic on First Street and Grand Avenue. On the kitchen's north wall, a door led to the side of the yard facing Grand Avenue. Carson walked through the door on to the lawn. Making his way toward the back of the house, he could see the replaced back porch window.

The back porch ran the full width of the house. The outer wall, a bank of windows, lined the seven-foot-deep area. Inside, a waist high counter ran the length of the windows. Under the counter shelves were packed full of an abundant variety of sun-dried, dirt-caked, flowerpots. Small hand tools and larger garden tools lay in and around the flower pots and shelves. In the corner of the porch, under the top shelf, an old beat up watering pail sat. He returned to the house, through the kitchen, and decided to investigate the attic.

The dark, hot, open, space area revealed old and broken household items at one end of the attic and was empty at the other end. The sharp angle of the roof made it hard to stand up straight anywhere except in the center where the roof met at its highest peak.

A church bell in the distance announced the time of six o'clock. Time to think about getting something to eat.

He remembered seeing a can of coffee in the cupboard when Esther gave him the tour. That would be one less item on his grocery list, and he'd be able to make his own coffee in the morning for breakfast. Above the stove, on the bottom shelf was an opened can of Folgers coffee, next to three more unopened cans and a five-pound bag of sugar. Peter obviously found a way around his rations. Just as he reached for the open can of coffee, his stomach growled, again, prompting him to forget about the coffee and get a good, hot meal in town.

As soon as he got back from eating a hot, hearty meal at Oscar Wilhem's restaurant, a relaxed mood filled the house for the rest of the evening. The next morning, a screaming, hot shower, with endless water, set the pitch for the day. Add on a cup of strong, black, hot coffee, and nothing could ruin his day. By that evening, his phone would be hooked up, and he'd be able to communicate with the outside world.

His hair dripped, still wet and gleaming as he walked into the kitchen. The clock above the stove showed 7:43 a.m. He looked outside the kitchen window. The town was engulfed in a dangerously thick fog. He guessed this happened often. His front door faced the Wisconsin River, only a short distance west of the house.

With a contented sigh, he plucked the coffee pot from the stove and filled it with water. The third heaping scoop of coffee revealed a lump. It wasn't coffee. He picked out a tiny, brown, cloth bag from inside the can. The bag was handmade from a small patch of brown muslin, with a fishing line draw sting. He started the gas flame under the coffee pot and walked to the table to investigate the tiny bag. Carefully, he picked the fishing line loose and dumped the content of the bag into his hand - a small gold key. It was smaller than his thumb nail. The ceiling light glared on the tiny key, making it hard to read the writing scratched along the spine. He turned the key at an angle. Suddenly, coffee spewed all over the top of the stove and onto the floor.

"Damn."

For a few minutes, the key lay forgotten on the table. After he cleaned up the coffee mess on the floor, Carson turned his attention back to the key.

He picked up the key and his cup of coffee and carried them over to the window hoping the softened, defused fog light might make it easier to read the scratches. He set the coffee on the sill while he examined the key. It looked like someone deliberately scratched an inscription on it. S-T-A-L-S. Was it a person? A code? What did it mean?

Absent mindedly he picked up the coffee cup and took a sip. When he replaced the cup, a small movement, from the sill, caught the corner of his eye. He picked up the cup and set it down. Again the sill rocked very slightly.

Curious, he played with the sill, watching it toggle back and forth, like a minuscule seesaw. On closer inspection, he saw a crack in the plaster that outlined the sill. In some places small pieces of plaster had already fallen off.

A shrill ringing interrupted the inspection. It rang four times, before he recognized the sound as the phone. For a moment he stood there confused. The phone wasn't supposed to be hooked until the end of the day. It rang three more times before he answered it.

"Hello." He wasn't sure who'd be on the other end.

"Hello, Mr. Grey."

"Yes."

"This is the Commonwealth Phone Company. We're just calling to test your hook-up and to tell you your party line number is 537."

"Thanks. Is there..."

The operator hung up on him without letting him finish his question.

He went back to the kitchen and the key. Why was a key buried in the coffee? How long had it been there? Who put it there and why? He decided to take it with him to the police station. He'd show Ben the key, give him his phone number and get directions to Floyd Whitefeather's.

****

Libby, the sheriff's department ever-dependable secretary, sat typing away at her Underwood when Carson walked into the police station.

"Can I help you?" A tall lanky man with 'Deputy Johnson' on his badge approached Carson.

"I'm here to see Sheriff Lyman."

"He's out on a call now. Don't know when he'll be back. Can I help you?" He offered again.

Libby walked between the two men to a tall black file cabinet.

"Nice to see you again, Mr. Grey." She continued with her task, doggedly digging through the center drawer, until she found the file she needed.

"Mr. Grey!" Deputy Johnson tripped over his own large feet on his way to shake Carson's hand. "I didn't know you were Mr. Grey. Sheriff Lyman told me a little bit about the case you two are working on. Let's go in here," he indicated to Ben's office, "where we can talk more."

Carson winked at Libby as she smothered a giggle, watching Deputy Johnson assume control of the station.

"Can I get you a cup of coffee? Libby here makes the best coffee in town. I'm not joking."

"No thanks. I've had my fill of coffee this morning."

Carson sat in the visitor chair as Deputy Johnson eased himself into Ben's chair.

"Are you expecting Sheriff Lyman to call and check in soon?"

"Probably not. He's at Lucas Wheeler's. Lucas calls about once a week." Deputy Johnson raised his eyebrows and shook his head. "Someone has rustled his cattle, he swears. It did happen once. Someone took a calf, years ago. Now, every time a cow goes through a fence and can't be accounted for, he calls here, sure it's happened again."

"Is rustling a problem here?"

"No. Not really. The problem is the condition of Lucas' fences. So, what can I tell Sheriff Lyman for you?"

"I need directions to Floyd Whitefeather's and I found this," he pulled the key from his pants pocket and gave it to the deputy, "in with my ground coffee this morning."

"It's a key."

"Yes. I know. It's a key. What do you think it belongs to?"

Deputy Johnson turned it over again and again while he examined it.

"I don't know."

"I was hoping Sheriff Lyman might be able to help me with that and tell me if there is any significance to the scratching on the spine."

Deputy Johnson held the key close to his face and turned it at an angle in the light.

"Let's see. S-T-A-L-S," he said. "It's not anybody's name that I know of, at least, not anyone around here. But it might be a place."

"A place."

"Yeah. The Catholic Church in town is St. Als. Short for St. Aloysius. Get it? S-T-A-L-S."

Carson took the key back from Deputy Johnson and waited, while the man wrote down directions to Floyd Whitefeather's.

"Thanks, I'll look into St. Als." Carson got up to leave. "One more thing." Carson wrote in the corner of the directions Deputy Johnson just gave him. He tore the corner off and handed it to Deputy Johnson. "Could you give this to Sheriff Lyman. It's my phone number."

"Ya know," Deputy Johnson blurted out putting Carson's phone number in a shirt pocket. "That key looks like it might belong to one of them little diary books like my daughter has."

"Diary book?"

"Yeah. That's what it looks like to me."

"Thanks." Carson took another look at the key before he put it back into the little muslin bag, then slipping the bay into his pocket.

As he walked to his car, a flurry of questions collided in his mind. A diary key? Who's diary? If not a diary, then what did it belong to? Did Esther put in there as some point and forgot about it? Did it belong to Laura? She admitted she spent a lot of time at the house. Maybe she needed to hide something from Peter. Or, was this one more enigma about Peter and his penchant for secrecy Carson would never understand?

Chapter Nine

Floyd Whitefeather lived north of Sauk City between Baraboo and Wisconsin Dells on an old back road.

Once Carson got to the outer limits of Wisconsin Dells, he knew he'd driven too far.

He'd heard of the Wisconsin Dells even before coming to Wisconsin, from travel brochures. In the 1890s, H.H. Bennett, Wisconsin Dells' favorite photographer, made the area a vacation hot spot for people in big cities like Chicago. Then local officials decided to flood the area and build a dam to encourage industries to set up shop. Not one business took advantage of the dam. Because of the dam, many of the locations Bennett took pictures of the Dells natural beauty would never be seen again.

The ground fog burnt off, and it promised to become another swelteringly hot and humid day.

Hay fields, on both sides of the road, lay flat waiting for the farmers to rake it into neat tumbled rows to dry: unlikely to happen today. The smell of freshly cut clover hung in the air.

Rounding a corner he swung down into the valley toward Baraboo. As Wisconsin Dells had its favorite son, so did Baraboo; Al Ringling, of circus fame, called Baraboo home.

If Deputy Johnson's alternate directions were correct, Highway 33, east of Baraboo, should connect with Highway A. So much for the comment, "You can't miss it." Carson knew he should have followed his gut instincts in the first place, instead of taking what looked like the easier route. Once on Highway 33, he had the road all to himself. Not wanting to miss the driveway to Floyd's, Carson drove at a slower speed and enjoyed the scenery.

According to the calendar, it was still spring for another week or two, and the abundant fauna and flora of the area was breath taking. Queen Anne's Lace, lilacs, violets, lilies, and an array of other wild flowers lined the road, making the ditches look like a rainbow banner. A young doe with her spotted twin fawns casually turned and looked up from their morning feeding in the uncut hayfield, next to a wooded area. Birds scooped up insects that hovered around the tall grass. The variances of green, from the leaves of different types of trees and grass would make a painter's pallet envious.

"I forgot just how beautiful the countryside can be," Carson said out loud.

So wrapped up in the scenery, he could easily miss Whitefeather's place. Ahead, in the middle of a field, stood a deserted barn, surrounded by tall pine trees and bushes. A car pulled around to the front of the barn and stopped. It was the sun's reflection off the silver car that caught Carson's attention.

Something about this didn't feel right. Carson cut the car engine and let it coast into the shallow ditch beside a fence covered in wild grape vines and ripe wild black berries. Slowly, carefully, he clicked the car door shut and crouched down next to the fence. He pried back the young, wet, malleable vines.

A car, identical in every detail to his, sat empty in front of the large, weather-beaten, double door barn. The barn's white paint had faded or chipped off with time, leaving it a washed out gray. The spider web cracks in the cement foundation showed layers of old caked mud. Dry, cracked and chipped barn boards cried out for repairs that would never be made. Centered above the double doors was another small door. Above that, a pulley attached to the barn. The frayed remains of a rope curled around and hung from the rusty pulley.

Suddenly, a tall darkly garbed man came out of the barn. The wide brim, dark hat, identical to Carson's, prevented him from clearly seeing who the man was. The man opened the car's trunk and rearranged some contents. He lifted a small wooden box. The weight of the box caused the man to walk awkwardly back into the barn. Within a few moments, he reappeared again. Back at the car trunk, he gathered up dusty burlap bags and a brown suit case and carried them into the barn. Again, the man went from the barn to the trunk. This time his burden appeared to be large and heavy, but Carson couldn't see exactly what it was.

Carson noticed the man seemed to be in a hurry and too preoccupied to pay attention to the surroundings. Carson doubled back along the fence row until he reached the woods. Then he ran through the woods and the adjacent field. The early morning fog had saturated the grass, making footsteps as quiet as possible. He ran to a row of bushes behind the barn for cover feeling sure the bushes would supply ample camouflage. Hunched low, he pulled a small leaf-laden twig away from a bush. Mosquitoes swarmed around his eyes and ears, biting any unexposed part of his body.

From this vantage point, he realized why the car parked in the front of the barn; the back of the building had no door. Over the buzzing in his ear, he heard the sound of a car engine starting. He stood up ready to run to the front of the barn. He had to see where the car was going. Just then, the car drove around the back side of the barn. Quickly, he ducked back down behind the bushes and hoped the driver hadn't spotted him.

An old truck, in need of a muffler, barreled down the road past the barn. Probably a local farmer. But, who was the owner of this car? Farmers don't drive cars like his. When Peter bought his car, he'd pulled a few strings and cashed in a few favors. He wanted his car to be special: the only 1941 silver Cadillac convertible coupe with black leather interior coming off the line in Detroit. He'd bragged about what having connections could do. Now a duplicate car was parked several yards away from Carson.

Also, farmers didn't dress like this man, either. In fact, his clothes were exactly like his; the same style of coat and hat in exactly the same color. Whoever this guy was, he chose this isolated spot for a reason and he didn't want to be seen clearly. And if he was seen, he wanted everyone to believe that he was Carson.

Now it was personal and hauntingly eerie. *Who is this guy and why is he going to such lengths to look like me?*

The driver walked back to the front of the barn the way he'd come, relaxed and less hurried.

As soon as he disappeared around the corner of the barn, Carson bolted to the opposite side. He meant to see the face of the other man, once they both reached the front of the barn.

But, when Carson approached the front of the barn he saw… no one. He faintly heard activity coming from inside. He reached for his gun snug in his shoulder holster and inched his way toward the barn door. Both hands supported the gun. He clutched it close to his chest and pressed his body up against the barn. Gradually, he crept his way to the open door. The damp ground continued to mute his footstep. The scraping from inside the barn became clearer.

At the open doorway, he stuck the barrel of the gun in first. Then he slid inside the door and quickly dove behind the closest object for cover. It took several seconds for his eyes to adjust to his surroundings as he peered over the empty oil barrel in front of him. Besides moldy smelling bales of hay, there were old cracked horse harnesses, pitchforks, ropes, anvils, and other farm equipment. Three small stalls followed by two larger paddocks lined the back of the barn. Loose piles of hay were strewn in the mow.

Shafts of bright light streamed in from the open door and bled between the wall boards. The stark contrast between bright light and murky shadows made it hard to find detail in anything. All the while he was getting his bearings, the scraping sound continued. Now he could distinguish it came from the largest paddock, at the back of the barn, in the corner opposite him.

In the back corner, the silhouette of a form began to take shape. Someone was digging a hole in the dirt floor. They had their back to Carson and seemed to be smaller than the man he saw outside, but, being bent over and in the shadows, made it hard for Carson to see clearly.

Desperately trying not to make any noise, Carson maneuvered, painstakingly slow, from one large object to another for cover, until he was only ten feet away from his prey. At the digger's feet, he saw the small trunk that was carried in earlier next to a large, brown, burlap bundle. The bundle seemed to be about five and a half feet long and loosely tied.

The intent digger stopped, and brought a hand up to the small of their back, and then straightened up to stretch. Carson's heart sank and a name caught in his throat.

"Laura," he whispered out loud.

The woman jerked up and froze at the sound of his voice. She turned enough to give him her profile.

"Laura. Why?"

Before she completely turned around, something hit him from behind. A tide of white, blinding pain overwhelmed him. He trudged forward a few steps, then fell next to the burlap bundle. The last thing he remembered seeing was the shocked, wide-eyed, dead face of the Wringer, Charlie Ballard, peeking out from a corner of the torn burlap.

****

Carson didn't know how long he'd been knocked out. He guessed not long. He knew he had to get out of there, fast. Smoke stung his eyes and filled his lungs. Pulling himself up onto a bale of hay, he coughed hard as the smoke thickened. Flames all around him eliminated all possible escape routes. It quickly became harder to breathe or see. The closed front door made the barn a tinder box that would be totally engulfed in flames within minutes.

It seemed like an eternity, but he finally stumbled to the front double doors. They were jammed from the outside. From the space between the doors, he could see a pitchfork pulled through the handles, making it impossible to get out. *Focus.* He thought to himself. *This is no time to panic.* Parts of the roof fluttered to the floor and ignited anything it touched. Eyes stinging from sweat and smoke, head pounding, he knew he had to find a way out now, or be burned alive.

He crawled over to a barrel and grabbed onto both ends, thankful it was empty. Now he had a battering ram. He looked through the smoke for the closest wall. Ignited debris, from the roof, fell onto his back starting his shirt on fire. He dropped to the ground in pain, but cognizant enough to know he had to roll on the dirt floor to put out the flames even though it wasted precious time. The heat intensified and smoke thickened with every second.

Desperation set in. Still light-headed from the hit, and eyes burning, he tried to take a deep breath, but it brought on a fit of coughing. Again, he grabbed the barrel at both ends, holding it over his head, taking several long strides to what he hoped was the closest wall. With every ounce of strength he had, he hurled the barrel at the wall. He barely heard the sound of wood splintering over the crackling fire within. He continued his forward motion, arms stretched out, until he felt the gap in the wall where the barrel broke through. The opening was barely large enough for him to crawl through.

The smoke had won. He collapsed, not knowing if he had gotten out of the burning building or not. Just before he slipped out of consciousness, he felt a burning sensation at his shoulders.

Chapter Ten

Four days passed, and Carson felt more than ready to leave the hospital; his doctor did not feel the same way. But, Dr. Bellany, begrudgingly, agreed to let him go home. Displaying a set jaw and a scowl, he drilled his signature on Carson's release form from Badger Hospital. Carson made an attempt to get out of bed as soon as the doctor's pen stopped moving.

"You're not released until this afternoon, Mr. Grey. Until then, you are going to stay in bed."

As soon as Dr. Bellamy left the room, Carson, again, tried to get out of bed. He barely sat up, before he began to sway off balance. A young nurse walking by the door saw him teetering. She rushed in the room and wrapped her arm around his back for support. Carson ignored her excessive hug as she eased him back down in a prone position.

"Let's get you back to bed," she insinuated a little too invitingly. "We can't have you getting hurt again."

She was helpful, too helpful. At first he was grateful, but he had since changed his mind. From the second he opened his eyes and realized where he was, *she* was always around. All the young single nurses paid him too much attention for his comfort level. No matter how he tried to be indifferent, this nurse kept showing up in his room.

"I'm being released today and need to call someone to pick me up. Can you make that phone call for me?"

"That's okay, nurse. You don't have to make any calls. I'll be taking Mr. Grey home." Neither Carson nor the nurse saw Ben standing in the doorway.

"How long have you been here?"

"Oh, off and on, the better part of four days."

"Really?"

"Really."

"Why?"

"Deputy Johnson told me about your visit when I got back from Lucas Wheeler's farm. Then the call came in that the old Metzer barn was on fire, and you were there."

"I'll get you some fresh water and be right back." The nurse smoothed over his bed sheet, folded back the blanket and fluffed the pillows behind his head. "If you need anything else, I'll be just outside the door."

Ben laughed. He walked into the room dragging a metal, straight-backed chair next to the bed.

"What's so funny?" Carson asked Ben.

"I don't touch anyone that much when I'm frisking them."

"What?"

"Never mind. How are you feeling?"

"I've been better. Could be worse."

The nurse bustled back into the room with a fresh pitcher of water. The conversation between the men stopped while she was there. Again, she fluffed the pillows and straightened the wrinkles out of the sheet covering Carson. She toyed with the curtains casting Carson an inviting smile and finally left the room.

"What happened out there at the barn?"

"I missed my turn to Floyd Whitefeather's when I took Deputy Johnson's directions. So I turned around and tried to get there going through Baraboo."

"Why didn't you go that way in the first place?"

"Because the other way looked easier. Then I saw a car. There is a guy driving a car, exactly like mine, and dressed like me, just like Esther said. I tried to get closer for a better look at him. I heard some noise in the barn and went in to investigate. That's when I was hit. That's all I remember."

Carson just couldn't bring himself to tell Ben about the woman in the barn. He wanted to hear from Laura what her involvement was and why.

"Your story puts a few more pieces together for me. This other car at the barn, was it exactly like yours - Peter Franke's?"

"Yes. Exactly like *my* car."

"No one said anything about this car to me before. Your car is pretty flashy for this part of the country."

Ben's eye brows furrowed and he stared out the window.

"Why would anyone think it was a duplicate car if we weren't seen together? People would naturally assume that it was me behind the wheel."

"They found charred human bones out there. Any idea who they belong to?"

"Charlie Ballard."

Ben heaved a long, sad sigh. He got up and went to the window, as if removing himself from the chair would also remove the responsibility of the phone call. It was easy for Carson to read Ben's actions. In the quiet, bucolic setting like Sauk City, murders upset the balance of nature. Lately, far too many dark, unexplained things happened here.

Dr. Bellamy burst into the room shadowed by Carson's nurse.

"Hello Ben. Did you tell him yet?" He stopped and turned to the nurse, who stood at Carson's bed side. "You can go now, nurse. Close the door on your way out."

She walked to the door and turned around for one more look at her patient. She opened her mouth as if to say something, but Dr. Bellamy's glare changed her mind. Reluctantly, she exited the room and closed the door.

"Not yet doc, but now I know whose body it was."

"Is anyone going to tell me what's going on?" Carson asked volleying looks between Dr. Bellamy and Ben.

"You're here, alive, because someone just happened to be on that road that morning in time to save your skin." Ben returned to his recently vacated chair and locked eyes with Carson. "He just happened to pick that morning to check in on his ill parents."

"Who was it?"

"Harold Maier."

"I'll have to thank him, before I go home," Carson calmly said.

Dr. Bellamy cleared his throat. "I can't allow you to do that."

Again, Carson looked at the two men for an explanation. Ben gave him the story.

"It seems Harold saw a cloud of dirt on the driveway ahead of him. When he cleared the woods, he saw your car parked on the side of the road and flames shooting out of the roof of the barn. He drove to the barn and saw you crawling through the side of the building. By the time he reached you, you were unconscious. He tried to pull you away from the burning building. But, burning shingles fell next to his truck's gas tank. The explosion threw him thirty feet, luckily away from the fire. He's been mostly unconscious ever since both of you were brought in."

"If he's unconscious, how do you know what happened?"

"Well," Ben continued, "partly by being at the site. We were able to piece together part of the story. Some of it came from Harold's delirious ramblings, until the medication kicked in. And then there's the statement taken from the milk truck driver, who called in the fire. He was on his way back from a pick up when he saw the flames and you and Harold. Now, with your account, I have more pieces of this story."

Carson returned his attention to Dr. Bellamy.

"How bad is Mr. Maier?"

"Fractured skull, four broken ribs, broken femur; his whole body is one big bruise. We were able to stop the internal bleeding."

"Marie has hardly left his side," Ben added.

"I ordered her to go home late last night," Dr. Bellamy said with authority. "She started to look as bad as her husband. I told her if she didn't get some sleep, I would admit her, and then she wouldn't be able to see Harold at all. That finally got to her."

The three men sat in silence for a moment. Sounds of muffled voices, shuffling feet and medicine cart wheels on the hallway floor filtered into the room.

The grievousness of the situation reiterated to Carson the urgent necessity to solve Peter's murder before any more innocent people were hurt or killed. The burden of Harold Maier's injuries and Charlie's death weighed heavily on him. He squirmed to sit up.

"Who's running Harold's farm?"

Carson nodded his thanks as Dr. Bellamy helped him sit up higher in bed.

"The whole community. The neighborhood wives are doing all they can for Marie and the kids. The men are taking turns doing the milking and fieldwork, around their own farm work."

Two knocks hit the door and it opened wide enough for Deputy Johnson's to stick his head through.

"Excuse me. Sheriff, I need to speak with you for a moment."

Ben stopped at the door.

"I'll be back to pick you up around two o'clock. That sound about right, doc?"

Dr. Bellamy nodded his approval.

The appointed time came and went and still no Ben. The only person pleased with the present situation was Carson's self-appointed, personal nurse. Dr. Bellamy initially intended to be with Carson when Ben came, but a hand injury at the plant required immediate surgery. He had no choice but to place Carson in the care of the nurse. Carson watched the clock, like a person on death row. He decided he would leave on his own, if Ben didn't show up soon.

When Ben strolled into the hospital, he took one look at Carson's *save me* expression, and quickened his pace.

"Thank you nurse, I'll take it from here." Ben grabbed the handles of the wheelchair and started to walk out the front door, before she had time to react. Carson could feel her immeasurable disappointment that he never looked back.

"You'll have to get used to less attentive care from now on," joked Ben.

"You mean I'll be able to truly get some rest." Carson laughed a feeling a freeness he hadn't felt in days.

The fresh air and direct sunlight were refreshing. He had block out the sun's bright glare with his hand until his eyes adjusted.

"Thanks, Ben, for extricating me from her clutches. A few more minutes with her, and I'd be guilty of a homicide. Where the hell were you, anyway? You said two o'clock."

Ben's chuckling annoyed Carson. He continued pushing the wheelchair to his car and was about to open the car door when Carson caught something small, fast and red out of the corner of his eye. Stevie Maier threw himself at Carson, fists flying.

"It's all you're fault. Because of you, my dad might die."

Flushed faced and winded, Marie caught up with her son. It took both Ben and Marie several moments to peel Stevie off of Carson, who could only stop the flying fists by holding up his arms to block the blows. Stevie took no notice of Ben trying to restrain him.

"None of this would have happened if you weren't here." Stevie continued through his tears.

"Steven, that's enough. We'll talk about this later."

Marie never looked at Carson or acknowledged his presence. She also never apologized for Stevie's behavior. Eventually, she calmed down the agitated boy. Ben released the tiger-boy to his mother, who took him by the hand, while they walked to the hospital. Marie talked in a quiet and soothing tone to Stevie all the way.

"She believes that too, doesn't she? She believes I'm responsible. I can't blame her, I guess. Does everybody else think that?"

Ben didn't answer the question. He helped Carson into the car and took the wheelchair back to the hospital. By the time Ben got back to the car, Carson was ready to continue investigating Peter's murder.

"Before you take me back into town, I have a favor to ask."

"What is it?"

"I need to talk to Laura Bradshaw. Can you take me to her place?"

"Sorry, I can't do that."

"Why not?"

Ben started the car and looked over at Carson.

"Because she asked me to keep you away from her."

"What? When was this?"

"The night before all of this happened. She called me at home and said you took her from work to lunch and grilled her on a lot a personal stuff."

"I was doing my job."

"Look, all I know is this: she feels that you crossed the line between personal and professional questioning. From now on, anything you want to say to her goes through me."

"You're not serious."

"Yeah, I am. Now, let's get you home. Don't worry about food. Libby's been beside herself with worry for you. When she worries, she cooks. I expect your refrigerator is full of casseroles of some kind, and there is probably an apple pie around there, too."

I can't believe she won't see me.

"One more thing. I was going to tell you this once you felt better, but now is as good a time as any; Floyd Whitefeather seems to have left the area."

"Great." Carson rubbed his forehead in frustration.

"How'd Libby get in the house?" Carson asked, breaking the tension he felt inside himself.

"I gave her a key. I got another one from Esther's sister so Libby could put the food in the house and see if there was any undue interest in the place."

"How do you mean, undo interest?"

"I don't know if the accident at the barn was just that or if someone tried to kill you. So I had you kept in the hospital for four days instead of three, with a little help from Dr. Bellamy. I also had the house watched, to see if anyone else was interested in it during your absence. Remember that broken window? Libby going inside was a way for me to see if anyone got in past my guard. She said the place was as clean as a whistle, so I pulled my guy this morning. It appears no one, besides Libby, cared about you being in the hospital."

Carson didn't feel like talking or listening anymore. All of his plans were eroding and there seemed nothing he could do about it. Laura found a way to make sure he couldn't see or talk to her and during his stay in the hospital, a person he needed to talk left the area. He felt like his hands were tied as far as Laura was concerned. She knew something and purposely never intended to share it. What was she doing at the barn and who was she with? The rest of the way home he looked out the car window watching cows graze in verdant, lush pastures, farmers making hay and rural country life calmly going on with its daily routine untouched by the ugliness of the murders surrounding them.

They pulled up to the front of Carson's house and stopped. Ben started to open his door, when Carson grabbed him by the arm.

"That's okay, Ben. I can make it from here."

"Tommy and I still expect to see you Monday night for dinner."

"I'll be there."

Carson grabbed his coat and hat and slowly climbed out of the car. He walked to the front door and watched Ben drive away. One step inside the front door, nausea washed over him, and he regretted not having Ben at his side.

Chapter Eleven

The house had been ransacked. Carson automatically reached inside his coat for the gun in his shoulder holster. Thankfully, Ben gave it back to him in the car. The memory of the last time he held his gun swiftly fluttered through his mind. Just as quickly, he banished the thought. He couldn't permit that memory to surface now. Whoever did this could still be in the house. All his attention and focus turned to looking for any sudden movement or unnecessary shadows.

Every piece of furniture, lamps and pictures in the living room were turned upside down and on the floor. He edged out of the living room and glanced into the kitchen, knowing there was no place for anyone to hide there. He saw the door leading outside still locked from the inside. With the exception of every cupboard drawer being pulled out and its contents dumped on the floor, the kitchen hid no one and suffered no real damages.

Still weak from the accident, every cautious step down the hallway was laborious. His lean frame used the wall for support as well as cover. As he closed in on the back rooms, he surveyed the bathroom from the hallway, using the medicine cabinet mirror to view the whole room - again, an empty room. That only left his bedroom and the adjoining back porch to check on this level of the house. He hugged the wall the last few steps to the bedroom doorway. Crouching down as low as his body would endure, he peeked around the door. The door leading to the back porch stood wide open.

He used the mirror on the dresser and saw an empty porch. He lurched to the opposite side of the door frame, inside the bedroom. The bedding, mattress, and pillows lay in a pile in the center of the room along with his clothes. The dresser drawers were pulled out and the closet door opened. There was one addition to the room's decor. Above the headboard frame, written in bright, red lipstick, a warning: SHE'S NEXT. His knees buckled, and a cold shiver ran down his back.

Stevie Maier's accusations rang in Carson's head. *'It's all you're fault. None of this happened before you came.'* Stevie was right. Somehow, his being there put innocent people's lives in jeopardy. Gentle, little Charlie Ballard, dead. And Harold Maier clung to life. They never asked to be caught up in this. Carson was now convinced he somehow played a part in this chess game. His next move could cost someone else their life: someone like Laura.

The sound of the front door clicking carried through the quiet house. Slow, deliberate footsteps made their way through the rooms Carson had just checked out. The footsteps stopped at the hallway. Carson steadied his gun. He heard the other person unlock the safety on their gun.

"I know you're in the bedroom. Come out with your hands above your head. My deputies are on their way."

Relief bathed over Carson at the sound of Ben's voice. He crumbled to the floor.

"Ben, it's me, Carson," he said in a weak drained voice.

"Carson, are you alone?"

"Yes."

Before Carson could get up, Ben entered the room, his gun drawn.

"Jesus, Peter, Mary and Joseph. What the hell happened here?"

"You tell me. I thought you had it guarded, and Libby said it was clean."

"I started to drive back to the station, and then remembered I forgot to give you Esther's extra key. You didn't answer my knock. I knew you were here. I looked in through the living room window and saw the mess. Then I called for backup."

"Thanks, Ben. Would you help me up? My legs aren't cooperating today."

Cautiously, Ben helped Carson to his feet. He walked to the closest corner in the room and turned over a forest green, winged back chair.

"You've got some explaining to do. What really happened here?"

"What are you saying? Look at the place. Someone tore this place apart."

"Conveniently, nothing is broken, just messed up."

"You think I did this."

"Maybe. I don't know. I don't know how you could in your condition, but maybe you're in better shape than you let on? What would you think if you were in my shoes? Libby came here this morning, and nothing was out of place. My guy saw no one come or go for four days and nights. I drop you off from the hospital, drive halfway back to the station then come back. By the time I get back here, it looks like a tornado went through. What am I supposed to think?"

"I don't know. Maybe you're supposed to think that I'm here to solve Peter Franke's murder."

The sound of the front door opening silenced both men. Simultaneously, their heads snapped up at the sound.

"Sheriff Lyman? Sheriff, are you here?" Deputy Johnson's hesitant voice cut through the air.

"Yeah, back here, in the bedroom."

Two sets of footsteps trotted down the hallway to the bedroom. Guns drawn, Deputy Johnson and another deputy tentatively entered the bedroom.

"We came as soon as could."

The other deputy offered no explanation and stayed purposely in the background. Carson watched him observe all the damage in the house and the message on the wall. Everything about him suggested average; height, weight, looks. He could easily blend into any crowd and no one would remember seeing him.

"Thanks, Deputy Johnson. I want you and Deputy Orlanger to pick up things here. I'll take care of Mr. Grey."

For a second, Deputy Johnson didn't move, his eyes still fixated on Ben's drawn gun. It was only when Deputy Orlanger poked him in the ribs and nodded toward the hallway that they departed.

"Don't make this any harder than it needs to be. I want to believe you, but look at it from my point of view as an officer of the law. Stand up. I'm going to cuff you. We'll leave nice and quiet and continue our conversation in my car."

Totally dumbfounded, Carson did as he was told.

Ben draped Carson's coat over his shoulder, hiding the cuffs. Carson couldn't understand what Ben was trying to do. Neighbors had seen Ben's car at the house before. Was this out of respect for him, or protection, or did Ben not want to look like the bad guy?

After being carefully secured in the front seat of Ben's car, Carson watched in amazement as Ben smiled and waved at the oncoming traffic, in his best folksy, business-as-usual manner. Without looking at Carson, he started the car and pulled away.

"Let's get a few things straight. I don't know if you are innocent or a crack pot. I know you were in Algiers when Peter Franke was murdered. You have the British Prime Minister as an alibi. I also know a young lady, who otherwise has an unblemished reputation in this community, calls me at home and begs me to keep you away from her. The very next day, you claim to find a mysterious key in your coffee. Then you manage to be found crawling out of a burning barn. You, and only you, saw this phantom duplicate car at the barn. You identified the corpse in the barn as Charlie Ballard. Ten minutes after you're home from the hospital, which was watched and visited by my people, I find you alone in it, and the place is ransacked. Have I left out anything? I can't legally charge you with anything, but I can make your life and this investigation a whole lot harder if you don't cooperate. You follow me?"

Instead of driving directly to the police station, Ben turned the opposite direction as if to give them more time to talk in the car. As they drove past the Bonham Theater, Carson couldn't help but notice the irony in the title of the current movie playing: *Somewhere I'll Find You*, starring Clark Gable and Lana Turner.

The undeniable circumstantial evidence of Ben's list gnawed at Carson. He knew what it looked like. He couldn't argue with any of it. Whoever was in that other car, at the barn, seemed to have a plan or vendetta against him? He also seemed to be one step ahead of Ben as well.

"Tell me, who knew I was being released from the hospital today?"

"Just the doctor, the nurse and myself. I didn't plan on running into the Maiers, so they know, and now, two of my deputies know. Why?"

"Someone else did, too."

"Well, whoever it was, if it wasn't you who tore your place apart, they won't be back. Either they found what they wanted, or they didn't."

"I'll play your game, but I want something in return."

"You're not in a position to be making demands."

By now, they reached the police station. They drove to the back side of the U.S. Hotel to use the back door, again avoiding undue attention.

"You don't even know what it is that I want." Ben remained silent. "No one is to know that I'm here, outside of your people. That other car will show up again, I know it."

Ben remained stoic.

"If this other person believes I'm out of the hospital, they'll come out of hiding and will eventually be seen driving that car. By the way, where is *my* car?"

"Your car is at my house, in my garage. I'm fine with your idea, with a few conditions of my own. Any and all phone calls you get or make, I approve of first, and I listen to the conversation."

"Agreed. I won't be making any calls or getting any. No one knows I'm here – right?"

"Sit forward and turn your back around to me, so I can take those cuffs off."

Obediently Carson turned his back around to Ben. He grimaced as Ben pulled his right shoulder further back to slide the key into the lock.

"One more thing." Ben waited until Carson finished rubbing his wrist and ready to listen. "None of this is talked about in Libby's presence. All she is to think is that I felt it better for you to recuperate here than at the house, around people who could help you if needed. She is to know nothing about the mess in the house, and you're to act as a guest around here, not my prisoner."

"Forced guest, don't you mean."

"I'll give your plan one week. If that other car doesn't show up, I'll book you in a heartbeat for the murder of Charlie Ballard and the arson of Metzer's barn."

With that said he got out of the car and walked around to Carson's car door. He gripped Carson by the upper arm with one hand and unlocked the building's back door. The pitch black interior flashed bright when Ben pulled on the light cord.

The back room of the police station held one lonely empty cell, complete with a sink and a hardly used cot, covered with a handmade patchwork quilt. The grimy miniature window allowed only the barest of light. The remaining area held discarded equipment and furniture to be used for parts or emergencies.

"Make yourself at home, since that's what it'll be for the next week or so. I'll have Deputy Johnson bring your clothes back with him."

****

Three days went by, and there was not a single sighting of the other '41 silver Cadillac coupe. In that time, Libby did her level best to put all of the weight back on Carson he lost in the hospital. Daily, she brought in a hot dish from home, so he would have at least one hot meal every day. Although he had other things on his mind, he had to admit, he looked forward to her meals.

William Denby called and talked to Ben, only because he couldn't reach Carson at the house. It wasn't until the following day that Ben told Carson about the phone call. Ben told Denby that Carson was still working on the case and hard to get in touch with. If any pertinent details came to light within the week, Denby could be assured of being informed.

Around lunch time on the fifth day, Libby went home to make a quick hot meal for everyone at the station. It became commonplace having Carson there. The radio played a Glenn Miller tune in the background. Deputies Johnson and Orlanger talked freely around him about their police business. The friendship between Ben and Carson remained strained. Most of the time, Ben sat in his office going over paperwork. Time was running out for Carson, and he knew Ben wondered if he made a mistake. If he had booked Carson for Charlie's murder, as soon as he was released from the hospital, maybe the deputies wouldn't be so casual around him.

Libby whirled back into the station casserole in hand. She seemed annoyed that none of the deputies cleaned off a place to eat. As fast as she cleared off her desk, the men replaced the same area with the contents from her basket. Just as she opened the lid to the casserole, the phone rang.

"Sauk City Police Department," she said replacing the lid with her free hand. "Sheriff Lyman, just one moment please." Using her hand, she covered the receiver and called out to Ben. "Sheriff, the phone is for you. Be quick about it. Your dinner is gettin' cold."

Ben smiled at her motherly scolding. He put his plate down and took the phone out of Libby's hand.

"Sheriff Lyman, can I help you? Whoa, just a minute. Start over, please, and go slow." He waited a few seconds before responding to the caller. "Are you sure? Where are you now? Okay. Do you know where we are? Can you come by now? Good, I'll see ya then."

Ben handed the phone back to Libby. His mood shifted. He openly smiled for the first time in days.

"Hope ya got enough for one more, Libby. I'm expecting a visitor. I think she might be hungry once she smells your cookin'."

In the midst of doling out the day's hot meal, a young woman breezed through the station door.

She had short black hair and black frame glasses, and she came across as the no-nonsense type. Her black pant suit hugged her tiny, wiry, five-foot-two frame. Before anyone had a chance to speak, the tiny dynamo shot her hand forward for a handshake.

"Sheriff Lyman. Thank you for seeing me on such short notice." Still holding on to Ben's hand, her eyes locked with his.

Ben became uncomfortable with the connection knowing everyone watched the exchange.

"Can I offer you coffee, casserole, pie?" Ben said awkwardly.

The young woman looked around the office at everyone.

"Oh, I am sorry. I didn't mean to interrupt lunch. I guess I forgot the time."

"That's okay, Miss... Osmond, is it? Let's go into my office and talk about your suspicions."

"Call me Bess, please," she said, blushing.

Between the second and third helpings, Ben had been forgotten, until he came out of his office and motioned for Carson to join them. Carson carried the chair he was sitting on into Ben's office, curious as to why he was being summoned.

"Thanks for joining us. Miss Osmond has quite a story. I thought you'd be interested in hearing it." Ben indicated a small space on the other side of Miss Osmond for Carson to place his chair.

"Really?" Carson answered curiously.

"Yes. She's here to fill out a missing persons report."

Carson threw Ben a confused look. He hadn't been in the area long enough to know anyone, let alone know if they were missing.

"Who's missing?" Carson asked.

"Carson Grey," Ben replied with a smile.

The young woman's face reflected total sincerity.

"Tell me Miss Osmond, do you know Carson Grey?"

"No, sir."

"No." He repeated her answer. "Then how do you know he is missing?"

"Sheriff Lyman, I'm very good at what I do. About two weeks ago, I learned an agent from Washington, Mr. Grey, arrived here to investigate the murder of another Washington agent, Peter Franke. I know Mr. Grey was staying at a boarding house here in town until about a week ago. From there, he moved into the same house Mr. Franke occupied. Then I heard he was involved in a barn fire and hospitalized for several days. From then on, no one has seen him. I have a problem with that part of it."

"What part is it exactly that you don't agree with?" Ben asked.

"From his supposed release from the hospital until today."

"Why is that?"

"Because I know he was in Madison five days ago."

"He was in Madison five days ago," Ben again calmly repeated her answer as if questioning her facts. "And how do you know that?"

"When I talked to the boarding house owner eight days ago, he said he'd hardly talked with Mr. Grey, but he described his car to me. It's a silver 1941 Cadillac coupe, and I saw it five days ago in Madison."

Sweet vindication. If only he knew for sure how the woman would react, Carson would have kissed her. Her knowledge of his life spooked him, but it was also going to spring him from Ben's forced hospitality.

"Why are you taking such a stake in Mr. Grey? Did you see him in Madison?" Carson asked.

She shook her head, finally taking her eyes off Ben long enough to answer Carson's question.

"My interest is professional. Men don't take women crime reporters seriously. If I can help Mr. Grey solve his colleague's death, maybe my colleagues, back in Madison, will start to see that I'm just as good at my job as they are. But, I never saw Mr. Grey that day, only the car."

"Miss Osmond, Bess," Ben grabbed back her attention, "do you know who this man is here on your left?"

"No." She answered totally sincere.

"I'd like to introduce you to Mr. Carson Grey - your missing person."

Her neck and face washed over in red. She tried to hide her embarrassment by stammering out her next question. "Mr. Grey, where have you been the last five days?"

Before Carson could answer, Libby opened the door and announced she would be out of the office for a short time: taking the dirty dishes and empty casserole bowl home. Should Ben need her, he would have to wait until she returned.

"That'll be fine, Libby. Go ahead, and do what you need to do." He knew she would be back in five minutes because she lived only a few blocks away and she hated missing anything.

She shot Ben one last glare before closing the door. They all listened to the fleeting tap of her shoes trotting across the office.

For a second, Bess Osmond seemed to forget that Carson hadn't answered her question. She opened her mouth again, probably to repeat the question, when again a knock on Ben's door stopped her. Carson hopped out of his chair and opened the door. Deputies Johnson and Orlanger blocked the whole frame.

"Lucas Wheeler has a yearling missing. He wants you out there right away."

"You and Deputy Orlanger go and see Lucas. Tell him something has come up. I'll call him later today." Ben nodded for Carson to shut the door, then he called through the closed door. "But first help Libby clean up."

He held up his hand, like he was stopping traffic, and tilted his head. A minute later, the front door to the police station opened and closed.

"Will you excuse Mr. Grey and me for a moment?" He got up and pushed Carson out the door closing it behind them.

"What are you doing?"

"Shhh," hushed Ben, "she could be useful to us – on a need-to-know basis."

"What? How?"

"She has access to things we don't. She did, after all, know an awful lot about your comings and goings. Being a woman, she's more likely to go unnoticed, and she sees things from a different perspective."

Carson threw his arms up in the air. "Well strike up the band for different perspectives – whoopie."

"Shhh. Carson, calm down." Ben pulled Carson over to the far corner of the station. "Now think. For one thing, I can stop you from talking to Laura Bradshaw, but there is nothing stopping her." He tilted his head toward his office. "I've got a gut feeling she can unlock doors we could never get through."

Carson composed himself and took a deep breath, expelling the air through his nose.

"Only on a need-to-know basis and only on peripheral matters. Then, I agree."

They quietly walked back into Ben's office. No one else was in the police station to hear the conversation, but still, they closed the door behind them.

"I'm sorry Miss... Bess. Mr. Grey and I had come to an understanding before we could continue talking with you."

"What kind of understanding?" Her voice filled with apprehension.

"One where we both agreed to set certain boundaries," Carson said firmly.

"Oh. I see," Bess' enthusiasm deflated.

"I don't believe you do. Mr. Grey and I have agreed to share sensitive information with you, because we think you might be able to help us find who killed Peter Franke."

"Really?" She replied too bubbly for Carson.

"But," he jumped in, "you are only to do background research investigating. We don't need anyone trying to be a hero... heroine."

Her eagerness contained, but her eyes danced at the prospect of being involved in the investigation.

"I understand. I hate violence. I'll do whatever you two need me to do." Her face and voice looked and sounded like a child promising to take on all the responsibilities of caring for a new puppy.

They spent the next hour briefing Bess Osmond on the case. There was no mention of the connection between Peter, Laura, and Carson. They didn't mention Charlie Ballard. All they related about the barn fire was that Carson had been injured and saved by a local farmer. The farmer, his family and the hospital were strictly forbidden to her. Ben would handle things there if need be. Finally, she understood, she couldn't have seen Carson in Madison – he was in the hospital, and Ben took him home from there.

"Well, one thing is for certain," she summarized, after the briefing, "you can't drive your car anymore."

"Come again?" Carson said.

"Someone out there knows all about you, and you're helping them achieve whatever it is they are trying to do. You're too obvious. Turn the tables on them."

Carson wanted to knock off the smug smile on Ben's face as the sheriff leaned back in his chair beaming. Ben's glowing *I-told-you-so* look and approving smile to Bess graded on Carson's patience.

"How do you propose I continue this investigation without a car?"

"I'm not suggestion you quit your investigation, Mr. Grey. I'm saying you do it without *that* car. Blend in."

"Go on, Miss Osmond," Ben encouraged.

"Bess, please."

"Excuse me," Carson interrupted, "would you elaborate on your *blend in theory?*"

"Ok. I've got an idea."

"No hero stuff, remember," Carson insisted.

"No hero stuff, right. My parents are in the Middle East now, like they are every summer. While they are gone, you can use their car. I'm sure they wouldn't mind."

Chapter Twelve

After some persuasion from Bess, Carson finally accepted her offer. She and Carson were going over the logistics of getting her parents' car when Deputies Johnson and Orlanger returned from Lucas Wheeler's farm. Their upbeat banter and jokes got too loud for Ben.

"Excuse me. I'd better see what all this commotion is all about," said Ben.

As soon as Ben opened his office door, Deputy Johnson bounded in Ben's office to relate all the details.

"He wants a full investigation into this."

"Into what?"

"There is a young heifer missing, sir."

"Are you sure it just didn't walk through his fence and is out running free somewhere, Deputy?"

"Afraid not, sir. Not this time," Deputy Orlanger continued. "There is evidence it was taken into the woods, and then loaded onto a vehicle."

"What kind of evidence?"

Once Deputy Orlanger began to speak, Carson quit talking to Bess and listened to Ben's conversation with his deputies. Carson felt that between the two deputies, Johnson was the more aggressive, while Orlanger the quieter, smarter, more likely to get all of the facts before forming a conclusion.

"Well sir, there are human footprints going into the woods from Mr. Wheeler's field, followed by a pair of hoof prints. About thirty yards into the woods, small trees and other plants are flattened, and there are tire tracks where the hoof prints end," said Deputy Orlanger, while Deputy Johnson shook his head in agreement.

"I'll be damned. Maybe Lucas isn't a crazy old man after all. That is the fourth or fifth animal that's gone missing this month. Libby!" he called to his secretary knowing she was probably in the back room.

"I didn't know there were others, or I'd have checked over the surroundings better," Deputy Johnson apologized.

"The other incidents happened in other counties. I want you two to write up everything you saw, then call the sheriffs in Dane, Adams, and Columbia County and compare notes. I want to know what the tire tracks are from. I want to know how long they've been there, how an animal might have been removed from the area. I want to know the last time Lucas was in his woods. Libby can help. In fact, have her call the Richland County Sheriff's Department too just to make sure they haven't had any reports of missing livestock." He shifted his attention to Libby who appeared from the back room when Ben started talking. "Libby, I need you to help Deputy Johnson and Orlanger with some phone calls. They'll update you."

Libby rushed to her desk and grabbed the phone book.

"Include in your report every detail you can think of: conversations, who were present, time of day, direction of wind, everything."

Orlanger and Johnson scattered back to their own desks with a sense of purpose and focus.

Ben sat back at his desk. "I think we finally got a small break in the case. It may seem unrelated, but I feel it's connected with Peter Franke's death somehow. So, what have you two come up with?"

"How can this be related?" Carson asked.

"I think our elusive friend may be desperate enough for food that he's helping himself to the local livestock. That's one way to get easy food and money. There are other reports in the area of missing livestock. So, what have you two decided to do?"

Carson sat too absorbed in what Ben had just relayed to answer. He tried to understand someone's motive to steal cattle when they had money from Peter's bank account. Is it the same person? Why take the risk of getting caught stealing? Maybe they already spent Peter's money?

"We've decided it would be best if I stayed here, in Sauk City, until tomorrow morning," said Bess. "Then I'll take Mr. Grey, Carson, to Madison to get my father's car. Mr. Grey has graciously offered me his house for the night. He said it would be no trouble at all for him to stay here at the police station tonight and walk to his house in the morning. Is that acceptable to you, Sheriff?"

The last thing Carson expected Ben to do was laugh.

"I'm sure it's all picked up and clean and you'll be very comfortable there. I accept the arrangement."

Carson threw Ben a nasty hard look.

"I'll use the rest of the day talking to a..." she checked her notepad, "Miss Laura Bradshaw. Carson thinks she's holding back important information. We think if I tell her that I am a reporter with the *Journal*, and that I'm writing a story on women's roles at Badger, she might be more inclined to talk freely."

"Well, Mr. Grey," Ben cajoled Carson, "is there anything you would like to add?"

"Yes there is, Sheriff Lyman," Carson threw back. "While Bess is talking to Laura Bradshaw, I'd like the two of us to pay a visit to Floyd Whitefeather's wife. If you will recall, he's been forgotten."

"Fair enough. I also want to stop out at Lucas Wheeler's. In light of the new information we've just received, I think a personal visit is in order."

****

Carson's last night, as a guest, in the Sauk City Police Station was anything but restful. He waited anxiously for Bess to return to the station and share what she found out from Laura, but she never showed up.

The third shift officer was all business and not very loquacious. Just as well. Since he couldn't sleep, Carson used the time to mentally review the afternoon.

The visit to Floyd Whitefeathers' ended up being a wild goose chase. Floyd, it turned out, hadn't run off trying to avoid any police questioning. He had been in the northern part of the state taking part in the sacred, annual Midewinin Ceremony. At first, he came off reluctant to say where he had been, knowing Midewinin teachings made people outside of the tribe uneasy. His evasive demeanor and the timing of his disappearance told Carson what he needed to know. As soon as he realized where Floyd had been, he quickly advised Ben to back off in trying to get any more information from Floyd. Growing up in Montana,

Carson had heard about the ceremony and respected it. He had no intention of interfering with Floyds culture.

When Ben asked Floyd what he meant at the bar by saying, '*stopping him in time*'. Floyd confirmed that he knew Peter Franke. Floyd heard that Peter was buying up a lot of land, some of it sacred land to his tribe. When confronted, Peter told Floyd he planned to dig up the land for new houses. By stopping him, Floyd meant by legal means. He called the U.S. Department of Interior, who also managed Indian affairs, to see if something could be done to stop Peter from digging up sacred grounds. Nothing sinister was meant by it.

"Why were you at the bar that night?" Ben asked.

"I was going to meet someone at the bar, then we were going to drive to the ceremony from there. I went inside to see if my friend was already there. He wasn't, so I decided to wait for him. I'd been fasting for the ceremony for several days. I guess I fell off out of my chair. Next thing I knew, Sheriff Lyman is standing over me, then he helped me outside."

"Did this other person show up?" Ben asked.

"He came here when he didn't find me at the bar."

"I see."

"Also," Floyd seemed unsure if he should say more.

"Yes," said Ben.

"Some weeks ago I had a vision. I knew it was meant for Mr. Franke. I told him about it and he just laughed at me. I'm still trying to understand the meaning. I saw a snake come out of the body of another identical snake. The snake tried to take a baby bird out of its nest. The mother bird, along with the help of an eagle, fought the snake. Then big waters came, and clouds covered the sun. I never saw what happened in the end."

Thinking about Floyd's dream helped Carson fall asleep, his last night in the Sauk City jail cell.

****

The second he opened the kitchen's side door, she made her first confession of the day.

"I owe you a cup. You really should get that window sill fixed. Before I had a chance to react my first cup of coffee landed on the floor."

"I know how you feel," Carson said, rushing through the kitchen. He barely glanced in the direction of the window sill, on his way down the hall, intent on enjoying his first shower in five days.

He called back over his shoulder, "Give me ten minutes, and I'll be ready to go. Could ya pour me a cup of coffee, too? I left the station before Libby came."

Feeling better than he had for days, a freshly showered and shaved Carson Grey entered the kitchen. His clean shirt casually slung over his shoulder. Like a magnet, he gravitated immediately to the cup of coffee on the kitchen counter waiting for him. He downed the whole cup in one long gulp. Then quickly he slipped into his shirt.

"Let's go. I need that car."

He was out the kitchen door so fast Bess had to run to catch up with him. Only one thing stopped Carson from taking off without Bess; she had the car keys.

"Slow down there, hotshot." She raced up behind him and led him to the passenger's side of the car, indicating to him where he was going to sit. "I'm driving. I know where we're going – you don't!"

To Carson's surprise, Bess Osmond was entertaining and animated. Her quick assessment of people and ability to hear what people were saying, by what they were not saying, was a talent usually found in one much older with more life experience.

She could also quickly read between the lines. Her blatant, honesty and bottom line comments always caught him off guard. Her audacity almost funny.

She trotted to the driver's side and slid in. Jabbing the key in the ignition, she gave Carson a "so there" look. They pulled out onto Water Street and from there they turned left onto Highway 12. Before they even crossed the bridge over the Wisconsin River, Bess started right in speaking her mind.

"So, is Sheriff Lyman married? He isn't wearing a wedding ring – a lot of guys don't wear them, you know. Who are the people in the pictures in his office, his sister or something?"

Carson laughed out loud.

"I believe he is widowed. Why do you ask? He's got to be at least ten years older than you. Why aren't you interested in somebody your own age?"

Totally un-phased by Carson's attempt to tell her to pick on someone her own age, she plowed on, "I guess I get this directness from my mother. My father is 18 years older than my mother. Years ago, my poor, unsuspecting father taught, and still does teach, archaeology at the university."

A smile spread across her lips and lightened her delicate features. She seemed to enjoy telling the story.

"About twenty five years ago, a fiery, Colleen Collins enrolled into his class. She was smart, pretty, young and knew what she wanted. She took one look at the newly appointed professor and never looked back. She said she knew she would marry him before the end of the first class. Dad says he came around to the same way of thinking about a year and a half later. Men are always slower at matters of the heart," she said matter-of-factly. "Anyway, they got married, had me, and now dad is head of the department. Every summer they go on digs somewhere. I get my determination from my mother and my fascination with crime and the dead from my father. You see, we women have this built-in standard that we look for in picking a mate. Some women give in and accept someone below their standard. I won't! I knew instantly that Sheriff Lyman possesses the traits that will compliment my strengths, and I have the traits that will compliment his strengths."

"You detect any weaknesses?" Carson couldn't help being amused and sarcastic.

"Just one."

"Just one? What is that weakness?"

"He appears to be happy and anchored in Sauk City. I don't know if I could be happy living in a small town."

Carson looked out the car window at the azure day and chuckled to himself. Poor Ben. Maybe he should warn him about her, but then, no. Ben always found it amusing when Carson got unwanted attention. Now it was his turn to watch Ben squirm from the attention, especially attention from this little pistol sitting next to him.

The drive to Madison took longer than Carson had anticipated, but he welcomed the opportunity to talk to Bess.

"What did you find out yesterday from your meeting with Laura Bradshaw?"

Bess remained silent, but he couldn't tell whether she was ignoring him or whether she didn't know how to answer him.

"Well, what happened?" he prodded.

"I have another confession to make," she admitted reluctantly. "I knew all about the relationship between Peter Franke, Laura Bradshaw and yourself. I've known about it for more than a week."

Carson's looked at her shocked and ready to say something to Bess, but she hurried on to explain.

"I really did believe you were a missing person. I had to act like I knew nothing. If I went in there and revealed how much I already knew, Sheriff Lyman would have shut the door in my face. I'd be treated like a meddling know-it-all reporter. I always felt there was more to Peter Franke's death. After hearing some of the details yesterday, I'm even more convinced that's true. I want to help in any way I can. Having met both you and Laura, solving this murder goes beyond advancing my career or proving my abilities to my co-workers. Do you believe me?"

"How did you learn about the connection between the three of us?" he asked sternly.

"I told you yesterday, I'm good at what I do. I'm not the only female crime reporter in the country, and I'm not without my resources. I have friends in Washington and New York. We help each other out whenever we can. We're all in the same boat."

The proof of her research ability made Carson reflective and quiet. Maybe Ben was right. She did seem to be able to get information.

He noticed they were in the town of Middleton. This was where Esther lived. They must be close to Madison.

"What did you find out yesterday in your interview with Laura?" he asked again.

Bess looked over her shoulder and changed lanes. More comfortable with her position on the road, she began. "I got to Badger late in the afternoon, and she was angry. Apparently, her boss never showed up for work and never bothered to call. That was the fourth time it happened, except, before he was just late for work. There were always some weak explanations as to why he was late, and he'd have lipstick on his shirt collar. So, this Owen guy, her boss, has a girlfriend named Jean."

"How do you know her name?" Carson tried to imagine Owen with a girlfriend.

"Because Laura said several times when he would be talking to her, he called her Jean. It could be that he was thinking of this other lady when he talked to her. Anyway, with him not showing up for work, that put more responsibility on Laura. The other ladies in the office look to her for answers. She said she had other responsibilities and shouldn't have to do Owen's job, too.

"Like I said, it was late in the day. She suggested we talk where she lives and to follow her home after work. So, I did. Geez, there were kids everywhere. She must have sensed my uneasiness around babies. We talked at a picnic table, under an oak tree, away from the house.

"At first, I think she didn't trust me. Eventually, she opened up a bit about Peter. My gut feeling is that she loved Peter, and still loves you both, but for different reasons. Does that make any sense? I can't say that I'd behave differently than she, given her situation. By the end, I found her to be warm, smart, protective and loyal, besides beautiful. I can see why you fell in love with her."

Carson blushed and felt a little unsettled. Bess' accurate insight and perspective were right on target.

"Do you think she had anything to do with Peter's murder?"

"Definitely not. It must be awful not being able to mourn for someone you love. Her eyes are so sad."

Bess turned off University Avenue, then south onto Randall Street, which veered off to the right and became Monroe Street.

"There, on our immediate right, is Camp Randall. This was one of the Union training camps during the Civil War. That cannon there was used in the training. Now, Camp Randall is where the University football games are played."

She crossed Regent Street and continued on Monroe Street where a little community opened up before them. Little mom and pop shops dotted both sides of the road for a few blocks, then it turned into a residential area. She turned and drove toward a pristine lake, then stopped in front of a multi-storied, redbrick, steep-pitched house.

"This is where your parents live?"

She laughed at the idea. "No. You know who lives in this house?"

"Obviously not, since I just asked you if this was your parents' house. I've only been in Madison for ten minutes. You're the one who is supposed to know where you're going."

She ignored his sarcasm. "This is Leo Crowley's family's house."

"Leo Crowley – *thee* Leo Crowley?"

"Oh, you've heard of him; the Former head of the Federal Deposit Insurance Corporation, FDR's man – yes, that Leo Crowley."

She checked her side mirror, then made a U-turn and drove back to Monroe Street.

"Okay," asked a confused Carson, "why did you show me that house?"

"Because, I want you to understand something. Even though I'm from what would be considered a small, hick town by DC standards, this small, hick town has its citizens who have helped shape this country on the national level. Mr. Crowley was a big man in this town before he became friends with Presidents Wilson and Roosevelt. He may work in the big city now, but he's from a small town - this town."

"And?"

"And... I don't know. I guess I want to say if he can do it, so can I."

"Just to let you in on a little secret, the place I'm from, in Montana, would consider Madison a metropolis."

He saw a big smile return to her face. She confidently navigated quietly through side streets until she pulled into a driveway on Emerald Street. The house had a half brick façade, with a semi-Tutor flare of architecture. Not ostentatious, but a house befitting a university department head. A mixture of single-family, sturdy-built homes and three-story flats made up the housing choices in the area.

"Come on in," Bess invited. "They keep the spare set of car keys in a kitchen drawer."

Professor Osmond and his wife chose expensive, but subtle, pieces of furniture. The whole interior was tastefully decorated. Many pieces of the furniture belonged to the Arts and Crafts era. All of the furniture complimented the polished hardwood floors. An expensive oriental rug covered the center of the room. Family pictures, taken all over the world, decorated the walls.

Carson felt he could be friends with the gray-haired man looking back at him from the picture with the pyramids in the background. Bess had her father's kind smile and the mischievous sparkle in her eyes from her mother.

"Here they are," Bess announced as she entered the living room jingling a pair of keys. "I'm sure the car's full of gas. I'll draw you a map so you'll be able to get back to Sauk City. Anything else you need?"

"Just do what you do best – research. No heroic stuff, okay?" He said, skeptical that she listened to a word he said.

Chapter Thirteen

Freedom and responsibility; reoccurring themes in Carson's life visit, yet again. Having Professor Osmond's car provided a necessary freedom. It also meant having another set of keys and more responsibility. He considered Peter's car, now his car, as a tool he needed to use in the investigation. If something happened to the car, no one but himself would miss it. Now he was using the car of a man thousands of miles away who had no knowledge of the exchange between his daughter and a stranger. His heart and head accelerated with the need to get back to Sauk City, but Bess' warning about speed limits rang in his head and his foot applied pressure to the brakes. The last thing he needed was a speeding ticket. How would he explain having a car belonging to another man whose address he didn't know? There was something else just out of reach in his mind: something Bess said, about her meeting with Laura. It softly whispered through his mind when she'd said it, but just as quickly it floated away. He hoped it would surface again soon.

The key found in his coffee represented another responsibility. It was important, somehow. He just needed to discover how. It had been about a week since he'd first found it. Then the barn fire, the hospital stay, and his extended "visit" at the police station. All those events kept the importance and the function of the coffee key out of reach. Now, he could put his time and energy into finding out what it belonged to and what the etching on the spine meant. If Deputy Johnson was right, then a visit to the Catholic Church was in order.

He still hadn't told Ben about the woman at the barn, or the note he'd found on the car windshield. Ben also didn't know the specifics about his and Laura's past relationship. Although, Carson suspected Ben knew more than he let on.

With remainder of the day he planned to visit Harold Maier at the hospital, and after that, he would finally get some food in the house.

****

Laura stood up and reached the small of her back arching backward as she rubbed the muscles. She looked down and around her feet satisfied with work she'd done in the garden. She wore an uncharacteristic pair of patched blue jeans. Pulling weeds didn't require the latest fashions from Paris. Using the back of her hand, she blotted the sweat at her hair line next to the red handkerchief covering her hair. She watched Mrs. Schultz finish sweeping the steps to the house. She smiled at Mrs. Schultz's proclivity for cleanliness. Suddenly Mrs. Schultz yelled out in pain as she reached the stair rail for support.

Laura charged out of the garden across the expansive lawn toward the house to help in any way possible. She watched Mrs. Schultz limp up the sturdy porch stairs one foot at a time, until she reached the porch's landing. Mrs. Schultz dragged her left leg behind her until she eased herself into the porch swing.

"Trudy," Mrs. Schultz yelled through the open screened window on her left. The urgency in her voice immediately brought a young lady to the screen door. Before she had a chance to ask, her mother answered the unasked question.

"I got stung by a bee. My foot and ankle swell up. Take da shoe off. Dare's no feeling in dat foot."

Obediently, the young lady quickly did as her mother asked.

Laura reached the stairs breathless just as Trudy took off her mother's shoe.

"What happened?" she asked.

"Mamma got stung by a bee. She's allergic to bee stings. It could kill her."

Mrs. Schultz waved her hand at her daughter, down playing the seriousness of the situation.

"Trudy, go in da house and get some ice and call da doktor. See if dare is anything else I should do - without going to his office. I need to talk to Laura. Now, go! Shooo!"

Hesitantly, the girl got up off the porch floor and went into the house.

Laura took one of the fan backed chairs on the porch and turned it around. Gingerly she lifted Mrs. Schultz' foot and set it down on the chair, before she sat down next to Mrs. Schultz.

"The weeds in da garden can wait one more day. God vill forgive us pulling veeds on a Sunday. Today, I need you to go to town and buy groceries. Trudy and I vill look after tings here."

"Okay. I know where your grocery list is. I'll just go up and change my clothes quick."

Trudy hurried through the screen door with ice wrapped in a dish towel and applied it to her mothers foot.

"I left a message with Dr. Crawford's wife. He wasn't home. She said she would have him call, as soon as he returns."

"Should I wait for his call to see if there is something I can get for you in town?" Laura asked.

Laura smiled at Mrs. Schultz who waved her hand at her like she was shooing away an insect. "You just go and change. Maybe he vill call before you go."

Laura's sense of fashion had drastically changed since moving to Wisconsin. She missed the days when she would spend the whole day lounging in a silk Noel Coward-like outfit. Here, they were simply not practical. Still, it was one thing to wear patched jeans to pull weeds: it was quite another to be seen in public in them. A simple summer dress would do nicely.

Ten minutes later, Laura studied her tall, tan, athletic form in front of a full length mirror. *I'm almost back to my old self.* Her hair was swept up in a French twist, and she wore a buttercup yellow dress with tiny blue flowers on the silky fabric.

Having a beautiful sunny day and being able to go into town seemed reason enough to get halfway dressed up. These opportunities were rare lately. Seeing herself in the mirror, and being happy with what she saw, lifted her spirits higher than they had been for weeks. She felt light and happy as she bounded toward the stairway. Halfway down the stairs the phone rang.

"I'll get it," she called to Trudy and her mother as she descended the last few steps.

"Hello," she answered with a smile in her voice.

"Hello, my love. It's good to hear your sweet voice. Did you find the cufflinks?"

A name caught in her throat, but she dared not say it. Peter was dead. Terror rooted her to the floor.

"Who are you?" she whispered into the mouthpiece.

"Come, come now. We know each other very well. Tell me, how's the legacy?"

"What do you want?" Tears blinded her vision.

The voice on the other end changed from friendly to cold and hard with a twist of sarcasm. "I want it all. Unfortunately, you're in the way, so is your old lover, Carson Grey." Again the voice turned to saccharine sweet. "Don't fret my sweet. In a short time, I will eliminate all the obstacles. I just wanted to thank you for helping me."

"Who are you?" she pleaded, again.

"Someone who's finally taking what's his."

The click on the other end of the receiver echoed in her ears. A million thoughts ran through her mind; pack up and leave, tell the sheriff, act as if nothing has happened and hope he, whoever, would go away.

Mrs.Schultz' voice dug into Laura's consciousness. "Is dat da doktar?"

With her heart still in her throat, she tried to answer back in her normal voice.

"No, Mrs. Schultz, it was for me; something to do with work."

"Land sakes," Laura heard Mrs. Schultz say, "Can't they get along without you for one day? I just thaut of one more ting to put on da grocery list."

****

As soon as Carson saw Dr. Bellamy walking down the corridor toward Harold's room, he picked up his pace. But Dr. Bellamy directed him into an empty room.

"Is Harold still too ill to see people?"

"Yes. He's out of the coma, but still sleeps a lot. He needs it to heal the ribs and femur. He still has a long way to go. Your visit will only bring unneeded anxiety. I'll let you know when he can have visitors. How are you doing?"

"Good doc. No more headaches. But, about Harold... it's not my intention to cause anyone more trouble. I just want Harold and his family to know how sorry I am about all of this."

"I know. They'll come around. They just need more time."

Carson left disappointed but relieved knowing Harold would be alright, in time. About the only good thing that didn't happen at Badger Hospital was that Carson never saw or heard the "helpful" nurse. It must be her day off or maybe she had a new victim.

Since his visit to Harold was cut short, he could now go and get some desperately needed groceries. The Kroeger Store ad in the *Pioneer Press* came to mind. If memory served, that store was close to his house.

A half a block from the store, he saw a parking space in front of the store. Before he had a chance to act, an oncoming car cut him off and pulled into the spot.

"Damn."

Further on the same block, another car pulled out and he quickly steered Bess' father's car into that spot. The annoyance he felt just seconds ago turned into a feeling of dumb luck. The driver of the car who'd cut him off was Laura. Should he follow her into the store? No. She had the restraining order on him, and he'd just gotten Ben back on his side. The last thing he wanted to do was jeopardize that friendship again. He decided to watch her from the car.

Just observing her for the first few seconds, he saw she acted preoccupied and unaware of her surroundings. She almost jumped out her skin when some kids on bicycles rode past her on the sidewalk.

He watched her slam into the door jam as she entered the store, almost as if she were drunk. Ten minutes went by, and Laura hadn't come out of the store. Another ten minutes went by and still no Laura. Carson got out of his car and nonchalantly walked up to the store window and looked in. He saw no sign of Laura. She didn't come out, so she still had to be inside.

He knew he would be causing trouble, but he had to know. He took a deep breath and walked into the store. Only two older women were there, waiting to be checked out, talking about the price of cake flour.

"Excuse me."

The women turned around in unison.

"Was there a young lady in here a few minutes ago? She had on a yellow dress."

"Yes. She went over to the window to look at something in the display, and then suddenly felt very ill. The clerk took her to the back room to sit for a spell."

The women said something else, but Carson never heard it. He walked behind the counter and through a door to the back of the store. An older man, carrying a case of Post Cereal, met him in the back.

"Can I help you, young man?"

"The woman in the yellow dress; where is she?"

"She left. She said she felt much better and left through the delivery door."

****

Laura's heart beat so fast and hard she couldn't think. Was it just a coincidence Carson was at the same store at the same time as she, or was he stalking her? She drove from the store as fast as she could: her mind numb. In her hurry to get out of town, she drove on the wrong side of the road, almost hitting an on coming car. She didn't see the silver Cadillac anywhere. How could he be following her without a car? The last thing she could cope with today would be a confrontation with Carson. He knew her well enough to sense something bothered her. She felt so full of turmoil at the moment she might have told him everything. Yet the voice on the phone had threatened his life, too. Thank God the other ladies and store owner occupied Carson's attention just long enough for her to leave.

Another thought made her shudder with fear. If Carson was watching her, maybe the person on the phone was too. Now she wished she faced Carson and told him everything. He had a right to know his life was also in danger. She resolved to go back to the store right away. If Carson was still there, she would tell him about the phone call. She knew one thing for sure; she had to make up her mind on how to best handle this situation and do it soon. Her decision could mean life or death to herself and everyone she loved.

****

Carson closed the door to a full refrigerator. He sighed at a job well done. He'd been in the house for over a week, and he finally bought some food. He grabbed the *Wisconsin State Journal* off the kitchen table and made his way to the living room and the sofa.

Just as he sat down, a knock came from the front door. Glancing out a window, he saw Ben standing at the front stoop.

"Hi." Ben walked straight in, not waiting for any invitation and didn't stop until he'd settled his body in a kitchen chair. "I wasn't sure you'd be here, especially not knowing what you're driving these days. Where'd you park?"

"On the street, a block away. I'm following your and Bess' suggestion."

"Mine."

"Yeah." Carson ambled over to the stove and grabbed the coffeepot. "You're the one who talked me into listening to her advice." He let the water from the sink splash into the empty pot. "Truth is I can't get the garage door open. It turns out Bess is pretty smart for her age."

"Sounds like you finally approve of her." Ben opened the cupboard and grabbed two coffee cups. "How'd your day with her go?"

"Great. I got a little tour of Madison along with some history. She felt compelled to point out Camp Randall and Leo Crawley's house, before she took me to her parents."

"Leo Crawley. Now, there's a character. My gut feeling tells me he had something to do with the plant being here in the first place."

"Yeah?"

"Yeah. Well, the reason I'm here, those tracks found at Lucas Wheeler's place were from a truck and not a tractor. I'm puzzled how no one heard or saw anything."

The blue flame under the coffeepot gradually generated enough heat to start a slow percolating under the pot. The aroma of strong coffee soon filled the kitchen.

"Well, at least you have some answers. I went to see Harold Maier when I got back into town. Dr. Bellamy updated me on his condition and..." Carson tentatively continued, "I saw Laura."

"I thought I told you..."

"Whoa. It's not like you think. I needed groceries. She just happened to be there at the same time. In fact, she cut me off to park in front of the store."

"You think she did it on purpose?"

"No. At first I thought it was just some idiot. She didn't know it was me she cut off. I could have been driving a fire truck, and she wouldn't have seen me."

"Why is that?"

Coffee spewed from the pot all over the stove and the adjacent countertop and on the floor.

"Damn," Carson muttered. "That's twice now that's happened. Half of it's on the floor."

Carson grabbed any and all dish towels readily available in the vicinity to sop up the mess while Ben jumped up to turn off the gas and remove the coffeepot from the burner.

After the spill was cleaned up, and the coffee poured, the conversation turned back to Laura.

"Where were we?" Ben asked. "Oh yeah, why do you think Laura didn't see you?"

"After she cut me off, I took the next parking space that came along. I never talked to her or approached her. I promise. I waited outside, in the car. Something clearly bothered her."

"Maybe she knew you were following her."

"No. Not a chance. How? She doesn't know what I'm driving. You don't know what I'm driving. She never knew I was there. I'm positive."

"You're positive."

Carson manners were a bit rusty, but he finally remembered to ask about the basics.

"Milk or sugar?"

"No thanks. If I change my mind, I'll help myself."

Even though Ben declined his offer, Carson went to the refrigerator and put a couple of drops of milk in his cup of coffee. "Are ya sure ya don't want any?" He raised the bottle of milk trying to change Ben's mind.

"Nope. I like mine strong and black."

Carson closed the refrigerator door and went back to the table. "Say, this reminds me of something."

"What?"

"That key I found in the coffee. I was planning to go to St. Al's tomorrow and do some clergy questioning. I'd like you to come along with me."

"Tomorrow. Not a good idea."

"Why not? We've already lost too much time."

"Because tomorrow is Sunday, and the Lutherans in Leland are having their annual Father's Day Play and Ice Cream Social. The public's invited. Knowing this community, Lutheran, Baptist, Methodist, Catholic, whatever, they'll all be there. They'll go there after going to their own church service first, of course. Then they'll mingle with the rest of the community. By the way, where is that key? I haven't seen it, only heard talk of it."

For a second, Carson stopped to think. He checked all his pockets, twice.

"It's in the pocket of the trousers I had on yesterday."

"You had that key with you the whole time you were at the station and never once showed it to me."

"I was there under protest, because you didn't trust me, and I couldn't trust that you wouldn't conveniently lose it or just dismiss it. Anyway, I changed and cleaned up so fast with Bess here, I forgot to keep it with me. Wait a second, I'll go get it." Carson left the kitchen to retrieve the key.

****

While he waited for Carson to return, Ben casually sipped his coffee and looked around the kitchen.

"Hey Carson, your window sill here looks like it need a little work"

Ben got no response, so he slid his chair to the window sill for a closer look. He placed one hand on the sill. It moved. He bent over for a closer look. He played with the toggling sill trying to find out how much weight on it made it toggle. It was worse than he first thought.

"I've got some plaster at home. I think that's all it needs," he called out again to Carson.

Ben leaned and reached over to put his coffee cup back on the table. In doing so, he knocked the sill askew from the window frame. It was then obvious; the sill was independent from the rest of the window frame. Carefully he lifted it away from the wall and set it down on the floor.

"Well, I'll be damned," he whispered to himself.

"What about the dam," Carson innocently asked entering the room with the tiny key in hand.

The angry look on Carson's face warned Ben he better have a good explanation.

"What'd you do? Now I'll have to find time to fix that," Carson complained.

"You knew about this?"

"Well of course I did. Even Bess noticed it. All it would have taken, before you totally tore it away from the wall, would be a little plaster – problem fixed. How am I going to explain this to Esther?"

That remark told Ben that Carson was talking about the window sill and not what he discovered.

"So you were going to plaster it back up?" said Ben.

"Yeah. This winter a lot of heat will be lost through that sill."

"That's great Carson, but I was referring to this." Ben reached down into the wall and pulled out a small metal box.

Dumbfounded, Carson looked at Ben, "What's that?"

"Don't know. I thought you knew. Why would anyone put a metal box of nothing in a wall? Let's take a look."

Ben set the small, dusty, box on the table and wiped the thick dust off with his wide palm, revealing a small lock on the side of the box.

He saw that it took Carson a heart beat of time to understand that he may be literally holding the key to the box. Without hesitation, Carson inserted the key. It fit. Quickly he turned the key, until they heard a click. Just as quickly, Ben flipped the cover of the box up. The box contained one item. There, in Peter Franke's handwriting, an envelope addressed to CARSON GREY.

"Talk about voices from the grave," Ben gasped.

Both men looked at each other for a second then slowly Carson's hand reached into the box and lifted the letter out. He read to Ben.

> **Carson,**
>
> **If you are reading this, it's because he has gotten the better of me. I knew you would find the key. I also know you are Laura's only hope. Don't let him take away her world. He is vicious and cunning. He will stop at nothing to get what he wants. Be careful,**
>
> **Peter**

Both men stood stunned and speechless for several moments, absorbing the message and warning from a dead man.

"This changes everything. Instead of coming to my place for dinner Monday, you're coming tomorrow. We need to lay everything out on the table and figure out who this mystery guy is, before there is anymore trouble. I'd like to deal with this now, but I promised Tommy we'd go to Fred's for supper."

"Do you think this person Peter's talking about has threatened Laura?"

"We'll find out tomorrow. She'll be joining us."

Chapter Fourteen

The day was perfect to Ben's way of thinking. It was June 20, Father's Day, and the weather couldn't be better. The humidity low, the sky a baby blue, and there wasn't a cloud to be seen anywhere. The birds even sounded happier. Ben's sister-in-law, Ruth, planned on going to the Leland Ice Cream Social and would be taking Tommy with her and Fred. Every kid in town would also be there. Tommy could find more than enough boys his own age to pull together a baseball game. From the kitchen window, Ben watched his neighbor finish mowing the lawn.

The sound of the bathroom door opened and wet feet padded across the wooden hall floor stopping at the kitchen doorway. Ben turned around, and there stood Tommy. Water still ran off his thick shaggy blond hair down his body, until absorbed by the towel wrapped around his waist. A small puddle of water collected at his feet.

"Do I have to wear good jeans to Aunt Ruth's?"

"Yes, and a clean shirt."

"Why?"

"If you don't go over there dressed like that, you know as well as I do she'll stop here on your way to the social for you to change. You might as well put the good clothes on now and be done with it."

"Ah geez," Tommy whined as he went to his room, leaving the puddle of water in the doorway.

Ben went back to scrubbing the potatoes and then set them on the counter to dry. Thankfully, he'd left Carson's place early enough yesterday to get to the store before they closed. Getting the food turned out to be the easy part; convincing Laura Bradshaw she needed to join him was another story. She gave him every excuse in the book why she couldn't make it. She finally conceded when he gave her the choice of either coming to dinner at his house or he would have a lengthy visit with her at the plant.

A door in the house quietly closed, and muted steps made their way toward the kitchen. Ben was on his knees digging in a lower cupboard for a large bowl as Tommy walked through the kitchen to the back door.

"I'm going now," Tommy announced.

"Yeah, okay." Ben looked up just as Tommy reached for the door handle.

"Whoa – stop."

"What?"

"What's that?"

"What?"

"In your hand."

"Dad, it's a baseball glove."

"I know it's a baseball glove. Where'd you get it? It's not the one I gave you."

"Oh. I got it from a friend."

"A friend? None of your friends can afford a glove like that."

"Not a kid friend. A grown-up friend."

Slowly Ben got onto his feet and approached Tommy. Being a cop made him suspicious of many things, but he was also a parent and a protective one.

"Can I look at it?" he asked, trying not to sound too wary or demanding.

Tommy flipped Ben the glove but kept one hand on the door knob evident he wanted to get out the door and end the interrogation. Ben recognized the fine quality leather and stitch work. He suspected the glove cost someone a pretty penny.

"So, tell me about this friend. How'd you meet him? How'd he know you play baseball?"

"He watches us play ball sometimes. One day we ended early. He asked me to play catch. He saw my old glove. The next day he gave me this one. Said it would help me play better. It has, too."

"I see. Hope you thanked him."

"I did. Dad, I gotta go!" Tommy shifted his weight from one foot to another looking out the door down the street.

"Okay, okay. One more question, and I'll let you go."

Ben handed the glove back to Tommy, who hugged it close to his chest.

"What's this friend's name?"

"He said his name is Holden."

A lightning bolt surging through him could not have been more shocking to Ben. He needed to stay in control and not scare Tommy.

"Tommy, I don't want you to talk to this Mr. Holden. Not until I've had a chance to meet and talk with him. Let me talk with him first. Then I'll determine if you can see him any more. Promise me you'll do this!"

"Okay, Dad. Can I go now?"

When Tommy opened the door wide, Ben pulled him back and gave him a big bear hug, lifting him off the floor.

"I love you, son. Don't forget that."

Ben set the boy back down to the floor and swatted his back side affectionately as Tommy dashed out the door. He watched Tommy run down the sidewalk, until he was out of sight. His first impulse was to put a kibosh on the social, but that wouldn't be fair to Tommy. Besides, there would be people all over the place. For insurance, he called Fred, and asked him to keep a close watch on Tommy. He knew if he asked Ruth, she wouldn't let Tommy leave her side. She was even more protective of Tommy than he. Before he hung up the phone, a knock came from the front door.

Carson stood there holding a pie. Ben wondered if Libby made it for him.

"Morning," Ben said. "You're early. Where'd you park?" Ben stuck his head out the front door, looking out on the street.

"Morning. You have an obsession about where I park. Do you realize that?" Carson took his hat off and looked for a place to set it.

"Sorry, comes with the job."

Ben saw Carson craning his head and guessed what he was looking for. He took Carson's hat and placed it on the back of the sofa as he walked back to the kitchen.

"I walked. You're only seven blocks away from my place."

"You don't want her to know what you're driving," Ben teased Carson.

"No. You only live seven blocks away, and it's a beautiful day for a walk," Carson defended himself quickly.

Ben smiled at Carson's sensitive reaction to what Laura might think.

"So, this is where you and Tommy live."

"Yep, my castle, such as it is."

Ben's lifestyle could be summed up in one word - comfortable. Nothing flashy or flamboyant; items were practical and comfortable or they probably wouldn't be in Ben's house. An overstuffed, rust-colored chair and sofa were the main pieces of furniture in the living room, along with a buffet and radio. Pictures of Tommy at various stages in his young life were everywhere. A wedding picture sat on the buffet. At a quick glance, Carson saw that Tommy looked very much like his mother.

Ben waited for Carson to gaze over the living room, then he proceeded to the kitchen, leaving Carson no choice but to follow. His kitchen looked as sparse and clean as his office. The only items on the countertop were a toaster and the recently washed vegetables.

"Since you're here early, I'm putting you to work," Ben said. "You can either peel the carrots or you can peel potatoes."

"I'll peel carrots. Where's Tommy?"

"Tommy left just before you came. He's at my brother's place for the afternoon. I'm sure he'll be going to the Leland Ice Cream Social."

"Your brother lives close by?"

Ben offered Carson a knife with a scene of a dog pointing at a pheasant etched in the ivory handle.

"Tommy only has to go to the end of the block, turn left, and it's the fourth house on the left."

"That's convenient."

The knife's sharpness apparent from the first touch of the blade to the vegetable. In no time, Carson had finished his task.

"Anything else?"

"Could you grab a towel and wipe up the small lake Tommy left in the doorway?"

"Okay. Then what?"

"Nothing. I'll just throw all of this in with the roast and everything can cook at once."

In no time they had the kitchen cleaned up. The vegetables joined the roast cooking in the oven. Ben set the table, while Carson mopped up the puddle on the floor. Both men sat in silence lost in their own thoughts, enjoying each other's company and the smell of a home-cooked meal in the making.

"I know it's none of my business," Carson started to apologize, but continued with the question, "but if everyone in town is at the picnic, why aren't you?"

Ben didn't answer right off.

"I haven't been inside a church or at a church function since Mary Jane's funeral. I don't want my personal feelings to prejudice Tommy, so I send him to church with Fred and Ruth. I think Ruth would like us both to go, but she respects my choices."

"Tommy's a good kid. You're doing a good job with him all by yourself. I've got one more personal question, then I'll never bring it up again."

Uneasy at what Carson's question might probe into, Ben got up with his cup and refilled it.

"I know when you married your wife she was already a widow with a young son. With her untimely death, you were forced to raise a young boy without his mother and you're not his natural father. How hard is that?"

Ben stalled answering, sipping his coffee. "Um, not bad. How hard is it? Kids don't have a choice who their parents are. Tommy was pretty young when Mary Jane and I married. We thought we would give Tommy a brother or sister in time. Then she got sick. We thought it was just a virus, but she never seemed to get any better. She finally went to the doctor. He did a lot of tests. Shortly after that, he told us she was very sick - terminal. A week later, she died. I think hearing how sick she was, she just gave up."

Ben walked back to the table and sat. "I don't know if I'm doing such a great job with Tommy or not. I try to teach him right from wrong by example. I hope that someday, when he has grown, he will pass on what he has learned from me. Having him in my life is my life. Not always easy, damn challenging at times, in fact. But not being his natural father isn't something I ever think about. I'm the only father he remembers, and he is my son."

"You're an amazing man, Ben Lyman. Not many men in your position would be so generous."

"I'm not generous, I'm selfish. Being able to have and see Tommy every day is like being able to see Mary Jane every day."

"Just the same, I don't think I could be a dad let alone raise another man's child. I'm too comfortable in my lifestyle to change it."

A car drove past the house honking its horn, then squealed around the corner. The diversion of the car got Ben up, again. He looked out the window and checked on the roast. Then he looked at his pocket watch, and grabbed two small hand towels. Just when he reached into the oven for the roast, a knock at the front door interrupted.

"Could you get the door? I think my last guest has arrived."

****

Laura nervously waited at the front door. She checked her hair in the reflection of the door window and second guessed her choice of dress and hairstyle. She wore her hair down and a powder blue silk dress with a single strand of pearls. She thought her dress might give the impression of being too formal.

If she were back home, she would have gloves on. Through the lace curtains, she saw a man walking to the front door. She took a deep breath to steady her nerves. She heard and watched the doorknob turn. The door opened, and all of her resolve disappeared.

"What are you doing here?" she said alarmed, "I mean, I didn't know you would be here."

The fact that Carson didn't react to her question or take his eyes off of her made her even more self-conscious.

Finally she asked, "Can I come in?"

"Oh, yeah, please, come in." Carson stepped back as Laura entered the living room. "Ben's in the kitchen. Follow your nose and you'll find him."

Ben had the roast on the table. He scooped the potatoes and carrots into their own bowls, when Carson and Laura entered the kitchen.

"Welcome. Take a seat at the table. Dinner will be ready in a second. I still haven't mastered making gravy."

He noticed Carson and Laura took seats opposite each other at the table.

"Hope you both brought your appetites," he teased. "There's plenty of food. Can I get anyone something to drink?"

His guests suddenly became shy. Laura requested water. Carson accepted coffee.

Throughout dinner Ben's attempt to initiate small talk received only a head nod or grunt. Finally he had had enough. He pushed his plate away.

"Okay, you two, we're here to share information concerning Peter's death. I thought a meal together would break down some barriers and make us more comfortable in each other's presence. I guess I was wrong. Since you're both unwilling to share polite dinner conversation, I'll jump right in and start with what I know. Feel free to correct me if I have any of the details wrong.

"About a month ago, I got a phone call from Harold Maier telling me his boy, Stevie, found a body in some woods. The body turned out to be that of Peter Franke. A few days later, you showed up." Ben looked at Carson. "Oh, the day Peter's body was discovered, you, Miss Bradshaw, abruptly left work without an explanation after receiving a phone call. I *will* have an answer to that question today before you leave! I know you two had more than a professional relationship in DC. Somewhere along the line, Peter Franke came into the picture."

Ben didn't miss the hurt look of betrayal Laura fired at Carson.

Ben continued undaunted, "Your boss, Mr. Denby, supplied me with much of the background information on all of you, although I probably would have guessed it sooner or later. Peter drove what he thought was a one-of-a-kind silver 1941 Cadillac. Turns out, someone else has one too: someone who tried to kill Carson."

Ben closely monitored the genuine look of shock and surprise on Laura's face.

"While Carson was in the hospital recuperating from injuries he got at the barn fire, another silver 1941 Cadillac was seen in Madison. I now know why someone ransacked Peter's house. But I don't know what the message means exactly. Excuse me a moment."

Ben left Carson and Laura sitting alone in silence. He returned with the small metal box and key.

"Maybe you can help us with the message, Miss Bradshaw." He set the box and key next to her. He ignored the momentary expression of panic on her face as she tried to read and understand his unspoken request. The key visibly shook as she inserted it in the lock. He moved to the other side of the table. He wanted to see her initial reaction to content in the box.

"It's addressed to you?" Her bewildered look turned to Carson.

"I know," he whispered. "Read the note."

Both men watched her reactions as she silently read the letter. They waited for her to read the letter out loud. It became obvious to Ben that Laura was not going to openly share what she knew, even after reading the letter.

"Miss Bradshaw," Ben's voice had an undercurrent of gentleness, "what does that reference to *taking her world away* mean?"

"I don't know," she replied softly, barely audible.

"Can you confirm the handwriting on the envelope belongs to Peter Franke?"

The way she nodded her head up and down, with her eyes closed and tears streaming down her face, she gave Ben the answer he wanted.

"Carson, I think it's time you tell us all you know. I'll let Miss Bradshaw recover from this shock for a few minutes."

Carson pulled the "IS SHE WORTH IT?" note out of his pocket and gave it to Ben, who had not seen it or knew of its existence.

"One night at the boarding house, I couldn't sleep. So, I got up to take a walk. This was on my windshield." He pointed at the note in Ben's hand. "At the time I didn't think anything of it. There was a wedding in town that night, and some of the guests also stayed at that boarding house. I met one of them in the parking lot. He was the bride's former lover; the one she said she'd wait for. She didn't wait. She married someone else. He was very drunk and bitter. I thought he got confused and put the note on the wrong car."

"Anything else?" Ben's tone sterner with Carson.

"Just one more thing. That day in the barn, right before I got hit from behind, I saw a woman digging in the back corner. She had her back to me. It was you," Carson said looking levelly at Laura's tear-streaked face.

"No! I never..." Laura denied choked with tears.

"I would know your figure and hair anywhere. When I called out your name, you stood straight up. Then you started to turn around that's when I got hit."

"No," she protested louder.

"Why didn't you tell me this earlier?" Ben said, annoyed with Carson.

"Because I wanted to hear from her why she was there. Then you told me she put a restraining order on me, so I couldn't confront her, until now."

Ben's frustration began to show. All of the miscues got in the way of the investigation. The gentle demeanor he'd extended to Laura earlier turned a bit harsher.

"Miss Bradshaw," he said in his interrogation voice, "I would like some answers. Where did you go so abruptly on the day Stevie Maier discovered Peter Franke's body? And why? Where were you on the day of the barn fire? Who is Peter talking about in the note to Carson? And what does the inference of *taking away your world*' mean?"

"I was at work the day of the fire. You can check that out. I was there all day. I never left my building. As for the restraining order, it was to keep Mr. Grey," she sneered Carson's name, "from harassing me." Her face contorted with anger.

"You mean from doing my job," Carson shot back.

"I have no idea who Peter is referring to in the note. Ask Mr. Grey, it's addressed to him. And *my* world is *my* business."

Ben ran out of patience. "Laura." His voice demanded attention. "Peter is dead, Charlie Ballard is dead, someone tried to roast Carson and by extension brutally injured Harold Maier, and now, I think someone is stalking my son trying to get to me. How many more people have to be hurt or killed just so you can hide some secret? Nothing can warrant this level of secrecy. Who is Mr. Holden?"

The name got the attention of Carson and Laura.

"Mr. Holden?" Laura's voice indicated a crack in her armor. "Mr. Holden is," she corrected herself, "was, a good friend of Peter's. Why do you ask? How do you know him?"

"You told me you didn't know him," Carson said pointedly.

"I don't know him – Peter did."

"I don't know him either. That's the problem. He shows up in town inquiring about renting the house Peter rented, and it seems he has taken an unusual interest in my son. All I know about him is that he's British."

"Has he hurt Tommy?" Carson asked.

"No."

"Yes, he's British. Peter said he met him, quite by accident, in London on one of his trips there. What has he got to do with any of this?"

Ben started to reply when he realized she had yet to answer where she went the day Peter's body was found. She had almost evaded answering that question again.

"I don't know yet. You still haven't answered why you left work on the day we discovered Peter's body."

He had never before seen so much venom in a woman's eyes. He had to force her or dare her to get the answer.

"If you're not willing to tell us, Miss Bradshaw, I'll say what you can't or won't."

Then he saw it in her eyes. He knew what and why she had fought so hard to hide. He also saw her determination. Her only chance to keep her secret was to call his bluff, but he was beyond any bluffing games.

"You left work that day," Ben began, "because your baby was sick. Isn't that right, Miss Bradshaw?" As soon as he said that he looked over at Carson to see his reaction.

"Oh my God, Laura," said a drained faced Carson. "It all makes sense now. Why didn't I see it; your slight weight gain and fuller figure, having to hurry home after work and having other responsibilities?

Ben's heart went out to Laura as she sank into her chair burying her face in her hands. The blue silk dress dampened with the deluge of tears. Carson looked like he'd been sucker punched by the news.

"I'm sorry. I wasn't totally certain until now. There are usually only a couple of reasons a woman fights so hard to protect a secret: either a man or a child is involved. Since the man is dead, it had to be a child, isn't that right, Miss Bradshaw?"

Still sobbing, Laura nodded her head at Ben's accurate revelation. "Yes, I have a son. He is almost seven months old, and Peter is his father."

Ben sat down next to Laura and held her hand. She heaved a heavy sigh. Slowly, she began to control her emotions. She dabbed her eyes with an embroidered, lace handkerchief she pulled from her dress pocket. She tried to smile as if relieved that the truth was finally out.

"Soon after I realized I was pregnant, I left my job.

Because Peter and I weren't married, my father disowned me, saying I had disgraced him and the rest of the family. I followed Peter out here to the Midwest.

"Our son, Carl, was born in Iowa. Peter worked there undercover as a Land Negotiator. We did plan on getting married. Then Peter was transferred here. He knew Land

Negotiators had a bad reputation here and he didn't want me to be a target of that hatred. He wanted to protect me. He thought if I got a job here and people thought I was a war widow, I would be treated better." She took a deep sigh as if exhausted.

"He called Denby and asked for a favor. The next day, I had a job at Badger. He got a house in town. I rented a room from Mrs. Schultz in the country. It was perfect for me. Mrs. Schultz babysat children for several other workers at the plant and was willing to watch my son as well. We were going to pretend we met here, get married and move on with our lives. Nobody needed to know the truth. We thought that we could get a couple of acres of land somewhere and build a summer home. I had no knowledge of all this other land he bought, I swear. Toward the end of May, Peter said he had to go back to Iowa for some unfinished business. That's the last time I saw him. The day you found Peter's body, Mrs. Schultz called me at work saying Carl was running a high fever. I left work to take care of him."

"Laura, why didn't you tell me this?" Carson pleaded.

"You hated Peter. That day you showed up at Badger, my heart was in my throat." She sat up to the table with a feistiness neither of the men expected. "The last thing in the world I would tell you is that Peter and I had a baby together. I'd been so careful for so long." Then she sat back in the chair depleted of the will to fight. "I couldn't trust that you wouldn't spill my secret. I'd be ruined."

"Is there anything else you haven't told us?" Ben asked sympathetically.

She nodded her head, and then looked at Ben. "Yes. A couple of weeks ago, someone left something in my car during the night. All the mirrors were moved, and the glove box contents were dumped on the floor."

"What did you find?" Ben asked.

"A pair of cufflinks. I gave them to Peter to wear to his mother's funeral. I never saw them again until that day."

"Something else happened yesterday, didn't it?" Carson insisted.

At first she acted like she wasn't going to answer Carson, then she opened up. "Yesterday, I got a phone call. He sounded like Peter and he... it was a man... asked if I found the cufflinks. I asked him who he was, and he said we knew each other very well. The way he said that made my skin crawl. He asked about the legacy. He was referring to Carl. He said I was in his way and so is Carson and that he would eliminate his obstacles. I was so frightened I didn't know what to do." She turned to Carson. "Then when I saw you at the grocery store, I panicked and ran."

"You saw me?" His voice full of incredulity.

"I didn't know if talking to you would make matters worse. I feel like this person knows every move I make. That's why I didn't want to come here today, Sheriff. I don't want to leave my son any more than I have to, and yet I have to protect him any way I can."

"Did the voice sound like Peter's throughout the conversation or did it sound like someone trying to sound like Peter?" asked Ben.

Laura closed her eyes as if replaying the phone conversation over again in her head.

"It sounded like Peter throughout. That's what really scared me." Her voice cracked. Another tear slip down her cheek.

"Did you hear anything else in the background?" Carson added.

"No."

Up until that last question, Carson interrupted very little. Ben could almost see the cogs in his brain plotting something. He didn't have to wait long, before Carson shared his plan.

"I have an idea," he announced. "Let me explain it, before you give me your answer."

Ben's skeptical expression accelerated Carson's explanation.

"Quit your job at Badger, leave Mrs. Schultz's and share Peter's house with me?"

Carson quickly continued, cutting off Laura's attempted rebuttal. "I'm not finished. If Denby can get you into Badger, he can get you out. He owes me a favor or two... at least. I can make the attic into a bedroom for myself, leaving you and your son the whole downstairs area. If this person has threatened your life and your baby's life, why live out in the middle of the country making it easy for him to do something without being seen? As Bess says, don't make it easy for him. At least being here in town you're only seven blocks from the sheriff's house and much closer to the police station than you are at Mrs. Schultz'. So, for safety's sake, if for no other reason, it makes sense. And Laura, who cares what the neighbors think! Your life is at stake. I think that has priority over perceived reputation. Since my life has also been threatened, we can look out for each other and the baby."

"I'm not happy with the idea, but it's better than the current situation." Ben nodded his head in agreement.

"I'm not comfortable with any of it. Or doesn't my opinion count?" Laura pouted.

"Are you comfortable with the idea of being at work not knowing if your son is safe at Mrs. Schultz'?"

Laura flashed Carson a flinty look, but she said nothing.

"Fine. It's settled. You'll move in tomorrow," said Ben.

Chapter Fifteen

William Denby's morning started off with an unexpected nonevent. His old, trusty alarm clock died in the middle of the night. Thanks to years – decades – of waking up at approximately the same time, regardless of an alarm clock, he would be only twenty minutes late. The alarm clock had been just a back up in case something really catastrophic happened. Always have a back-up plan was his motto. Unfortunately, mass transit's back-up plan meant taking the next available train, making his arrival to work even later.

He walked down the long, dark corridor of his building until it changed direction. He turned right into another long, dark corridor that led to his office.

Through the opaque window in the door, he saw the outer office, where the secretary pool worked, lit up. Even though it had been many years since he'd been in the field, the old instincts kicked in. Instantly, his hurried gate became a slow, deliberate prowl. His rubber-soled shoes made soundless contact on the tile floor. He pressed himself up against the wall. When he was close enough, he pressed his ear next to the door. He heard a muffled voice inside.

Quietly, he tested the door handle to see if it would respond to his touch. It did. He burst into the outer office.

"It's not like him. Just a minute. Here he is now," said a secretary to the person on the other end of the line. She covered the mouthpiece with her hand. "It's Mr. Grey, sir. He sounds quite anxious to talk to you."

Denby dashed into his office.

"Denby here."

"You're late." Carson sounded agitated.

"What's wrong?"

"More than I have time to go into right now. I need you to come up with some excuse and get Laura out of Badger, today."

"Today!"

"Her life, her son's life, which you conveniently never told me about," Denby smiled but said nothing, letting Carson rant, "and my life have been threatened by someone who sounds, at least on a phone, like Peter Franke. She's scared to death. She's moving into the house with me, but we need her out of Badger today! Tell them whatever you want, just don't cause any suspicion. One more thing, find out everything you can on a Brit named Holden, James Holden. All I have is a name. Laura confirmed Peter knew a guy named Holden."

Denby scribbled down the name on the corner of the first piece of paper he could find.

"Holden. Okay. Why?"

"He showed up here, but stays in the shadows. I don't have a good feeling about this guy."

"You haven't given me much to go on. Ask Laura if she remembers anything else about him."

"Okay. That's it for now. I've got a lot of things to do here before she and her son get here. I'll update you later."

The click on the other end of Denby's phone marked the end of the conversation, leaving Denby with a new problem. Who of his over worked staff could he drop this extra burden of researching Holden on? He looked out his office and saw the early bird secretary clicking away at her typewriter, totally unaware that she was sitting in the unlit end of the office.

"Sandra. Sandra," Denby repeated as he walked back to the outer office. "Sandra." She popped her head up from her typing.

"Yes, Mr. Denby."

"Why are you here so early today?"

"I have a doctor's appointment this afternoon. I sent you a memo last Friday. The night janitor let me in this morning."

"Hmmm."

Sandra was a good worker, efficient and thorough, but the office gossip. He dare not trust her to research Holden.

"That's right. I forgot." He turned and walked back to his office.

Finding a believable excuse to get Laura Bradshaw out of Badger, on such short notice, might be very touchy. Especially, since she would still be in the area where anyone could run into her at any time. The extra hour he had, by being on Eastern Standard Time versus Central, allowed him a small cushion to come up with an excuse. He sat down and stared out his window intently thinking of an exit excuse for Laura. He didn't notice the other offices light up or hear the other agents and secretaries filter into work. A knock on his office door broke his concentration.

"Excuse me, Mr. Denby, but there's a reporter to see you," said his personal secretary.

"Send 'em to the press corps," he responded automatically.

"They asked specifically to talk to you – by name. They said they were here to help Agent Grey."

Talking to anyone from the press had never been part of Denby's job. Any and all inquiries were passed on to the State Department's own press corp. Dropping his name and Carson's changed the usual protocol.

He looked from the window to his secretary with a curious frown, "Send them in then, Millie."

The chubby auburn haired secretary pushed her glasses up on the bridge of her nose as she closed the door. Seconds later, another staccato knock pelted his office door.

"Come in."

Denby stood up behind his desk ready to greet the visitor. He was unprepared for who walked through the door.

Bess Osmond confidently strolled in as if she belonged in this office. He couldn't ignore the piercing blue eyes framed by her short black hair.

"What can I do for you, Miss…"

"Osmond." She answered his open-ended sentence as she pumped his arm. "I'm a reporter for the *Wisconsin State Journal* in Madison, Wisconsin, but that's not why I'm here. I just told your secretary the reporter thing to get in here."

Her serious, blunt, honest answer amused and impressed Denby. The sincerity and frankness probably made her good at her job. At least he believed her.

"Then why are you here?"

"That's a long story."

Denby checked his watch for the time. He still had about twenty minutes to come up with a reason to get Laura out of her job.

"Okay. As long as it doesn't take up too much time. I'm a busy man."

Bess took the chair Denby indicated. "I'm a crime reporter in Madison. When the discovery of Peter Franke's body was made public, I did my own investigating of sorts. I tried to shadow Mr. Grey's movements. I never saw him or met him at first. I just knew where he'd been staying... that sort of thing. Anyway, then there was the barn fire, and Mr. Grey was reported to be in the hospital. Yet, I saw his car in Madison the same time he was supposed to be in the hospital. I found out later, when I actually met Mr. Grey, that it wasn't his car I saw in Madison."

"Wait a minute, wait a minute, a barn fire?"

"Yes sir. Mr. Grey was in the hospital for several days, and another man is still in the hospital as a result of the accident. You did know about this, didn't you?"

"In a way. You just used different words than Carson. He told me there had been an incident, you say a barn fire. Proceed." He checked his watch.

Bess rushed on, "Anyway, I went to the Sauk City Sheriff to report Mr. Grey missing, because I thought he was. That's when they filled me in on what happened. I'm a very good researcher, Mr. Denby, and we – Mr. Grey, Sheriff Lyman and myself – agreed that I would do research on the case, and they'd do all the dangerous stuff. Except now, I'm here as a friend, a concerned friend, and not a reporter."

"You still haven't told me why you are here."

"Oh! I have a hunch, Mr. Denby. When I interviewed Laura Bradshaw, she confided that Peter Franke acted erratically, like two different people at times. This started to happen around the same time as his mother's death. I think Peter Franke mentally snapped when his mother died. I've read medical reports of this sort of thing happening. Something traumatic happens that triggers another personality. Remember, they just assumed the body belonged to Peter Franke, because some of his personal effects were found close to the body. The body was, in fact, too decomposed for a positive ID. I came here to get as much information as I can on Peter Franke."

Denby sat back in his chair, mulling over her request.

Carson had just said someone who sounded like Peter on the phone had threatened Laura, her son, and himself. Maybe this young lady was on to something they never thought of. Denby sat up leaning forward with his elbows on his desk.

"Miss Osmond, I'll grant you your request, but there are several conditions. You can see Peter Franke's personal file, I think that's what you want." Bess frantically nodded her head in the affirmative at his comment. "But only Peter Franke's file. The information you find will not be published anywhere at any time, and the files and anything in the files never leave this office, and you have to be willing to do me a favor. This is an 'I'll-scratch-your-back, you-scratch-mine deal'."

Denby waited for some reaction from Bess.

He got no reaction.

"I just got a call from Carson this morning. He wants me to dig up all I can on a Brit named Holden. That's all we have so far, a name. All of my people are stretched to the limit with their workload. You said you are good at research. We'll see. Find out who this Holden is for me. Carson said Laura confirmed Peter knew Holden, so you'll probably find it mentioned in Peter's files. By helping me out with this, you are helping Carson and Laura. Do we have a deal?"

"Yes, sir." Bess jumped to her feet ready to seal the deal with another handshake.

"Millie," he spoke into the intercom on his desk.

"Yes, Mr. Denby."

"Can you come in here for a second?"

He waited for her answer. A quick knock at the door was the only warning, before Millie entered with a stenopad in hand and a pen.

"Millie, Miss Osmond will be helping out here for..." he looked over at Bess for an indication of how long she planned on doing research for him.

"Let's say three days for a start," Bess answered Denby's questioning stare.

"Put her at Emily's desk. I believe she's on vacation this week."

"Yes, sir," Millie replied.

"Right, and give her any files and records she asks for. She'll be reporting directly to me."

"Yes, Mr. Denby. Miss Osmond, follow me, please."

"Thanks, Mr. Denby. You won't be sorry, sir," Bess said as she followed Denby's secretary out of the room.

The door to his office hardly shut before Denby began dialing his phone.

"Sheriff Lyman speaking."

"Bill Denby, here. I got a call from Carson about an hour ago. He asked me to come up with an excuse to remove Laura Bradshaw from her job, effective immediately, because of a threat on her life. You know anything about this?"

"Yes, I know about the threats. One of my deputies is escorting her into town now."

"What kind of an excuse can we use to remove her without causing any suspicion?"

"What about chicken pox?"

"Chicken pox!" Denby exclaimed.

"Yeah. It's highly contagious. She could say she's been exposed and doesn't want to possibly spread it through the plant. It could be devastating to the work force. And she doesn't want to spread it through the house where she lives."

"That will only buy us a couple of weeks of time."

"My gut feeling is that's all we'll need. Did Carson say anything to you about a man named Holden?"

"Yup. I've got your reporter friend working on it in exchange for information on Peter Franke."

"Reporter friend?"

"A Bess Osmond."

"Ah, Bess. I shouldn't be surprised to hear she found her way to DC. I am surprised that she went without consulting with either me or Carson. She clearly isn't afraid of going to the top to get answers."

"I see. Well, I guess I'll call Laura about the chicken pox excuse, since it's the only one we've got."

Denby hung up wondering if he was doing the right thing. Standing and looking out of his office window, he reviewed the roster of problems in Wisconsin. Moving Laura could add to the list. She would be closer to police protection – that was a plus. The threat maker would be less likely to try anything in town with neighbors all around. Carson was also threatened. Having everyone under one roof might just be the worst thing possible. Carson may not be as willing to be away from the house for long periods of time, and that could hinder the investigation. The biggest question was Laura and Carson themselves. Having been romantically involved in the past could cause one or both of them to not pay attention to the present. They couldn't help but cross paths everyday. He wondered what the terms of the living arrangements were.

****

For the first time in a long time, Carson was nervous. It was one thing to suggest an idea, quite another when the consequences of the suggestion could change your life. At one time, he saw himself spending the rest of his life with Laura. That was before she'd left him for Peter; that thought still stung him. Before this case, he reconciled his life would be that of a confirmed bachelor.

There were other women, of course, but they regarded Carson the same way he regarded them - a nice diversion. There were never any strings attached to make life complicated. Outside of work, there were no demands on him or his time. He could understand how Denby never got around to having a family outside of the office. While part of him feared becoming Denby, another part was more afraid to answer the question "what if?" when it came to Laura.

Did she want things to be the way they were between them before or after Peter came into her life? If she agreed to try and get back together, would it be because she really cared or because she was looking for a father for her son? She'd dropped him once. What would stop her from latching on to the next rich guy who came along?

Carson zapped out of his reminiscent daze and looked at his watch, 10:30 a.m. Laura would be there any minute. He scooped up the last of his clothes from the dresser and headed to the door. He stopped and looked back over the room trying to see it through her eyes. Would she notice or approve of the added lock to the door connecting to the back porch? Would she want to rearrange the room? Was it clean enough? He decided it was good enough and marched through the hallway to the stairway that led to the attic.

****

Laura paced in her small rented room fuming. She hadn't got any sleep the previous night. The baby had a fever, and fussed all night. She still didn't like Carson's plan. The peaceful floral wallpapered room did nothing to calm her nerves. Her agitation transferred to Carl. Singing to him didn't seem to help. Eventually, he fell asleep and she put him down for his morning nap earlier than usual.

Now, she had to phone Owen with the trumped up excuse of being exposed to chicken pox. Sheriff Lyman and Carson were taking advantage of her vulnerability. Did they really expect her to live in the same house with a man who hated her son's dead father?

"Are they even thinking about what's best for Carl?" she vented, watching Carl sleep. "Do they really expect all of us to stay cooped up in that little cracker-box-sized house day and night?"

The sound of a car driving up to the house stopped her pacing. She looked out the window, thinking it was Carson. Dust kicked up behind the car and flew out across the adjacent fields, powdering the corn stalks. The car stopped under the oak tree next to her own car. For several moments, the driver didn't move. Finally, a man stepped out of the car. The long arms and torso didn't seem to fit his legs, yet Laura felt sure, if need be, he was probably fast. His fluid movements were cat-like.

She watched him walk up to the front porch as he took in every detail of his surroundings. As his gaze swept across her bedroom window, she stepped back, hoping not to be seen.

Mrs. Schultz met him at the porch door. Their conversation took no more than a minute or two. Then she heard the heavy footsteps of Mrs. Schultz lumbering up the stairs. In the whole time she'd lived there, Mrs. Schultz came to the third floor only one other time – to show her the room.

A light tap on the door announced her presence.

"Laura, dare is a nice yung man downstairs to see you." Mrs. Schultz's muffled voice crossed the barrier between them.

Laura quickly looked over at Carl sleeping peacefully in his crib. Out of habit, she checked herself in the mirror.

"I'll be right there, Mrs. Schultz."

The heavy footsteps plodded back down the hall, then slowly descended the stairs.

By the time Laura arrived on the front porch, the young man sat sipping iced tea sitting on the porch swing. At her entrance, he stood up quickly, not sure where to put the glass. Not in the mood to entertain, she inwardly enjoyed watching his uneasiness in her presence. She didn't bother offering to take his glass.

"And you are...?"

"Deputy Orlanger, ma'am."

"Then why aren't you in uniform, Deputy?"

"Sheriff Lyman didn't want me to upset anyone by coming here in uniform."

"I see. He doesn't trust I can drive into town on my own? Or, he thinks I'll leave town and he sent you here to make sure that didn't happen? Isn't that right, Deputy?"

"I don't know, ma'am. You'd have to ask him." Deputy Orlanger shuffled his feet looking down unable to look at Laura.

Too tired to spar, she resigned herself to her fate. She would direct her wrath on those who deserved it - Carson and Ben.

"Well, since you're here, you can take the suitcases I've packed, and the crib, which are upstairs, third floor. I'll take the baby with me. While you're getting those things, I'll say my goodbyes to Mrs. Schultz and Trudy. Then I have a phone call to make."

Chapter Sixteen

June was rapidly coming to a close and the weather hinted of a continued hot and humid July. The farmers would be happy, Carson thought. Corn grew best in heat and humidity.

The old adage of "knee high by the fourth of July"; a phrase of standard to measure the crop's progress came to Carson's mind. To his eyes, the corn looked well beyond knee high. As he drove past Badger, he tried to imagine how the area looked before the government built the ammunitions plant. If not corn fields, then maybe hay fields or farm houses. Farmers would be busy in their fields. It occurred to Carson that the economic windfall to Sauk County could only last as long as there was a war. A huge paradox existed; the more powder they made and shipped out, the sooner the war would be over. As soon as the war ended, there would be no need for Badger and thousands of employees would be out of work. The big question was: were they working so hard to end the war or end their employment?

During the past week, he filled his time talking to almost every tire recapper in the area and got nowhere. Between the recappers and the filling station attendants, no one remembered seeing a silver 1941 Cadillac coup. This mystery man would need to fill his car up with gas and possibly need his tires recapped. How was he getting around the gas ration allotment? Only two gas stations had any recollection of such a car, one in Monroe, about fifty to sixty miles south of Sauk City and the other in Randolph, about sixty miles northeast of Sauk City.

Neither time could they remember anything about the driver - only the car! The gas station in Monroe placed the incident about a month ago. At first, Carson thought the attendant just generalized the occurrence. Time in the past melts into itself.

"I remember because it was my birthday," responded the attendant in Monroe. "I remember yelling back to Pat, my boss, that if he wanted to get me something for my birthday, I'd like a car like that one. We joked about it for a week."

Frustrated and hungry Carson stopped at a road side diner outside of Sauk. He started to believe this line of thinking only wasted valuable investigation time. Carson asked the waitress if there were any rural gas stations or recapers in the area that didn't get much business, a customer, not the waitress, had an immediate answer.

"You could try the ol' Berry place. You might have to wake ol' Junior from his nap to help ya, but his place is as small and hidden as any filling station you'll ever find."

Carson took the directions to the ol' Berry place. He thanked the customer, grateful for the information, yet half mad at himself for having to chase down this Junior Berry and waste more time.

To find the Berry place, Carson needed to drive a few miles south west of Sauk.

The man at the diner said to look for the "Rainbow House" on his left, and then take a left onto Skunk Hollow Road. At the next intersection, turn left again. Then look for what looked like a trail into a farmer's field. As soon as Carson pulled onto the trail, he immediately regretted it.

To say it was a trail would be charitable. The bottom of Bess' father's car thudded against the hard, bumpy, uneven ruts. Carson shifted the car into first gear and slowly crept to the crest of the knoll where he saw what might laughingly be called a filling station.

"No wonder it gets very little business; just getting here could destroy your vehicle," Carson said out loud.

Sure enough, sitting in a weather beaten, wooden, straight backed chair with only its hind legs touching the floor on a porch as it leaned against a seedy shack, an older, heavy man slept. Even as Carson pulled up to the pump, the man in the chair didn't move. It wasn't until Carson got out of the car and slammed the door before the old man opened one eye lid.

"Excuse me," Carson called out to the man. "Do you mind if I ask you a few questions?"

The chair thumped, as it made hard contact with the porch. From the wary look on the man's face, Carson sensed Junior Berry might be less than willing to answer any questions. He pulled out his government ID card and showed it to the man.

"I ain't done nuttin' wrong," he calmly said, still reading the card.

"No. I'm looking for someone who drives a particular car, a silver Cadillac coupe. Have you seen him?"

"Why? He done sompthin' wrong?"

"Don't know. I'd like to talk to him."

The little man seemed to relax knowing he wasn't in trouble and the reluctance lessened.

"Yeah, I seen 'im,'bout a month ago. Became a regular. He come every three, four days then quit. I ain't seen 'im for more'na week."

Carson sat down on the top step of the dirty, wooden porch. Maybe if Junior felt elevated in any way to the government man, he would be more talkative.

"Do you remember anything about the driver? What did he look like? Did he happen to mention where he was coming from or going to?"

"Na, na, nothin' like that. Kept to hisself, he did. He wore his hat down low, but one time he drives up without his hat on. He thinks I'm sleepin. I got a look at his face before he put his hat on."

Then Junior quit talking and closed his eyes. Carson had been around too many characters like this one.

"We'd appreciate anything you could remember."

"We – the government?"

"The government, yes, but I meant Sheriff Lyman and myself."

Just saying the government wouldn't be enough. That was big brother, the nameless, faceless bully. Adding Ben was insurance. Ben was close. He had a familiar face and the local authority.

The wily smile vanished from the little man's face. Dropping Ben's name had done the trick.

"He were a younger fella like yourself, maybe younger; tall like you and strong. The last time he were here, he weren't driving his fancy car. Had a truck with a calf in back."

"Did you ever wonder or look at his gas ration ticket? That's a lot of gas for a person to use, especially since you said he came here regularly."

"Yeah, I looked - once. They was government stamps. I don't ask questions. A man's gotta make a living."

"You said he was strong. How do you know?"

"He filled up seven, five gallon cans full o'gas. Said he'd be away for a while. Well, he picked up all but three cans at once. He put'im them in the back of 'is truck with the animal. His lady friend took the rest of the cans."

"Lady friend?"

"She were a looker." He smiled at the memory. "Tall, trim and blonde."

"Do you remember anything else about him?"

"Let's see." The old man looked up and shielded his eyes from the encroaching sun light on the porch. "He had shorter, yeller hair. When he talked to his lady friend, he called her Shatzi; 'Hurry up Shatzi,' 'Get in the truck Shatzi,'" the old man mimicked the orders heard from the stranger. "He talked like he owned her. Him fuss'in so much."

Junior pushed his chair and again let it lean against the shack. Either he was through giving away free information or he couldn't remember anything else.

Carson hardly noticed the car's bottom slamming against the ground as he drove back to the main road. Junior Berry's information only gave Carson more questions and no concrete answers.

On his way back to Sauk City, he decided to pay a visit to Badger and have a little talk with Owen. He really wanted to see how things were going without Laura. He felt no guilt pulling Laura out of her job. He knew he did the right thing – regardless of what Laura thought.

As expected, he was stopped and detained by the guards at the main entrance. None of the current guards were familiar, and he no longer drove the coupe.

"Can I see your driver's license, sir?"

He handed the young man his State Department ID card along with his driver's license.

A big, black Plymouth barreled toward them from inside Badger and roared past. The driver slammed on the brakes and skidded to a stop just short of reaching the highway. A dust cloud followed. Then the car screeched away toward Sauk City. The outbound traffic guard joined his companion by Carson's car.

"One of these days those brakes won't work for her.

Then what'll she do?" the guard said.

No one sat behind Laura's desk. Two other women sorted mail, while a third woman seemed to be looking for something in a large pile of papers. Owen had his office door closed, but Carson could hear him talking.

One of the mail openers noticed Carson and stopped her task. She ripped off her protective sleeves and discreetly dropped them on her desk, as she shuffled past it toward Carson.

"Can I help you?"

"I'm here to see Owen, Mr. Anderson."

She gave Carson a discouraging look. "Oh, I'm sorry. Mr. Anderson is very busy today and can't be bothered. We have to come up with all the production numbers for the month, again. He's on the phone with Washington right now, trying to get us more time."

Carson reached into his inside suit pocket one more time and produced his State Department ID card.

"Oh. I'll get him right away." She rushed to Owen's office, rapped on the door, and popped her head inside.

"Excuse me, Mr. Anderson. There is someone here from the State Department to see you." Then she whispered to Owen, loud enough that Carson heard. "I think it's the same man who upset Laura that day."

Owen told her something Carson couldn't clearly hear. She nodded her head then closed the door.

"He'll be with you soon. Please wait there." She pointed to the empty desk, formerly used by Laura, and hurried back to open the mail, grabbing the protective sleeves on the way.

He didn't wait long. Moments later, Owen popped his head out of his office door.

"Where's Jean?" He asked no one in particular.

"She just raced out of here a minute ago. Said she had to go into town for something," answered the woman still intently digging through the piles of paper.

Hearing the name Jean perked Carson's attention. Bess said Laura had complained Owen confused her with someone named Jean. Coincidence, maybe, but it didn't take Owen long to replace Laura. Did he replace her with his girlfriend?

"Ah, Carson." Owen approached Carson. "Nice to see you again. Come into my office."

Once in the office, Carson's eyes darted around the folder-laden room. Owen stopped, as of trying to decide which pile of folders to move to make space for Carson to sit. The phone sat on the floor by Owen's feet.

"That's okay, I won't be long. I know you have a lot of work to do. Your secretaries told me about the report."

"That's frustrating," he sighed. "It just disappeared." Owen dropped in his chair.

"I only have a couple of questions to ask you. To your recollection, did Peter Franke ever mention the name Holden?"

"No, no. That name doesn't seem familiar to me at all."

Owen stared at the ceiling tapping his steepled fingertips together.

"Did he ever talk about his plans for the future?"

"Once in passing, he did say – oh, what was it now," Owen's look shifted from the ceiling to his feet, "something about learning the ins and outs of his father's business."

"Did his temperament change? I mean, happy one minute and angry the next?"

"No. Not so much minute by minute, but more like week to week. He'd be here one week and be his usual self, then the next week, when he wasn't supposed to be here, he'd show up with a real short fuse."

"What do you mean, not supposed to be here?"

"He'd say to me on a Friday, 'See ya in a week or so. Got business out of town next week.' Then he'd show up on Monday or Tuesday and act mean and superior around everyone."

"I see."

Carson let Owen reflect a bit more on Peter's behavior. "Tell you what, I'll leave and let you re-do your production report, but think about my questions. If you can remember any other odd behaviors, let me know."

Carson got up to leave, but stopped by the door.

"I understand you've already replaced Miss Bradshaw," said Carson idly brushing lint off his hat.

"Yes. Luckily, I knew Jean, Miss Barber. She'd been looking for an office position. We're lucky to have her. She's very qualified."

"I'm surprised she didn't already have a job."

"Oh, that's because she just moved here. In fact, she is moving again this weekend – so she can be closer to work. That's the kind of employee every boss dreams of."

"Then you're one lucky man, Owen." Carson finished brushing his hat.

As soon as he walked several feet into the outer office, Carson pretended to tie his shoe. He looked around. The woman who had been digging through the pile of papers must have given up on her quest or found what she needed. She sat at her desk. The other two women were not around. He cleared his throat to get her attention.

"Yes?"

He walked quietly over to her desk.

"I may be out of line here, but Mr. Anderson just mentioned that his new secretary would be moving this weekend. I was hoping she was here, so I could offer to help her – seeing how she's new to the area and all."

"Oh, don't worry about Jean. I'm sure she's rustled up enough help – new to the area or not."

"You sound like you don't approve of her."

"Don't really know her. Owen brought her in the very afternoon Laura left. I guess it pays to *know* someone. At least he's coming to work on time. He just doesn't seem her type at all."

"How do you mean?"

"Well, she's – I don't know – not a fast woman, if you know what I mean, but compared to Mr. Anderson – she's a fast woman." She muffled a giggle. "But then, my mother still doesn't understand what I see in my husband, Lyle. And we've been married for twelve years. I guess that's what makes life interesting."

Carson saw the other two secretaries walking back to the Admin building through the window.

"I just thought I'd offer to help, but you're probably right."

He met the other ladies at the front door, smiled innocently, put his hat on and left Badger.

Chapter Seventeen

Carson decided to share with Ben all he leaned from Junior Berry and Owen. It beat the alternative of going to his house – and to Laura.

"Mr. Grey, is there something I can do for you?" Libby sat at her desk knitting. "The sheriff's out for a bit."

"I don't think so. I hoped Ben would be here."

"I must tell you the news. Deputy Johnson and his wife have just learned they will be welcoming an addition to the family sometime in late December or early January. I've already got one booty knitted and I think I can have the other knitted plus a blanket by the fourth of July, barring any major obstacles between now and then."

"That's great, Libby. Be sure to tell Deputy Johnson congratulations for me. Could you leave Ben a note for me? Tell him I have some interesting information for him that I think he'll want to know."

Now he had no choice but to go to the house and spend the rest of the evening with Laura. He knew she had supper ready and waiting for him. Since she couldn't work and felt confined to the house, she had become a domestic prisoner. He knew she didn't like the living arrangement. Her movements and conversation were still guarded with forced politeness.

The late afternoon air felt still and clouds began to form in the west. *Let it pour* he thought. Maybe it'll clear the humidity. The air felt still, and it had gotten heavier since he arrived at the police station.

He wondered how the baby seemed little affected by the heat. So far, Carl was the only one who adjusted to all the changes with the least amount of objections.

Carson parked the car in the tiny garage behind the house. It had only been two days since he forced the rusty hinges open enough to allow the car in. He chose that task as an excuse to do something outside, while Laura sulked in the house.

Walking to the house, he noticed all the shades were drawn and newspapers were pinned to the bottom of the curtains completely cheating the sun's rays from entering the house. He grabbed the door knob - locked. His heart quickened. He slid the key into the lock and quietly opened the side kitchen door.

The house interior felt at least five to ten degrees cooler than outside, and something smelled delicious.

"Laura," he said softly.

"We're in here," she answered from her bedroom.

He walked down the hallway to what used to be his room. Happy baby gurgles accompanied Laura's gentle voice. Sitting in the middle of the bed were Laura and Carl. She had Carl propped up with pillows facing her. She tickled him under one of his three, chubby chins and on the bottom of his thick bare feet. Carl's giggles were infectious, and Carson couldn't help but smile seeing the diaper-clad baby squirm with joy at his mother's touch. For the first time since she'd come to live in the house, Laura seemed relaxed. Her hair pulled back and put into a high ponytail. She looked cool and comfortable in her cotton top and shorts. Finally, she saw Carson standing in the doorway.

"We just woke up from our afternoon nap and had our third cool bath today, didn't we," she said poking Carl in his little soft tummy, bringing on another fit of gurgles.

Laura bounded off the bed, gently picking up Carl and shifting him over to the opposite hip while she straightened the bed sheet with her free hand.

"Let's show Carson what else we did today so he won't think we're both a couple of lazybones," she cooed to Carl as they left the bedroom and walked toward the kitchen.

Carson followed them happy to see Laura content in her role and surroundings. He hoped she meant to serve whatever smelled so good, until he saw a homemade three layered chocolate, frosted cake on the kitchen counter. He had been too preoccupied when he'd entered the house to notice it.

"We have to celebrate tonight. Somebody is seven months old today." Laura kissed Carl on his cheek and nuzzled his neck.

The phone rang in the living room, momentarily stopping the fun. Carson saw Laura's body tense and the fear in her eyes. He walked into the living room to answer the phone.

"Hello. Yes, just a moment. I'll go get her." He laid the phone down and walked back into the kitchen. Laura busied herself setting the table with one hand while holding Carl.

"It's for you," he said when he entered the kitchen.

She froze holding the flatware. The smile left her face.

"It's okay. It's Mrs. Schultz."

As soon as he said Mrs. Schultz he saw her relax and the smile returned. On her way into the living room, she plopped Carl in

Carson's unsuspecting arms. Each seemed just as surprised as the other. Carson fully expected Carl to let out a monstrous wail at any moment and shed big crocodile tears. Instead, the little boy just looked up at him with his big blue eyes that reflected total innocence and trust.

By the time Laura picked up the phone, Carl had grabbed Carson by the nose. Carson laughed and poked Carl in the stomach as he had seen Laura do many times. The result was the same: drooling giggles from the baby. Carson had Carl seated in a highchair, that they'd found in Ben's attic, when Laura returned.

"Is everything all right?"

"Mrs. Schultz was just wondering how we were doing – any signs of pox yet?"

"I'll get the pillows for the highchair."

Carson left the room long enough to get three small sofa pillows. He propped them on either side and behind Carl while Laura carried the baked potatoes, meatloaf, corn and tossed salad to the table.

She separated a thin slice of meatloaf into tiny pieces and then did the same with part of a baked potato.

"I hope you like cold meatloaf sandwiches. I made enough to last for days. I don't want to turn the oven on if I don't have to in this heat."

Carson wanted to tell her that she wasn't obligated to do any cooking but settled with the safe answer.

"I happen to really like meatloaf, cold or hot."

She rewarded him with the kind of smile that comes from being satisfied and appreciated. When she looked up, his eyes locked with hers for a few seconds. Carl whimpered and broke up the moment. Half embarrassed, Carson turned his attention to his own plate, while Laura busied herself cooling Carl's food by blowing on it.

Carl became a thankful diversion. Spoonful after spoonful, he gobbled up the food as if he hadn't eaten in days. Like a baby bird waiting for its next worm, Carl's mouth opened for more food before Laura had a chance to get the spoon back to the bowl and fill it. Finally, satisfied, he played with the spoon. The mood, again, turned stilted.

Even though Carson finished eating, he decided to wait for Laura. She seemed to use Carl's eating habits to put off any discussion between them. She watched her son play, while she slowly ate her meal.

"Can I put a piece of cake in front of him?"

"Sure. It's his cake," said Laura.

At first, the cake puzzled Carl. When he realized he was allowed to play with it, he attacked the cake. The fat palms of his hands hammered it. He squeezed cake between his pudgy fingers. He smeared it in his hair and the rest of his body. Several crumbs even made it into his mouth. He loved being the center of attention.

Both Carson and Laura laughed at every facial expression he made squeezing and smearing the cake all over. With no more cake in front of him, Laura got up.

"All right, young man. It's time for bath number four."

Carson sat alone in the kitchen, sorry that the fun had ended. Carl provided an outlet to laugh and relax.

He thought about what Junior Berry said. Should he tell her and ruin the first pleasant evening they shared since she came to the house? No. She needed to be happy tonight. She needed to believe things would be all right in the end.

Sounds of baby laughter and water splashing filtered into the kitchen.

A loud crack of thunder shook the house signaling what lay ahead for the rest of the evening.

The cold shower he took helped lower his body temperature. Exhausted from not getting any restful sleep for the past three nights, he fell asleep immediately.

Rain pelting the roof, and the wind howling outside helped deepen the much needed sleep.

He is slowly following the faint snaps of broken twigs in a steep, heavily wooded hillside. Small spots of sunlight filter through the leaves and dot the ground like reflections off a chandelier. A thick carpet of moss covers the ground and fallen trees. He is too anxious to appreciate the natural beauty of the surroundings. The tree-covered ridge prevents a clear sight of anything but more boulders and trees.

Gradually, he realizes he is holding a rifle and crouches down behind a huge boulder, waiting for the sound of the next snapped twig. No sound comes. Cautiously, he stands up and, still fiercely gripping the rifle, begins to climb up the steep grade of the mountainside. Then it happens. Another twig snaps somewhere behind him. Swiftly, he turns around and raises the rifle to his shoulder, ready to fire at the cause of the sound. Out of nowhere, a blood-curdling scream pierces the silence.

Although the scream could have easily come from the cougar that had been following him, it bore a touch of human quality. A thick, sickening feeling momentarily overtakes him. He is too numb to move. Somewhere from the depths of his being, his subconscious takes over. Adrenaline pumps through his veins as he hurls himself back down the steep mountainside. Speed, agility and fear carry his feet over the booby-trapped ground at a rate even he finds hard to believe.

Another scream rents the still air. Fear is diminished by a small degree. The second scream is close and feels more animal than human; still he forges on through the thicket. He has to know. He is drawn to a tiny clearing that he knows leads to a cliff. At least from the edge he'll have a better vantage point of the valley below. Every step closer to the ledge of the cliff, his feet become heavier. His heart still races, but his head, like his feet, sense dread. Each step closer to the ledge is agonizing. He has to know.

The valley below is untouched, but at the bottom of the cliff lays Ewan, his ten-year-old little brother. His throat has been ripped out. For an eternity, it seems, he stands there in utter disbelief. Out of the corner of his eye, a tawny patch of color blocks a dot of sunlight from the trees to his right. In one fluid movement, he turns around and raises his rifle at the cougar he knows is there. The cougar is in midair, leaping at him from the trees. He pulls the trigger, killing it instantly. The dead, limp body grazes the cliff ledge before it, too, falls over the side, landing next to Ewan. Overcome with grief, he falls to his knees and screams at the forest in futility. "Why did you follow me? Why didn't you listen to me?"

Carson woke up with tears streaming down his face. His heart racing, his head pounding, but screams still ring through the house. It took a couple of seconds to register the screams were coming from downstairs - from Laura.

Downing the stairs, three steps at a time, he flew. As he reached the bedroom door, a flash of lightning fully illuminated the silhouette of a man standing outside her room in the porch, clearly holding a knife. Laura's body, pressed against the bed's head board, clung to the wailing baby. Her wide-eyed terror and continued screams didn't faze her antagonist. Carson turned the lights on, and heard the intruder run out the back porch.

He pried her squeezing arms open long enough to take Carl and replace him with pillows. She was too terrorized and in shock to be rational or even notice. After he took the crying baby back to his crib, he returned to Laura. Grabbing both shoulders, he tried to calm her and force her to look away from the porch. Finally, he shook her so hard she gasped for air. Recognition sunk in. She threw her arms around his neck and sobbed in his shoulder.

Seeing this strong-willed, beautiful woman reduced to helpless tears, and his own nightmare still fresh in his mind, he whispered a promise to Laura.

"I won't fail you like I did Ewan," he professed rubbing her back in an effort to calm her down.

She said something he couldn't make out. With her face buried in Carson's chest, he had a hard time hearing whatever she was saying. She clung to him like he was her only hope for salvation. His attempts to calm her down finally started to work and her repeated statement became clear.

"Don't leave us. Please, don't leave us."

He knew at that moment he could never walk away from her or her son. They needed him as much as he needed them.

"I won't let him hurt you or Carl."

He grasped her shoulders and pulled her away from him. Her frightened eyes looked up at him for comfort. He leaned down and gave her a long, gentle kiss then pulled back.

"Believe that."

Chapter Eighteen

Carson, Ben and Deputy Johnson combed the back yard, especially in and around the back porch. Sheets of ragged rain and howling winds acted like a demon preventing them from finding anything. After an hour of walking over the yard, the only bit of evidence they had was a broken pane of window from the back porch door.

"Looks just like the last broken pane," Ben said to Carson. "This time he used a night storm to block out any obvious noise or from being seen. He knows someone is in the house and, to be more specific, he knows Laura is in the bedroom."

Water dripped off Ben's rain gear. It marked his path through the kitchen where he stood by the side door.

"What does he want from us?" Laura pleaded rocking Carl back to sleep.

Ben shifted his attention to Laura. "I'm hoping you can tell us. What threat are you and your son to anyone?"

Deputy Johnson returned to the kitchen, from the direction of the bedroom, with a hammer in hand.

"Whoever he is, he won't be entering through the back porch again. I've boarded up all the windows and the door." He looked at Laura. "There won't be any sunlight coming in, but there won't be any intruders either – at least not from that area of the house."

"One thing is for sure." Ben turned the door knob. "The honeymoon is over. He knows where you are, and he's becoming more desperate. I don't think there's anything we can do - let him come to us. All we can do is be ready for him. There's nothing more we can do here tonight. I'll check in on you in the morning."

A gust of wind swept into the kitchen as Ben and Deputy Johnson exited and disappeared into the stormy night. Carl squirmed in his sleep, as the wind streaked through the house.

"I think it's safe to put him back down."

"Yeah, I think I'll go back to bed too." Carson started to walk in the direction of the attic.

"No!" Laura abruptly responded with fear. "I mean, stay down here with us – just until morning. I'd feel better if you did."

"Laura, there's a light on in every room of the house. He's not coming back here tonight, trust me."

"Please," she begged, "just until morning."

Carson wrapped his arm around Laura and Carl leading them back to the bedroom.

Carson didn't hear Ben's knock on the front door the following morning. He was too busy trying to keep Carl on his feeding schedule. Ben's second effort paid off. Carson opened the door looking a bit rushed. Before either of them had a chance to say anything, Carl's tantrum pulled Carson's attention back.

"All right. I'm coming." Carson called back to Carl in a hushed voice. "Sorry, Ben, duty calls."

Carson hurried back to the kitchen. Carl sat with more food on him than in him. Try as he might, Carson could not keep up with Carl's demands.

Ben's smile with what he saw annoyed Carson. Either he was being mocked or Ben recalled when Tommy was this small.

"Where's Laura?"

"Still sleeping, I think – or did I hear the shower start?" Carson replied between catching dribbles of cereal escaping from the sides of Carl's hungry gobbles.

"Maybe you should feed him more often," Ben joked from a kitchen chair, far enough away from the show to not be caught up in it.

"It's his second breakfast. He's a bottomless pit." Carson tried to negotiate the spoon to Carl's mouth without the little, pudgy, flaying hands hitting it.

"He's a growing boy," chimed in Laura walking into the kitchen, her hair in a towel.

"Carson, he's supposed to eat the food, not wear it."

"Tell him that. Why can't he sit still?"

Laura released Carl from the high chair, trying to hold him out and away from her clean clothes.

"Because he's seven months old, and you're supposed to be the adult here. Come on mister, we have a date with the bathtub."

Carson waited for them to leave the room.

"Any second thoughts about them living here?"

Carson ignored Ben's inference. He waited for the footsteps to disappear into the bathroom and the sound of water running. Then he faced Ben with a sense of urgency.

"I need to tell you what I found out yesterday."

"Libby's note said you seemed a bit anxious to talk to me yesterday. I take it you found out something about our mystery man."

"Yeah. Seems he used an old, out-of-the-way place to get his gas. A place called Berry's."

"Sure, the Berry place," Ben replied, "I should have thought of that place. Wonder how he found out about it?"

"Junior Berry told me our guy came every few days, but he hasn't seen him for more than a week. He said that he got a look at the guy. This could be our break. The guy is about my age, maybe younger, around my height, blond and strong. The most disturbing information is what he called his lady friend."

"Lady friend, eh?"

"He referred to her as 'Schatzi'."

"That's German for sweetheart, isn't it? What's disturbing about that?"

"A couple of things. First off, if it's Holden, he's British. Why would he use the word Schatzi? Secondly, that's the pet name Peter used to call Laura. Ben, everything about this guy screams Peter Franke – age, height, blond, strong. I didn't want to say anything around Laura until I talked with you. Last night wasn't a good time. Also, the last time he got gas, he was driving a truck with a calf in the back."

"Well that ends one mystery for me."

"I'd like to go back out there today with you, but I don't think Laura feels safe being here by herself anymore."

The sound of voices coming from the direction of the bathroom prevented further conversation. Both men listened to Laura talk to Carl as they made their way back to the kitchen.

Laura loved the role of motherhood. She looked happy and comfortable, yet Carson recognized the invisible cover of protection mothers extend to their children. Her rapt attention to

Carl was easy to understand. She had the added pressure of protecting him from a would-be assassin.

She plopped the diaper-clad baby on the floor next to Ben's feet, and then got a cool glass of water from the sink. At first, Carl objected to being set down, but something interrupted his objection. He chose to attack the shoelaces within his reach. They all were amused by how engrossed Carl seemed to be with Ben's shoelaces.

"Sheriff." Laura settled into a chair without Carl noticing. She proudly rubbed Carl's full head of blond hair, "Remember that box you and Carson found here in the kitchen?"

"Yes, I remember."

"You seemed to think I should know something more. Well, just now, when I was bathing Carl, I was thinking how fast time has flown. He's now seven months old, doesn't seem possible. Then I thought I haven't seen Carl's birth certificate since we left the hospital. Peter said he'd take care of it and put it somewhere safe."

"Sanctuary," whispered Carson.

"Did Peter ever mention where he'd put it and why he thought it needed to be somewhere safe? Safe from what?" Ben asked the last question more to himself than as a question Laura could answer.

"I don't know. We never talked about it again. I trust Peter did just that – put it somewhere safe. He always said he wanted to take over his father's business, and someday it would become Carl's. I suppose he gave it to his lawyer."

"But you don't know for sure?" Carson leaned his elbows on the table.

"No, I just assumed."

"Was Peter a religious man? I mean, did he favor one religion over the other – go to services anywhere?" asked Ben.

"He was brought up Roman Catholic, but we, as a couple, never attended church anywhere together. I don't think he went anywhere alone, either."

"Maybe he visited one church."

"Ben, are you thinking what I'm thinking?

By now, Carl grew bored with Ben's shoe laces. Having untied both shoes, he sought his mother's attention. He whimpered when Laura got up and walked away to the refrigerator. But when he saw the bottle in her hand, his attitude greatly improved. Wholeheartedly, he accepted the bottle as Laura lay him in her arms.

"The same day this place was ransacked, Saint Aloysious had a break in. I didn't hear about it until two days later. Father Stanton didn't report it. As far as he could tell, nothing was missing. Apparently, one of the cleaning ladies heard about the break in. She reported it to Deputy Orlanger. She knows the good Father is getting on in years and his eyesight isn't what it used to be. So, when he said nothing was missing, the cleaning lady wasn't too sure. She wanted to report it, so that, in the future, if something isn't in its place, at least we'd have an idea when it might have happened."

"Smart cleaning lady." Laura rocked Carl.

"Do you think Peter gave someone Carl's birth certificate, and that's why the church was broken into?" Carson asked.

"Only one way to find out."

****

The original three day stay in DC evolved into more than a week. When she wasn't helping Denby, Bess spent time at libraries reading every psychology article that would support her theory on Peter Franke. She wavered between exhaustion and exhilaration. Besides doing the research on Holden for Denby, she found herself filling in for some of the department secretaries on several occasions. The last few days were the most mentally demanding for Bess. She read scores of confidential files on Peter Franke and as many files on all his assignments and written reports. Her ability to analyze and correctly interpret information amazed and even impressed Denby. She was flattered when he told her she could work for him, should she ever want to change occupations.

The core of Peter's family history fascinated her. All of their sad deaths only confirmed her belief that Peter Franke mentally snapped after his mother's death, especially, since it made him the only survivor in the family. She suspected the guilt and burden too much for him to handle.

When she questioned Denby, he responded with certainty

Peter never knew how or when his brother and real father died. He doubted Peter ever knew he had a brother.

None of Peter's written reports came across as being depressed. Report after report detailed meetings, times, places and who attended the meetings. His attention to detail and recollection in his reports came across in a matter-of-fact manner.

Toward the end of the pile of reports, she noticed a slight difference in his style of writing. As the reports became more current, the details of people, places and things became more cryptic. When she pointed out this change of habit to Denby, he told her he too noticed the change, but attributed it to just a change of style in his written reports.

"All agents change the way they write their reports a little from time to time."

She decided to accept what Denby told her, until she read the report: *November 14, 1941, London – Saint Paul's Cathedral.*

......met up with JH in chip shop. Holden is a huge surprise to me. I trust him with my life. He....

The name "Holden" jumped off the page at Bess like a firecracker. Without thinking, she burst into Denby's office with the news, running right into him. The look of surprise on his face reminded her of what she had just done.

"Oh! I sorry Mr. Denby, but I've finally found Holden!"

Denby's expression remained blank.

"Holden – Peter Franke's friend. The man Carson asked you to find out about?"

Recognition finally spread across his face.

"Holden. Really. Where?"

Bess flashed the report open in front of his face before he finished asking.

"See, there, Holden is mentioned in this report."

"Yes, Miss Osmond, I see. Is his name mentioned anywhere else?" Denby took the report out of Bess' hand.

"Well, I just found this one... so far. There are still more reports to read through, but doesn't this help? I mean, now we know he exists. That's probably not his real name, but it's a place to start."

Denby didn't respond in any way. Engrossed in reading the report, he tuned Bess out.

"This does help, doesn't it, Mr. Denby?"

Slowly he replied while still reading. "Yes, this helps. Bring in all the rest of Peter's reports you haven't read, and we'll go over them together." He reached for the intercom system on his desk.

"Millie."

"Yes, Mr. Denby," a voice squawked back.

"Call Quigley and tell him I won't be able to make the meeting. Something's come up. Then write me a memo to call him tomorrow."

"Mr. Denby," the voice asked, "is Miss Osmond in there with you?"

"Yes, Millie, she is. Why?"

"There is a phone call for her out here. What should I do with it?"

Bess mouthed to Denby to have Millie hold the call.

"It's okay, Millie, Miss Osmond will get her phone call out there. She's on her way out now."

Fifteen minutes passed before she finally returned with her arms over flowing with files.

"Is something wrong?"

"No." She spilled the unread reports on his desk. "Nothing's the matter. I'm just a bit confused."

"About what?"

"According to the Department of Commerce, Peter Franke's stepfather's business started doing business with Germany."

"Where did you get your information from?"

"That phone call. Mr. Denby, my sources are quite reliable. I'm sure the information is correct."

"How much longer were you planning on being here?"

"Now that we've found Holden, I'll leave tomorrow. Besides, my boss in Madison is ready to fire me. I've used up all my good excuses."

"Okay. I'll go over the reports and look for more references to Holden. You use your sources and see who is calling the shots at Peter's stepfather's business. See if it ever dissolved, who their customers are and, if you can, see if it's a front for something else. This whole thing doesn't feel right to me."

"Could this really mean that I'm actually right; Peter Franke is alive, and trying to kill Laura Bradshaw, their son and Carson Grey?"

****

Outside of a few tree branches strewn over the ground of Saint Aloysius's church, no other damages were apparent. The flowers around the rectory had been flattened overnight, but they would survive. A willowy, white-haired woman knelt before them. Her knotted arthritic hands lovingly patted the recently replanted flowers. Seemly pleased with her efforts, she rubbed her hands together, then slowly dragged one of her kneeling legs in front of her and pulled herself up into a standing position.

She appeared to be a volunteer gardener for Saint Al's church. She addressed them first, as Ben and Carson walked up behind her.

"Well, Sheriff, you got me; caught me burying my life's savings in St. Al's flowers. Guilty."

Carson smiled genuinely taken in by the spirited, wrinkled-face woman with impish mischief in her twinkling eyes.

"Ah, Sally, I knew it'd be only a matter of time, before I caught you up to something nefarious. Unfortunately, I left my cuffs in the car. I guess I'll have to let you off with a warning this time. How'd you know it was me?"

"Your shadow preceded you, Benjamin." Her eyes twinkled with glee at his inquiry. "My goodness, you're supposed to be the one who knows all the tricks. Suddenly, I don't feel so safe." She winked at Carson. "Who's the good lookin' fella with you? Another deputy, I hope. Those other two you have are hopeless in the looks department."

"Sally, you don't really think I'd hire this guy? Not now, knowing how you feel. I'd lose my best girl."

Their arms intertwined as Ben nonchalantly escorted her back toward the church.

"Say, Sally, do you know anything about the break-in here at the church about ten days ago?"

She nodded. "I do. Wasn't here that day myself; home making strawberry jam or I would have been here. Irma Hathaway called me about it. Said she was thinking about reporting it, even though Father Stanton didn't think it necessary."

Carson picked up his pace, until he reached the other side of Sally.

"Sally," he diverted her attention from Ben, "can I call you Sally?"

"You're that other government fellow. You're the one Irma was sputtering on about."

"Yes, I guess I am. Did this other woman happen to mention if anything was actually taken in the break-in?"

By now, the threesome had stopped walking and stood in front of the rectory. A man dressed in black, half a block away, walked toward them with an arm full of groceries. Short, stubby, with pale skin Father Stanton looked as if he enjoyed carrying his burden.

The threesome waited for him to meet them.

"Not much happens around here that Irma doesn't know about. She said, 'as far as she could see, nothing from the Rectory was missing,' but they left the place in such a mess she couldn't be sure."

Father Stanton finally reached them slightly winded and thankful for the chance to rest.

"Hello, Sheriff," he said slightly winded. "I thought it was you. I wasn't sure until just a few seconds ago."

One of the grocery bags found its way into Carson's arms. Ben took the second bag.

"Hello, Father. This is Mr. Grey. He and I would like to talk to you about the break-in here at the rectory."

"I'd almost forgotten about that. After Irma reported it, we never heard anymore about it from your office. I thought it wrong of her to bother you. Let's talk inside and get out of the sun."

Sally stayed behind.

"I'll be going now, Father. The flowers should make it as long as we don't get another storm like last night. Nice to meet you, Mr. Grey. And Benjamin, next time carry your handcuffs with you."

The interior of the rectory was dark and cool. The bottom half of the walls were covered with mahogany wainscoting. A floral design of wallpaper went from the top of the wainscoting to the eleven-foot high ceiling. An old, dark, Oriental rug covered the floor. Neither Ben nor Carson had ever been inside the home of any religious minister or priest. It had always been like an invasion of privacy.

Directly inside the front door a dark varnished, wooden staircase carried the eye to the second floor. To their immediate left the receiving room, furnished with several comfortable overstuffed chairs waiting for them. Father Stanton led them into the room and invited them to sit.

"I'll take these groceries to the kitchen and be right back with some refreshments."

Carson and Ben sat quietly observing the room when Father Stanton returned, carrying a tray with a pitcher of lemonade. They waited until he served them their drinks and sat down before they started asking questions.

"Our interest is in the break-in, not so much to see if anything is missing, although I'd be interested to hear if you discover something gone. Our interest is because of a coincidence of another break-in that day," explained Ben.

"Coincidence?"

"Father, I'm living in the house Peter Franke lived in before he was murdered. The same day of the rectory break- in, my house was also ransacked."

"I see."

"No, Father, I don't think you do."

"Yes, I do. You think the same person broke into both places looking for something specific – something Mr. Franke wanted kept in a safe place."

Father Stanton's clear understanding of the situation left Carson speechless.

"Yes, I do have something that Mr. Franke gave me for safekeeping. He came to me about four months ago and gave me an envelope to keep for him. I thought it highly unusual. He wasn't a member of the congregation, but I sensed something troubled him. Perhaps he was even afraid of something. So I agreed to keep the envelope. He said he no longer felt he could keep it safe by himself and then said if anything should happen to him, a Mr. Hewes would retrieve it and know what to do with it. I'm still waiting to hear from this Mr. Hewes."

"Did Mr. Franke ever say who Mr. Hewes was or confide in you who or what he was afraid of?"

"Sorry, Sheriff, he never expanded on that."

"This envelope he gave you, do you know what its contents are?" Carson's fingers were white from gripping his glass so hard.

"I do. I'm puzzled why anyone would break into a rectory for something as common as a birth certificate and some notes."

****

Director Denby never made it to his meeting, and he never made it home that day. He and Bess Osmond spent the whole night reading reports, phoning various government department heads, combing over tax returns and trying to figure out the connection between Peter's reports and his father's company records.

According to the tax forms from the previous few years, Franke Import/Export scaled back their productivity slightly from the years leading up to 1941. But the current records at the U.S. Commerce Department showed a decided increase in business volume in the past few months. When they called Franke Import/Export, they discovered the manager, director and company attorney and department heads were all new at the jobs.

Denby and Bess repeatedly pored over the files and reports, sorting out the useful information from the useless.

"He only mentioned Holden five times in eighteen months," lamented Bess. "Does Holden have anything to do with Franke Import/Export?"

"The answer's here. I know it is," Denby insisted. "I'll go over these reports as many times as I have to, until we find the answer."

Frustration started to wear them down. Denby felt bad for Bess. She wasn't used to this level of excavating for answers. He watched her pace the office: rubbing her eyes and squeezing the muscles at the back of her neck. She tried clearing her mind, anything that would help her see something she'd missed in the past twelve hours. Her actions briefly reminded him of Allen Clarke. A small pain tugged at him. The sound of her voice brought him back to the present.

"Okay, so, what do we have for sure?" Bess asked.

"For sure, we have a lot of information that looks all above board and legal. No mention of Holden."

"Arghh!" She stared out the office window into the black void of the night. "Are there any more files or reports we've missed?"

"The only files that aren't here are support files."

"Support files?" She said confused.

"Files that confirm what we have in front of us."

"Can we get them anyway? I have to look at something new before my head explodes."

"Sure. The files I'm talking about are in the cabinet, next to Millie's desk. Here are the keys."

He threw her the keys and Bess scurried out of Denby's office, leaving the director alone with his thoughts. The real reason he felt reluctant to quit was because he knew Allen Clarke's death was somehow involved in all of this. The sting of Allen's death still hurt Denby more deeply than he'd like to admit. He hoped solving this puzzle, would give him and Allen's family some answers.

When Bess returned, with a pile of thin files, Denby mentally sighed at how many support files she had in her arms. As she carried them into the office, a paper clipping with a picture slipped from one of the files and floated to the floor. They both followed the photo's descent. The other open reports, tax forms, files and pictures already completely covered Denby's desk. The only place to lay the new files seemed to be in the chair Bess just vacated.

The photo on the floor was Marianne Himmel Szescy Franke, age 25. Bess picked it up.

"She was beautiful. Where'd you get the photo?"

Bess handed the photo over to Denby's outstretched hand. He looked at the picture.

"We do a background check with all of our agents, photos and all, and in Peter's case, because of his heritage, we felt it wise to dig deeper than normal. He started working here only a couple of years ago. Once we realized his mother's direct Germany background, we were skeptical about hiring him. We can't be too careful when it comes to this line of work."

Denby handed the photo back to Bess. He kept combing over the files. Bess seemed captivated by the articles and pictures from the new files. The sixth file had her rapt attention. It contained the history, in photos, of Peter's civilian life: college rowing team, fencing team, family Christmas vacations in Europe and earlier childhood.

Further down in the file, the photos took a decidedly darker turn. A collection of German newspaper articles and pictures lay before her. The grizzly interior of a blood-spattered bakery with a sheet-covered corpse riveted her eyes to the photo.

"This must be about Peter's German father," she said staring at the picture.

Several more German newspaper articles followed. Denby looked up when she came to a photo he knew well. He's seen the photo many times. It became part of Peter's background check; information received from Interpol, before Denby hired him. Although it disturbed him at the time, he felt sure Peter knew nothing about it. He could see that the picture absorbed Bess' attention. Eleven partially charred skeletons lay on a tarp next to a burnt house. Under the picture were the names of the victims. He knew by heart the names of each victim and that the seventh skeleton on the tarp belonged to Josef Szescy. The way she looked at the picture disturbed him.

"Find something, Miss Osmond?"

"I'm not sure. I think I've found something, but I can't put my finger on it. My father always taught me to look at the details. He'd say 'It's in the details where secrets are revealed.' This photo is... funny."

"Funny. How?"

"Here." She got up from the floor and jabbed the photo in front of his face. "Do you see anything odd?"

Denby had seen the photo many times over the years, but this time he gave it more scrutiny. His eyes kept floating back and forth from the skeletons to the burnt house. Suddenly he became animated.

"Here. Look at the picture of the house. In the background is Josef's motorcycle. Now, really look at skeleton numbered seven."

Bess hovered over his shoulder studying the photo as instructed until she saw it.

"Oh... my... God!"

Chapter Nineteen

Ben hardly understood anything Bess jabbered over the telephone. She confirmed Holden existed and Peter wrote about him in several of his reports. Her unbridled excitement flowed through the phone line. It reminded him of how Tommy acted on Christmas morning.

"Okay. We'll get together with Carson and Laura once you get back...mm hmm, mm hmm. When can we expect to see you... mm hmm, mm hmm. Well, have a good flight back. We'll see you later then, Bess... uh ah, uh ah, yeah. Okay. Bye, Bess."

He glanced down at the envelope on his desk from Father Stanton. He needed to talk with Carson or Laura. One or both of them had more information, whether they knew it or not.

"Libby," Ben called out, "when you get to Carson's, tell him to come here as soon as possible. Tell him Bess called from Washington. She and Denby discovered Holden."

Even though no answer came from Libby, he knew she wrote down everything he said. A minute later, he heard the front door close.

Ben had the documents, previously in the care of Father Stanton, all opened in full display on top of his desk: Carl's birth certificate, a letter addressed to Mr. Hewes, Peter's will and personal notes.

The notes listed dates, times, and places, all neatly broken down in four columns. Perfectly understandable Ben thought considering the type of work Peter did, yet a lot of the notes had odd abbreviations he didn't understand. Carson mentioned Peter's penchant for secrecy and note-taking.

The entries starting November 1942 up until weeks before Franke's death perked Ben's interest. Every other Wednesday night at 10:30 p.m., Peter recorded an entry referring to J.H. After talking with Bess, Ben now could assume J.H. was James Holden.

As far as Ben could tell, those were the only initials that would interest Carson. But then, Carson would have a better feeling for what was important, since he knew Peter and Peter's idiosyncrasies.

Fifteen minutes later, Carson slipped into Ben's office unnoticed.

"Where'd you come from?" Ben said surprised.

"The front door. You did ask me to come. Or was Libby wrong? Sally's right, your powers of observation are shaky."

"Where's Orlanger?" Ben ignored the jab.

"He's at Libby's desk manning the phone calls. At the moment no one appreciates Libby more than Deputy Orlanger. Thanks for keeping this stuff here for me. I don't feel like I can keep it safe at the house, especially after the storm."

"No problem," said Ben. "Pull that chair around here. I need your opinion on something."

Carson carried a chair around to Ben's side of the desk. Ben rolled his chair aside, making room for him.

"Is this going to take long? Owen Anderson was on the phone with me when Libby came. He sounded anxious and wants to talk to me and you as soon as possible. Oh, by the way, could Libby stay with Laura when I'm with you? Laura still doesn't like being alone at the house."

Ben nodded.

"Owen will either have to wait or come here. I need you to decipher this document. It's one of the documents Peter gave Father Stanton for safekeeping."

Ben slid the sheet of paper with the four columns in front of Carson.

"Since you knew Peter professionally... you did train him, didn't you?"

"Yes."

"I need you to see if there is any correlation in here, besides the ones I've marked."

Carson's eyes scanned down the columns, then across, looking for any hidden messages.

"While I'm deciphering, as you put it, call Owen and tell him what you just told me," Carson said. "Say, did you have any luck getting hold of Peter's lawyer, Hewes?"

"I'm expecting a call back from Franke Import/Export. Speaking of them, Bess said she discovered some juicy information. She's flying back today and wants to talk to you, me and Laura tonight." Ben walked to the door of his office. "I'll use Libby's phone when Orlanger's done."

Ben briefly left his office leaving Carson to concentrate on the documents.

"Find anything?" Ben asked Carson while entering his office.

"Not much. KG is Kew Garden, STPL is Saint Paul Cathedral, KB is Knight's Bridge, HP is Hyde Park and BB is Big Ben, I think. How about you?"

"Owen said he'd be here a little later. He'd come now, but something came up. Can I look at that again for a moment?" Ben pointed to the birth certificate on the desk.

A rap on the office door was followed by Deputy Orlanger entering.

"There's a phone call for you, Sheriff, at Libby's desk."

"Thanks, Henry. I'll take the call in here."

Orlanger transferred the call immediately and Ben answered on the first ring.

"Sheriff Lyman."

The expression on his face became more serious as the one-sided conversation went on.

"Thank you for calling me. I appreciate the information." Said Ben then hung up the phone.

"Something wrong?"

"We now know why Hewes never showed up at Father Stanton's door," said Ben.

"Why is that?"

"He was found dead in his bathtub six weeks ago, of an apparent heart attack."

"Interesting."

"It does fit in with something Bess said on the phone. She said that it sounds like nobody knows who's in charge at Franke Import/Export."

"Who was that on the phone, then?"

"Chief Hornby in Alexandria, Virginia. I guess my call to Franke Import/Export spooked their secretary or she didn't believe me. She called their local police station to let them be the bearers of bad news."

Carson stood up, checked the clock on the wall, then made his way to the door.

"Where are you going?" Ben asked.

"Since Owen won't be here for a while, I thought I'd use the time and get a few groceries Laura asked me to pick up. I'll be back before Owen gets here."

"Do you hear yourself?" Ben couldn't hide his smirk.

"What?"

"Just a few days ago, at my house, you told me you didn't think you could ever be a family man. Yet here you are today concerned about the time and getting groceries."

"I won't fail on my responsibilities, and besides, there is Carl to think about."

****

When Carson dropped off the groceries, Carl was down for his morning nap. Libby had taken the opportunity to show Laura how to make her famous cherry/apple pie. At the first opening of escape, Carson made his excuses and quickly left.

As soon as he entered the police station, he knew something was wrong. Nobody was in the office. Libby's phone's shrill ring went unanswered. The ringing mixed with the sound of the back door slamming and footsteps running back and forth. Finally, Ben and Deputy Orlanger came in the office from the back and acknowledged Carson but were too bent on readying themselves to talk to him.

"What's happened?"

Both Ben and Deputy Orlanger ignored him.

"Ready?" Ben asked to Orlanger.

Deputy Orlanger nodded, then disappeared out through the back door.

"What's going on? What happened?"

"There's been an explosion at Badger. A car blew up. The place is in an uproar. Everyone wants to leave, but they're afraid their cars might blow up, too. Someone reported hearing gun shots being fired."

"Let's go. I'm going with you."

****

The plant's own fire station had already contained the vehicle fire and secured the surrounding area by the time Ben, Deputy Orlanger and Carson reached Badger. All that remained of the car was a bent, charred, steel frame. In the driver's seat sat a skeleton with its mouth open as if screaming for help. Although the initial fire had been put out, smoke still seeped from under the belched hood. A ring of people, ten deep, wearing looks of shock and disbelief, surrounded the vehicle. No one seemed too eager to go back to their jobs, no matter how much they were reprimanded by their supervisors. The gathering crowd parted for Ben and Deputy Orlanger, as they walked through to the burnt out car that encased the corpse.

Carson didn't need to view or inspect the body. His gut instinct knew it belonged to Owen Anderson. Instead of heading to the smoldering wreck, he scanned the crowd looking for any of the women who worked for Owen, especially the one who he talked to several days ago. She wasn't there. Not wasting any more time scanning the dazed mourners, Carson moved from the outer fringes of the crowd and gradually edged his way to the Administration Office. There he found the same three women who had been there days before. They stood at the windows with tear-stained faces and damp handkerchiefs in their hands, staring at the throngs of people outside. Owen's new secretary was not among the faithful. Only the woman he'd talked to earlier show any attempt to pull herself away from the window when he entered the building.

"It's Mr. Anderson, isn't it?" he asked in a consoling manner.

She acknowledged his comment with nod of her head.

"I was afraid of that."

Tears rushed back into her eyes at his statement. She opened her mouth to speak, but not a sound came out. Her emotions got the better of her, she started to cry again.

"It happened so fast, I'm sure Mr. Anderson never felt anything," Carson whispered to her as she buried her head into his chest. He looked back out the window, hoping the women were unable to see the hideous expression left on Owen's skeleton.

"Where's Mr. Anderson's other secretary, Jean?"

The weeping woman in his arms pulled back from Carson revealing a totally different attitude. Not anger, but pure hatred covered her face.

"That evil witch! She's the reason he's dead."

"What do you... what do you mean?"

"Earlier, right after Owen got off the phone, she went into Mr. Anderson's office and slammed the door behind her. Then all we heard were loud voices. I did hear them mention Laura's – Miss Bradshaw's – name and your name. Jean carried on something terrible. Then she left, slamming his office door and the front door when she stormed out."

"Did you see her leave Badger?"

"No, we kept our heads down. It was none of our business; we just happened to be caught in the middle."

She started to cry again, dabbing her eyes.

"Poor Mr. Anderson."

"How can you say she was responsible for his death?"

"Because," the youngest of the group spoke up, still standing at the window, "not long after she left, Mr. Anderson came out of his office very upset. He had me find that production report. The one we had to redo and some other things from Jean's desk."

The secretary next to Carson finished the story. "Then he grabbed the papers and announced he was going to see the sheriff. One minute later – this."

She hardly finishes the last sentence before another series of tears replaced the words.

Even if only part of these accusations were true, Ben needed to interview these ladies and get their statements. Whatever information Owen felt he had to share with Ben and himself, it no longer existed. It was part of the pile of ashes outside the front door. Maybe one of these ladies would have some insight as to what Owen knew or suspected. And, if these ladies were right, Jean was just as dangerous as the man driving the other coupe.

"Would any of you say that Jean resembled Miss Bradshaw in any way?"

The question took their minds off the commotion outside for a moment. Collectively they looked at each other as if challenging one another to speak first.

"She is about the same height and size as Laura, come to think of it," the younger secretary commented.

"Her hair color is a bit darker than Laura's, but I'd still say it's blond," said the secretary, who until now had not spoken.

The younger secretary moved away from the window, dabbing her eyes dry.

"Sometimes when she wore her hair up and pulled off her face... there were more than a few times I caught myself calling her Laura."

From what they said, Carson felt sure this woman, Jean, must be the same woman he accused Laura of being that day in the barn. And the same woman Junior Berry saw at his filling station. Carson wondered what her connection to all of this was. Did she purposely use Owen as an *in* to the plant? What did she need to have access to?

Carson just started gathering more information from Owen's secretaries, when Ben came through the front door.

"I need to see Mr. Anderson's office."

"Is it safe to go home?" asked the youngest secretary.

"Yes, ma'am. I believe this was an isolated incident."

The older secretary pointed Ben to Owen's office.

"Mr. Anderson's office is right through that door there. I'll clean off his desk for you."

"No," said Ben. "We've got to go over it for evidence. His office is off limits until further notice."

Soon police from all over the county inundated the plant. If not involved with helping disperse the crowd, every able-bodied officer was involved with the monumental task of getting statements from every person present at the time of the explosion. Ben, Deputy Orlanger and Carson remained in Owen's office looking for any clues that might lead them to where Jean went and why she left in such a hurry. None of Owen's secretaries knew why he needed to talk to Ben and Carson.

At 9:30 p.m., they sealed off Owen's office door and went back to Sauk City. A small band of gate guards vigilantly kept the press at bay. In the morning, reporters, police and plant workers would be back at Badger, picking up where they left off. No explosion or loss of life would shut down Badger – the war took precedence.

Bess, Laura and Carl were waiting for them at the police station when they arrived. The women tried to sort out the events of the day from the gossip being retold all over town. Deputy Johnson played with Carl while they talked. Carson's eyes met Laura's when he entered the station. He shook his head at her tear-welled eyes to answer her questioning stare.

"I brought Laura and Carl," Bess said. "I hope you don't mind. Deputy Johnson said it would be all right to wait here, since we planned to gather here tonight and talk."

"Have you already told Laura why we're all here?" Ben asked.

"No. I wanted everyone together."

"Laura, Bess has been in DC with Denby. She's been doing research for us and him," said Carson.

"What specifically were you looking for?" Laura asked.

"I went to try and find out who Peter Franke was and to understand him better."

"Let's all find ourselves a chair and a place to sit." Ben yawned with exhaustion.

While everyone gathered chairs, placing them in a circle and looked for a table, Laura excused herself and Carl to quickly change his diaper. Then she grabbed a bottle out of her purse to give him.

"I'll start and get us all up to date," said Ben. "Yesterday, Father Stanton, at Saint Al's Catholic Church, admitted that Peter Franke had given him an envelope for safekeeping. The envelope contained Carl's birth certificate, a letter addressed to Peter's lawyer, Mr. Hewes, and some personal notes. Mr. Hewes was instructed, or I assume instructed, to relieve Father Stanton of the envelope should anything happen to Peter. The reason Mr. Hewes never came for the envelope is because he died shortly before Peter died."

"How convenient," Bess blurted out, then blushed. "I'm sorry, but isn't it just too well timed?"

The rest of the group remained quiet.

"There is one thing in his personal notes that bothers Carson and me. Peter had contact regularly with someone whose initials are J.H."

"Bess, you and Denby found the name Holden mentioned in several of Peter's reports didn't you?"

"Yes, five times."

"Peter kept his own personal notes hidden. He had contact with this J.H. every other Wednesday night while here in Sauk City and in Iowa, right up to the Wednesday before his death," Ben explained.

"This should help you redefine when he was killed then, right?" asked Laura hopefully looking at Carson and Ben for an answer.

Ben reflectively nodded in the affirmative.

"Another question was answered today at the plant," Carson interjected. "About a week ago, I accused Laura of being the woman in the barn the day of the fire. I've come to learn it wasn't you. I'm sorry." Carson looked over at Laura. "It appears Owen's new secretary, or girlfriend, is that woman. Your former co-workers claim she is responsible for Owen's death. Where she is currently, we don't know. The other secretaries stated that this Jean and Owen got into an argument this morning. She left Badger slamming doors and hasn't been seen anywhere since."

"We've notified all neighboring law enforcement concerning her. Don't worry about her, Laura," Ben reassured her. "We'll find her."

"That's interesting, but I think my news will knock your socks off," Bess announced, squirming in her chair. She looked quite pleased with herself at the anticipation she created. Her pregnant pause was longer then Carson wanted to wait.

"Are you going to tell us, freely, or do you expect me to bribe you, like other reporters?" He said angerly.

"All right, all right," said Bess. "Your findings about Mr. Hewes relate to and explain a few things. Mr. Denby checked into Franke Import/Export. We found out that the people in key positions are all new. If Mr. Hewes is dead, that would explain why they have a new company attorney, even if his death is just too convenient for my money. When we asked who was in charge, the acting director said he didn't know for sure. He said he gets all of his instructions by telephone every Thursday. Now isn't that interesting, in light of what we just learned about Peter and his Wednesday phone calls?" She sat up rigidly in her chair. "Are you ready for the eye popper news?"

"Bess, you're scaring me. Please, let's get this over with so I can get Carl down for the night," pleaded Laura.

"When Mr. Denby and I couldn't find any other mention of this Holden. I asked if we were looking at all the files they had on Peter Franke. You see I was still going on the assumption, and I'm still pretty sure, that Peter Franke suffered from a mental breakdown, triggered by the death of his mother. When Mr. Denby and I were going over Peter's support file, we came across one that had photos from a German newspaper. I sensed something wasn't right. Mr. Denby found the discrepancy. The person or corpse they identified as Josef Szescy was not Peter Franke's identical twin brother. Peter Franke's brother, Josef, was not killed that day. He may still be alive. All of the other bodies were identified by families, leaving one body, which they assumed to be Josef Szescy. But no one identified his body because he had no family in Germany."

Chapter Twenty

Laura wavered in her seat and dropped Carl's bottle.

"Peter has a brother?" She said in a weak voice.

"Do you know what you're saying?" Carson angrily replied to Bess's shocking announcement.

"I'm saying the newspapers, Interpol, whoever in Germany, tagged the wrong guy that day. Germany is a dangerous place to be right now. Maybe Josef Szescy is dead by now, but the skeleton in the photo couldn't possibly be Josef for the most obvious reason."

"Which is...?"

"Peter Franke is, or was, about your height, Carson, right? Well, the skeleton in the picture was hardly any taller than I am."

"What has this got to do with Peter? Why is this news important?" Laura asked.

"It's not." said Ben. "I don't think it has any bearing at all on the happenings here. All you've given us is a lot of facts, unrelated facts. I don't see how any of it tells us who Holden is, where he is, or who killed Peter Franke. Franke Import/Export has nothing to do with what's going on here. Peter may have sick, we don't know. We're jumping from one conclusion to another. It's throwing us off our main objective and clear thinking."

"I, on the other hand, think this is very significant. I think Peter found out he had a brother and found him, or Josef may have found Peter." Bess sat back in her chair sulking. No one seemed enthralled with her conclusion or with her research's findings.

"If this Holden is Peter's brother, why the name change or British accent?" said Laura.

"I agree with Ben," said Carson. "Why don't we all go home and sleep on it. We're trying to make this information fit into each of our own theories. I need to clear my head, too."

****

If he didn't know every crack on the ceiling before, he knew them now. It was 3:18 a.m., and Carson had yet to embrace any sleep. His eyes had adjusted to the darkness of the bedroom hours ago. Since the storm, his sleeping arrangement changed, he hoped permanently. Laura asked him to move down into her bedroom. How could he refuse? Seeing the web of plaster cracks on the ceiling reminded him of the case. Each crack was like a clue leading to the main crack, in this case, Peter Franke.

Carl whimpered in his sleep. Laura's reflex reaction was a sigh. She rolled even closer to Carson, yet both she and Carl remained asleep. His first impulse was to turn on his side to face her, and then pull her closer to him so he could wrap his arms around her. Better judgment intervened. When Laura lay Carl down for the night, she commented on how exhausted she felt.

226

She fell asleep immediately. So he remained on his back staring at the cracks in the ceiling plaster. Finally, he drifted off.

The room, still dark due to the boarded-up back porch, felt hot and stuffy. Both Laura and Carl were awake and out of the room. Carson assumed the time to be around seven o'clock.

Muffled laughter drifted into the bedroom from the kitchen.

"Shhh. You'll wake him up."

Carson swung his legs over the side of the bed, pulled on his trousers and walked bare footed to the kitchen.

"It's about time. I was afraid I'd wake you up when I put him down for his morning nap."

"What time is it?"

Carson's eyes swept up to the wall clock that displayed 9:20 a.m.

"Why didn't you wake me up?"

"I thought about it, when Ben called earlier. But since you slept soundly through the phone ringing, I told him that you were still asleep. He said not to wake you. Were you going with him today?"

"I thought about it."

"While you're deciding, I'll put Carl down." She picked Carl up off the kitchen floor. "There are some scrambled eggs for you on the stove."

The eggs probably tasted good, but the conversation with Laura, about Peter's complete family's story, replayed through his mind. He'd put it off long enough. Just when they were reaching a comfortable routine of being in each other's company, Peter Franke, from the grave, inserted himself into their lives, again.

Laura soon returned to the kitchen. She peeked around a sun-faded newspaper hanging over the window and sighed.

"Another hot day. I can't believe we're barely into July, and it's already this hot."

Steamy water filled the sink as she took apart several bottles, before immersing them in the sudsy water.

"Laura, let the dishes soak. We need to talk about last night."

She reluctantly dried her hands on a dish towel and sat tentatively at the table.

"Laura, how much do you know about Peter's past?"

"All I know is he had a mother and stepfather. The rest of this, having a brother, I've never heard before."

"I believe you. Peter never was very forthcoming about himself, unless he could brag about something. I'm going to tell you the whole history of Peter's life. I guess I should start with his mother before he was born."

To his surprise, Laura gave him her full attention. She didn't balk at the idea. She listened.

"Peter's mother was born to a poor family in Germany. Still a teenager, she found herself pregnant by the local baker's son. She married him, they had twin boys, and a year later they divorced. Each parent kept one of the sons. Marianne, Peter's mother, made her way to New York. She found a job and met Peter's stepfather at a social function. Peter's real father was murdered in his bakery. Some suspect Peter's brother, Josef, of the murder. It looked like a robbery gone bad. The only things missing were money and a ring, nothing else. Did Peter tell you any of this?"

She shook her head but said nothing.

"Josef all but disappeared from the earth after the murder, until 1937. He worked as a guard at a Nazi camp around Grafenwohr, Germany. His body, or what Interpol believed to be his body, was discovered along with ten other Nazi officials in a house fire. We now know they mistakenly identified Josef, because his motorcycle was at the house, and one of the corpses wore the ring previously owned by Josef's father.

"No," she whispered, "he told me nothing of this. He would have told me, if he knew. We shared everything."

It still stung to hear Laura talk about the closeness she'd shared with Peter. Deep down, Carson had to admit she loved Peter, but he knew she also loved him.

His mind went back to the plaster cracks on the ceiling. Again, every small crack represented a clue or a person. All of them connected to a main crack – Peter Franke.

"Peter kept all of those contacts with J.H. a secret from you; maybe he kept other things from you too."

"No," she insisted, adamantly defending Peter's memory.

"You once told me that Peter acted like two people, his temperament changed; he'd say one thing one day and deny it the next day. What if his behavior did have something to do with his mother's health? Maybe he was just sick and no one knew."

Laura slightly nodded her head as if agreeing to a logical explanation for his behavior. The fact that she didn't automatically argue the point, but actually seemed to find merit in it, surprised Carson.

"Why would Peter want to hurt me, or Carl?"

"Laura, if he was sick, maybe sicker than anyone knew, maybe he didn't know what he was doing. At least it's an explanation. In the meantime, try to remember conversations you had with him that might give us some insight. I've decided to stay here with you today and not help Ben."

After calling the station, Carson called Denby to update him and to see if any sensitive information surfaced such as information from MI-5 or Interpol regarding Josef Szescy or Holden. But, it looked like Bess shared everything, and he didn't learn anything new.

Carson then looked around the house for things he could do. Things that would give Laura and him space to be alone with their own thoughts, yet keep him close by in case something came up. The task of cutting the lawn seemed an appropriate choice.

A year's worth of dirt and grime covered the small, square window panes in the garage. When Carson pried open the garage door, sunlight flooded in. The air inside the small garage smelled like an old furnace gone bad – hot and oily. Otherwise, the building appeared to be in relatively good condition. Even the whitewash paint looked to be fairly recent. Esther took good care of her property.

Whoever cut the lawn last – he presumed Esther – had made sure the blades were cleaned off, and sharpened. Carson rolled the lawn mower out from the formerly dark inferno into a bright scorching one.

The grass was long and thick. Carson couldn't remember the last time he cut grass. He did recall it used to be his private time. The time he would let his mind wander and dream about leaving Montana, about the life he would have without worries or responsibilities.

For no particular reason, Carson chose to cut the grass in the front of the house first. The sharp blades made short work of the front yard.

The larger back yard would take more time. Barely half way through the back yard, his shirt already stuck to him with sweat. Once finished with the lawn, the garden beckoned to him to pull the crop of weeds.

"My lawn needs to be mowed."

Ben stood outside the yard, leaning on the whitewashed picket fence. Grateful for the break, Carson wiped the sweat off his brow and met Ben by the fence.

"Libby told me you called. I called Denby, too, right after I got back from Badger. Since you're already here, he wants you to investigate Owen's murder as well. I told him I thought both murders may be related."

"On your way home for lunch?"

"I'm on my way to watch Tommy play ball for a bit. Wanna come along?"

"What I really want is a shower. Has Tommy seen any more of Holden?"

"Don't think so. Hasn't said so."

"Say, I have a question for you."

"Okay."

"I heard your deputies talk about the Riverview Ballroom. Is it really a good place to dance?"

"Sure is. Mary Jane and I used to go there a lot."

"Hmm. I'm thinking of asking Laura to go there with me. She needs to get out and relax."

"That's the best place around here to dance."

Carson walked back to retrieve the lawn mower. He pushed it half way back across the yard, when one of the wheels clicked on something silver. The small reflection off the object caught both Carson's and Ben's attention.

"Well, now, this is something the wind didn't manage to blow away the other night." Carson picked up the object.

Ben walked around the fence over to Carson.

"Blow what away?"

Carson held up his hand. A small, one-and-a-half-inch by three-inch silver object, partially caked with dirt, gave off a sharp reflection in Ben's eyes as Carson twisted it in the sunlight.

"What is it?" he repeated.

Carson placed the small object into Ben's outstretched hand.

"It's a cigarette lighter."

Using his thumb, Ben rubbed away the dirt from the front panel, revealing the initials J.H.

"This only means Holden *may* have been here the night of the storm. We don't know how long this has been here. He could have dropped it that day when he talked to Esther."

"True, but she never mentioned him being in the back yard. He was here, and Laura has cause to be afraid."

After Ben left, Carson returned the lawn mower to the garage. In the small confines of the garage, Carson looked for something to scrape the grass from the underside of the lawn mower. He didn't see Laura holding Carl standing in the doorway.

"Could you watch Carl? I have to go for a walk. I'm tired of living in a cave."

"Sure. I'd like to shower first. Don't go far."

****

The Wisconsin River ran parallel to the sidewalk Laura walked on. It felt liberating to get out of the house, even if only to think and breathe the hot air. The river glimmered under the direct sunlight like a rhinestone-covered dress. Laura desperately wanted to jump in and play in the water. The top looked glassy smooth, but Laura had recently read a warning in the local paper and heard from the ladies at Badger about how the rushing currents beneath the Wisconsin River were deadly. The deceptively smooth top concealed a killer underneath, waiting for its next victim. As inviting as it looked, she knew she couldn't do anything risky anymore. Now she had Carl to think about.

On the next block, across the street, she saw a spot under a tree where she could sit. She crossed the road. Her thin-soled loafers felt the heat emanating up through them. The shade under the oak tree was welcome added by the slightly cooler air next to the river.

This was the first time in weeks she didn't have to worry about Carl. It felt good to be unencumbered. Carl was the best thing in her life, and she wouldn't change her life for anything. He had brought meaning and focus into her life, yet the task of motherhood overwhelmed her at times. How was she going to raise him on her own? Right now she couldn't allow her mind to go there. She had to think about conversations she and Peter had shared.

She stared at the bright shimmering water for a short time. Gazing at it gave her an almost hypnotic feeling. Unfolding like little snippets of life through a photo album, memories of happier, more carefree days, seeped into her mind. She remembered picnics and canoe rides, the day she introduced Peter to her parents and the day she found out she was pregnant. She lingered on those memories. Then her recall turned darker; Peter's crude comments about her body's changes during her pregnancy, his temper tantrums, and the time he hit her for correcting him.

The tree's shade had moved, while she'd been in her trance. How long had she been sitting there, thinking in the sun? Tears flowed freely now down her sun burnt face. The sting of the past and the tears against her burnt face felt like an external and internal brand. She wiped away the tears and decided to go back to the house.

An unnerving silence greeted her when she walked through the kitchen side door. The clock on the wall said it was 2:15 p.m. She hadn't been gone as long as she'd thought. Tiptoeing across the floor, she got as far as the hallway, when she saw why it was so quiet in the house. Carson and Carl were cuddled up together asleep on the sofa with Carl between Carson and the back of the sofa. Both were breathing deeply and soundly.

Suddenly, she felt nauseous. A sudden feeling of shakiness moved her to get a cool glass of water and sit down. As she closed the refrigerator, a figure out of the corner of her eye caught her attention.

She swallowed a scream at the base of her throat and her knees were about to buckle when she realized the shadowy figure in the doorway was Carson. The amused look on his face made her angry.

"Carson, you scared me half to death!"

She leaned against the cupboard for support and to recover from the shock.

"I didn't mean to scare you. Have you looked in a mirror?"

"No. I just got back from my walk. You and Carl were sleeping so soundly, I thought I'd sit in here until you woke up. Why?"

"Because your face is very sun burnt. Go take a shower and cool down. Go on. Carl isn't going anywhere. Neither am I."

She nodded her head in agreement and drank the whole glass of water before slowly making her way to the shower.

"When I'm done, we can talk about Peter if you'd like," she said with a small smile and sadness in her eyes.

Carson looked back at Carl, who had rolled on his side. Laura was already down the hall and closing the bathroom door when the high shrill ring of the telephone pierced through the quiet house. Carson blasted across the room to answer it by the second ring. He ripped the phone out of its cradle.

"Hello."

Several seconds went by with no answer. When a voice did respond, Carson felt bolted to the floor.

"Do you really think they're safe with you?"

Peter's voice sarcastically teased over the line; his hollow, cold, timber tone, mockingly sinister. Carson now understood why Laura was so terrified after hearing it.

"Do you really think I'll let you harm them?"

"I knew it would only be a matter of time before she'd run to you. Too bad it won't matter in the end – for any of you."

Carl whimpered, then rolled on his back and fell back asleep. Carson couldn't believe anyone could intentionally hurt such an innocent being as Carl.

"You tried to kill me once and failed – you'll fail if you try again. What do you want from us?" Carson hissed.

"Ever the champion. I have a message for Laura. Tell her the next time she goes for a walk to wear a hat. The sun can be murder."

There was no time to respond. The voice on the other end hung up. The empty silence and the looming threat repeated in Carson's head. He'd barely put the phone back in its cradle when it rang again.

"You won't get away with it," Carson spat into the phone.

"Did I get you at a bad time?" said Ben.

"I'm sorry. I just had a chat with the same person who threatened Laura. She's right. He sounds exactly like Peter."

"What'd he want?"

"Nothing. Just threats. I think he likes frightening people. Hear from Denby?"

"Yeah, that's part of the reason why I'm calling. MI-5 never had anyone working for them named Holden, and so far, Interpol has no trace of Josef Szescy. They believed he died in 1937."

"Hmm."

"The other reason I'm calling is the Madison police just called. They have the body of a woman who matches our description of Owen's missing secretary. Since I've never seen her, I'm taking one of Owen's other secretaries to help identify the victim. I'm waiting for her to arrive now. Wanna go along?"

"How'd she die?"

"Strangulation."

"Pick me up on your way out of town. Ask Libby if she wouldn't mind coming over here; I don't want Laura left alone, since she is being watched."

Singing came from the bathroom, accompanied by footsteps in the hallway.

"I've got to go," he whispered into the receiver.

As quietly as possible, Carson hung up the phone. Unfortunately, he wasn't quick enough or quiet.

"Who's that on the phone? Ben?" Laura walked into the living room rubbing her hair with the towel in her hand.

"Yeah. MI-5 said they never had anyone working for them named Holden."

"Really." She looked lost in her private thoughts for a few seconds. "I remembered something today about Peter."

Carson glanced at Carl, and then guided Laura, by her arm, into the kitchen. Even though she'd just had a cool shower, her skin radiated warmth through her yellow cotton blouse. He sat her at the chair farthest away from the kitchen door, hoping her voice wouldn't carry into the living room.

It didn't matter. Carl woke up and could hear them. His "I'm famished" cry got immediate attention. Carson broke for the couch, before Laura changed her mind. In one fast swoop, Carson was back in the kitchen, opened the refrigerator, and had plucked out a bottle and stuck it in Carl's mouth before either Carl or Laura knew what happened.

"He won't take a cold bottle, especially after he's just woke up," Laura chided Carson.

The hungry little baby clung onto the cold bottle as he greedily gulped the milk.

"I guess he instinctively knows this will help cool him down. We forget he gets just as hot as we do."

"He needs to be changed." Laura started to get up.

"Change him later. It won't hurt him to wait this one time. Now, what did you remember?"

To Carson's surprise, instead of looking down at the table or floor, she looked at him squarely in the eyes as she recalled an instance with Peter.

"Once, around the time his mother was very ill, right before she died, he told me how important family was to him and that he wanted to marry me and start a family. Then about a week later, I said something to him in passing..." Laura looked away for a second, as if trying to recall the incident. "Oh, I remember now. I asked if I could get a dog, after we got married. I've always wanted a dog. It would be a test to see if we were responsible enough to have a family. Father would never let me have one when I was growing up. 'Too much work,' he always said. Well, as soon as I said that, Peter became very angry, saying awful, mean things to me."

"Mean things like what?"

Tears welled in her eyes. She caught a tear as it rolled down her face.

"He said 'no' and yelled at me that I would be the last person on earth he'd ever want to be tied down with. That life was too short to waste on children or a family. If I ever got a dog, he would torture it in front of me to teach me a lesson. He said I was just a diversion, until he got tired of me. All the while he was throwing things around my apartment, breaking them. He said his life didn't really start until October of '41 and there was no room for me in his new life. That conversation happened in January of 1942."

Carson sat quietly, letting her talk through the memories even though they were painful.

"He said it was on that trip to London, when both of you had all those meetings with Prime Minister Churchill, that he realized he wanted to be involved with changing the world. Being involved with the decisions that could alter history excited him."

Carson sat so engrossed with her story he forgot he was holding Carl, until the bottle fell to the floor. Before he could react, Laura grabbed Carl out of Carson's arms and held him over her shoulder patting his back.

Carson got up and paced around the kitchen floor, rubbing his forehead, trying to piece together her story. Something nagged at him, but he wasn't sure what.

"He liked the idea of being involved with worldly decisions, yet wasn't he going to quit the State Department to run his father's business? It doesn't make any sense," Carson said.

"I reminded him of that. I said that that would tie him down as much or more than a family."

"What did he say to that?"

"He punched me in the face. Three weeks later, I found out I was pregnant."

Chapter Twenty-One

Ben and Carson sat in the front seat and talked most of the way to Madison. Betty Murphy, the more talkative secretary from Badger, sat in the back, mute the whole way.

All of them had their car windows rolled down, letting the hot air whirl around the interior in an effort to fight off the oppressive heat. The wind made Betty's hair whip at her face. Not once did she try to restrain it. Her blank expression never changed during the drive. Her hypnotic stare finally broke when Ben reached around to the backseat and touched her arm, announcing their arrival.

It was four o'clock when they arrived. The full impact of the sweltering heat hit them like a wall the second they stopped the car.

The red brick, three-story Hotel Washington, located six blocks from the state Capitol, next to a train station, clearly the dominant building at the corner of West Washington Avenue and Regent Street. It had Christmas tree shaped parapets at the corners and center of each side of the building and bay windows beneath the side parapets. A band of lighter colored stone separated each floor. Quions accented the windows and parapets. The south corner wasn't a corner at all: diagonally cut, it made for a unique entrance into the hotel. An abbreviated veranda welcomed guests into the hotel.

Outside the hotel, several parked cars butted up to the building. Carson assumed they belonged to the police, but they could just as easily belong to patrons of the tavern at the west end of the building.

Ben helped Betty out of the car and escorted her into the lobby. Carson followed silently behind. Inside the lobby, six of Madison's finest stood around quietly talking amongst themselves. The scene reminded Carson of a football huddle. One of the policemen saw Ben as soon as they entered the hotel. The huddle broke up. The observant officer approached Ben, Betty and Carson.

"You the Sheriff from Sauk City?"

"Yes. I'm Sheriff Ben Lyman." Ben swept his arm around to Betty and Carson. "This is Betty Murphy and Carson Grey. They're here with me to identify the body. Where is it?"

"At the morgue."

"At the morgue! Why was I told to come here if the body is somewhere else?"

"Because Chief Kraemer wants you to see the room and help answer a few questions. Besides, the body was beat up pretty bad. The Chief wanted it sent to the morgue before it decomposed any further. We took a lot of pictures of her before we took the body away. You can still go to the morgue, if you want. The pictures are up in the room with the Chief."

"Where's the room?" Ben asked still annoyed.

"Up in 312. If you take the stairs, it's the sixth room on your left.

The policeman dropped the cigarette he'd been smoking on the floor and stamped it out. Immediately, he lit up another one and rejoined his buddies as Ben, Betty and Carson made their way to the stairway.

Two men carrying a large, black case came out of room 312 as they reached the third floor. Only Chief Kraemer remained in the room.

He wore a uniform like the men downstairs, but the badge on his chest identified him as the Chief. He turned from the window when Ben, Betty and Carson entered the room. Just under six feet tall, his physique suggested a man who took pride in staying in shape. He appeared to be in his forties, with graying temples.

By the way he closely observed them; Carson suspected a military background. Chief Kraemer quickly glanced at his watch then addressed his audience.

"Judging by the amount of blood and skin under her fingernails," he carefully walked across the littered floor, trying not to step on any of the scattered debris. "She put up one hell of a fight before he finally got her." The killer should have noticeable scratch marks and cuts on him."

Chief Kraemer finally crossed the room to shake hands with Ben.

"Is this the way you found the room?" Ben asked.

"Exactly. Two of my guys just finished dusting for prints. Oh, I ah," Chief Kraemer maneuvered to the bed and picked up a folder, "I suppose you'll wanna take a look at these." Chief Kraemer handed Ben a folder full of pictures.

"I had the lab rush the photos for you."

Carson and Betty were invisible to Chief Kraemer. He addressed all of his side of the conversation to Ben.

Ben barely scanned the pictures before handed the folder to Carson.

"Those photos are meant for you to view, Sheriff."

"I appreciate that Chief Kraemer, but Mr. Grey and Mrs. Murphy are here with me to identify the body. Mrs. Murphy worked with the victim and Mr. Grey was," Ben cleared his throat, "briefly acquainted with her. I've never met the victim."

Kraemer appeared annoyed and not in the habit of sharing business with civilians. Ben's explanation of the presence of Betty and Carson put a mark against him in Kramer's eyes.

"Mr. Grey is here on behalf of the War Department. I'm assisting helping him with another murder case. We think these murders may be connected to the other in some way."

While Ben introduced Carson, Betty's eyes lingered on the photos, loosely held in Carson's hands.

Carson noticed her drained face and shallow breathing. He caught her as her knees started to buckle, flicking the photos back on the bed and ushered her to a chair by the window. He opened the window for some fresh air.

Ben glanced back to the photos scattered on the bed.

"I take it by the look on your face you can now positively identify the victim." Sarcasm laced Chief Kraemer's voice.

"What? Er. Oh. It's just that she looks remarkably like someone else I know."

"To get that kind of a reaction it must be a close resemblance. Good. I've a few more surprises for you."

"Breathe deep and focus on that tree over there," Carson instructed Betty.

"You shouldn't have brought a woman up here in the first place. They have no business at a crime scene," Kraemer sneered.

The callus remark passed ignored.

"Like I said, the room is as we found it. The surprises are in the dresser." Kraemer continued, his voice dripping with condescension.

"Which drawer is it in?"

Chief Kraemer smiled a priggish superior smile, then navigated his way through his crime scene, until he reached a three-sided mirrored dressing table. He opened the top right-hand drawer and collected all the contents.

"These are the personal effects of hers. I think from those you can help us identify her."

Three letters were addressed to Jean Montgomery in Madison, Wisconsin. One letter stamped January 1942 addressed to Jean Lennox at Knightsbridge in London, and one post stamped June 1943 to Jean Hardy, Washington, DC. There were pictures of Jean with a man, a dead ringer for Peter Franke. The pictures were taken at a pub somewhere in the UK and one in the Scottish Highlands. Also included with the personal effects, a small hand gun, wrapped in a white handkerchief, cinched with a fine wire. A hand mirror and hair brush completed the menagerie of items.

The brush and mirror were not important, but the gun and letters greatly interested Carson. One by one, he read the letters, starting from the oldest to the most recent. The letters were full of names, places and facts that tied in with Peter's notes. In short, the letters were instructions for Jean to carry out; people she must make connections with and places to go for further instructions. Each letter ended with a promise of how all of the objectives were *necessary for the cause* and how they would be *rewarded* in the end. Each letter signed off with *Forever Yours, Josef.*

When Carson finished reading the last letter, he handed them to Ben to read uninterrupted.

"So he's alive. Bess was right." Ben rubbed his temples.

"None of us could have ever guessed Josef was behind all of this. How could we? We all thought he was dead, until yesterday. Even so, the German photos only showed that the skeleton couldn't be Josef. Besides, when Peter was alive, maybe he was in on this, too. And just maybe, the body was Josef's, and Peter is still alive. Or maybe the body belonged to no one you knew and Peter's personal effects were left there to derail us, and both Peter and Josef are alive and working together."

Chief Kraemer inserted himself into the conversation. "Are you planning on sharing any of this with me, or are you going to keep me in the dark? Who is this woman and the man in these pictures with her?"

Carson could see Ben tensing his jaw. Carson knew he would probably never see Chief Kraemer again, so what Chief Kraemer ultimately thought of him didn't matter. Ben, on the other hand, might have to deal with this guy again in the future. He quickly answered to give Ben time to cool down.

"We only knew the victim as Jean. God only knows what her real name is. I think if you run her fingerprints through Interpol, you might get your answer. The man in the picture is either the man whose murder I'm in Sauk City to investigate or his twin brother."

"Sounds intriguing. What can I do?" asked Chief Kraemer inserting himself in the investigation.

"Nothing. Sheriff Lyman and I are a team, and we're not accepting any new members at the moment, but I'll be sure to put you on the list should we decide to expand."

The room vibrated with tension. Both men understood and loathed each other.

"Sheriff." A meek voice came from the window. Betty's face, still drained of color, tried to stand up. "I'm sorry, Sheriff Lyman,

I didn't think I'd be like this. I don't think I'll be able to look at her body at the morgue after all."

"That's okay, Betty. You won't need to. Carson and I will do that on our way out of town. We know it was Jean."

It didn't take them very long at the morgue. Collectively, they only wanted one thing: to get home as fast as possible.

Unfortunately, the ride back to Sauk City was delayed. Ben's front left tire needed to be recapped immediately making it necessary to find a filling station, or they wouldn't be getting home that night.

"I should have taken care of this sooner. I knew that tire was bad," apologized Ben. "I'm sorry to keep you even longer, Betty."

"That's okay. You're probably doing my husband a favor. He never knows how to deal with me when I'm around death. He says I take it too hard," she said with a faint smile looking at Ben from the rear view mirror.

Carson smiled listening to Betty. He understood her perfectly. As a little boy, he always became melancholy for days whenever he heard of someone in the community dying or he found a dead animal in the mountains.

An old voice echoed through his head: "You'll have to harden up and grow up some day. I won't have a son of mine seen crying in public over a dead animal."

A month later, his father walked out on his family, leaving Carson no choice but to grow up and be the man of the house at the age of nine.

It was minutes to closing time at the filling station when Ben pulled up. The attendant expected Ben to ask for gas, not recap a tire. Disappointment crossed his brow. If Ben hadn't been wearing his uniform, Carson was sure the attendant probably would have told him to go elsewhere or come back tomorrow.

"Tell ya what, I'll pay ya double," offered Ben.

That seemed to pacify the attendant well enough. Before he started the job, he quickly went back inside the station and turned over the "OPEN" sign in the front window to display the "CLOSED" side.

Carson chose to sit in a chair outside the station's front door while Ben and Betty went for a walk. He welcomed the opportunity to enjoy a quiet moment and think. There was so much new information to absorb and sift through. His mind almost reached the saturation point.

This started as just a routine investigation. Then Laura came back into his life. Was Peter dead or alive? This investigation had almost cost Carson his life. Someone was still threatening his life and those he loved. If something happened to Laura or Carl, he didn't think he could ever recover. His emotions and attention were being pulled in opposite directions simultaneously.

The station attendant worked as fast as possible. Carson could only imagine what was running through the young man's mind. An out-of-town police officer shows up with another man in the front seat and a middle-aged woman in the back. When they got out of the car, the sheriff stayed with the woman. The attendant probably wondered what she'd done and if she was dangerous. She had to be, why else would she be escorted by two men?

As the attendant finished up with the tire, the phone in the station rang. Quickly, he grabbed the closest rag and vigorously wiped his hands.

Carson listened in on the attendant's side of the conversation.

"Well, where'd you call... here? Obviously, I'm still here if I answered the phone."

The attendant wedged the phone between his chin and shoulders and kept wiping his hands as he listened to the caller.

"How can I be there and here, too? I can't be at two places at once. I'll get there as soon as I'm done here."

Ben and Betty came into view from the station window as he uttered the last sentence.

"I'm almost done here. I'll be home as soon as I can. Bye."

Carson quickly paid the garage attendant and met Ben and Betty at the car. He was suddenly very eager to get on the road.

"We'll get you home straight away, Betty. Ben can drop me off after we've taken you home."

The closer they came to Sauk City, the more anxious Carson became. Finally, they arrived at Betty's house. Her husband came out on the porch to greet the car and gather is wife. He waved to the men in the car as they drove away.

"They're a nice couple, Lyle and Betty: hard working, honest. I went to school with Lyle, known him all my life. He becomes more like his father every time I see him," said Ben waving back out the window.

"I'm sure they are. Ben, back there, at the filling station, right before you and Betty got back, the attendant got a phone call. He said something that finally unlocked that nagging feeling I've had for weeks."

"What'd he say?"

"He said, 'I can't be there and here, too. I can't be at two places at once.' You said something like that, too. That night at Goerk's tavern. You said, 'Seems your Mr. Franke led a double life.' It was right there in front in me."

"And?"

"That's the key! Owen, Denby and Laura told me things that didn't make any sense. I never connected everything, the dates... until now."

"Whoa, whoa, whoa, slow down. Told you things like what? What dates don't connect?"

Carson took a deep breath. He tried to control his excitement and concentrate on what he wanted to say.

"Pull over somewhere so you'll be able to listen and follow me."

Ben stopped on the side of the road under a huge oak tree as the sun began its race toward the horizon.

"Okay. Denby and Laura both talked about when Peter left for his mother's funeral. Denby said Peter went to Switzerland – London - somewhere, to get his mother's body and had a private funeral for her in Virginia. Laura said she gave Peter a set of cufflinks before he left for the funeral. She never mentioned anything about Peter going overseas to get his mother's body."

"It could just be an oversight. She might have forgotten to mention it."

Undaunted, Carson continued. "Then Owen said he noticed Peter's temper change. On a Friday, Peter would say he'd be gone for a week because he had to go to out of town. But Peter would show up on the following week acting mean and abusive."

"Maybe something happened over the weekend that canceled his trip out of town."

"Then why didn't he just tell Owen that?"

"Carson, you both work for the government. He was here undercover. If his instructions came from Washington, he couldn't just spill them to anyone who asked."

"Then just say a change of plans. Twice Laura talked about times when Peter was supposedly in London with me."

"Supposedly?"

"Yeah. Last November I was in London with Commander Eisenhower and Mark Clark. Peter wasn't with us. I'm sure. I remember, because we were invited to the traditional, annual banquet of Lord Mayer of London. That was the weekend Churchill ordered the church bells to ring for the first time in two and a half years. Peter wasn't there. I know it."

"Laura's human. She may have gotten mixed up with the dates."

"I don't think so. She was quite clear when she told me that she needed him with her last November. Turns out, that's when Carl was born. Peter wasn't with Laura at Carl's birth. He told her he was in London. In one of their fights, he told her his life began in October 1941. He met Holden in October 1941. If my memory is right, during his time with the department, he said he needed to take one more trip with his ailing mother. Did he go to London with his mother in October 1941, and that's where he met Holden - Josef?" Carson's last statement was said out loud, more for himself than Ben.

"Carson, what are you getting at here?"

"Don't you see? 'I can't be at two places at once.'" He repeated the attendant's statement. "I think all those instances of Peter's personality changes are because it wasn't Peter. It was Josef."

"Are you saying Josef inserted himself into every aspect of Peter's life and no one picked up on it?"

"Oh, they picked up on it all right. Every time Owen or Laura would remind the man, who they thought was Peter, about something he'd said earlier, that's when the uncharacteristic temper would flare. He, Josef, had been tripped up, and being mean and angry was his way of covering up."

"Okay. Let's say you're right. That would mean that Josef had been in Peter's life since..."

"Since October 1941. Through all of those meetings and Wednesday phone calls, Josef learned about every aspect of Peter's life. We don't know where Josef was when Peter called him all those Wednesday nights. Josef could have been close by – in the area."

Both men sat silently in their seats processing the possibility.

Just sharing, out loud, what had been brewing in his mind the last hour solidified to Carson the answers to all of the loose ends.

"Oh my God!"

"What?" Ben followed Carson's stare out the front window, looking for whatever troubled Carson.

"Oh, my, God," Carson repeated.

"Carson. What's the matter?"

"I just remembered something else Laura told me. She said that Peter told her how important family was to him. Later, Peter, or so she thought, insulted her, and said she was the last person he would be tied down with. Three weeks later, she found out she was expecting Carl. If Josef inserted himself in Peter's life, that would include Laura. Who's Carl's real father? It would tear her apart to think it might be Josef."

Carson looked out the passenger-side window and sighed in helpless frustration.

"Carl's true father is the man who will have the privilege of raising him. I need to think more about this. It's getting pretty late, and I still need to pick Tommy up from my brother's. I think Tommy and Helen are up to something. Every July 4th, they always have some surprise for me. I need to pick him up before they decide to reenact the signing of the Declaration of Independence. Besides, I don't like the way those clouds are banking up in the West. I think we're in for another long night."

When they pulled up in front of Carson's house there were no lights on.

"That's odd," Carson noted. "It's too early to put Carl down for the night and too dark to not have the lights on. Laura always has the lights on, especially after that last storm. She would wait up for me no matter what time I got back. Where's Libby?"

"There's probably a good answer to all of your questions. I'll go in with you, this time."

Carson knew in the pit of his stomach something was terribly wrong. Every step closer to the house, the heavier the feeling of dread filled him. When they reached the slightly ajar front door, his suspicions were confirmed.

Both men, on instinct, reached for their guns. At Ben's nod, they both rushed into the house. Silence and darkness greeted them. Hesitantly, Carson turned on a light. Under an overturned chair, a small ankle and black shoe lay on the floor.

Ben rushed around the end table, effortlessly throwing the big chair out of the way, and knelt next to the body on the floor.

Carson picked up an overturned lamp and turned it on. Libby lay on the floor with a small pool of blood under her head.

"She's alive," said Ben relieved. "She's been beaten unconscious. That bastard will pay for this. Check the rest of the house. I'll call the station for back up. She needs to go to the hospital."

Carson didn't need to be told what to do. He slowly inched his way down the hallway toward the bedroom and bathroom end of the house. But he knew it was just an exercise; Laura and Carl would not be there. HE had them. The message on the bathroom mirror validated Carson's fear.

"YOU CAN'T SAVE THEM! YOU'RE TOO LATE."

Carson's bellow of anguish prompted Ben to forget about Libby for a second and he rushed to Carson's side.

"We'll get him! You've got my word. We'll get him."

"Damn right we will. If he disturbs one hair on either of their heads, he'll pay with his life."

"As soon as they get here for Libby, we'll go after him."

Carson continued looking for clues while waiting for Ben's men. He returned to the living room finding Ben, on the phone, and frantic.

"There's no answer at home, Helen. Are you sure he's not there?" Ben's face washed with anxiety and small beads of sweat formed at his hair line.

"Helen, when was the last time you saw him?"

Stoned faced, he hung up.

"Tommy never showed up at my brother's this afternoon. They haven't seen him. I'm the last one to see him at lunch. They assumed he was with me. He's not answering the phone at home. I need to find my son."

Deputy Orlanger and another man rapped on the door as they entered the house. Immediately they spotted Libby on the floor. Slowly, gently, Ben carried Libby's tiny body to the back of Deputy Orlanger's car.

"Take her to Baraboo as fast as you can. As soon as she is admitted, get back to the station." He started to walk to his car then stopped. "Tell them to take good care of her. GO!" Orlanger and friend jumped in the car and sped off. "Carson, you're coming with me!"

Ben blasted from Carson's house to his own in record time. Each of them lost in his own private hell. Like Carson's house, Ben's was also dark. They approached the house with guns drawn. No words needed.

On top of the incredible sense of loss and emptiness, Carson felt the burden of guilt. If HE took Tommy as well as Laura and Carl, it was his fault.

Ben's front door also left unlocked and opened.

"Tommy," Ben hesitantly called, desperately hoping for an answer. None came. He turned on a light and ran toward Tommy's bedroom. Carson went to the kitchen.

Ben showed up in the kitchen holding Tommy's baseball glove with a blank look on his face.

Carson stopped reading a note he'd found.

"This is Tommy's. He took it with him everywhere. He must have been taken from here by force."

"He was. His abductor left this." Carson held out the note for Ben.

Ben looked at the note expressionless, not making any attempt to take it from Carson.

Carson read the note to Ben.

"He's with me. It's unfortunate your son has to pay for your mistakes. You should have never gotten involved. Now he'll go down like the others."

Chapter Twenty-Two

Ben couldn't get back to the station fast enough. They had to figure out where HE took Tommy, Laura and Carl.

Ben and Carson came to a screeching halt in front of the police station narrowly missing the building. Junior Berry was there waiting for them. He had been there for hours – pacing. He'd declined all offers to tell anyone his purpose for being there. He would only talk to Ben. What he had to say could only be said to the Sheriff.

Ben didn't have time to listen to what Junior wanted. That's what he had deputies for.

"Sheriff, I have to talk to you."

Ben cruised past Junior into the station. He had more important things on his mind. Time was wasting.

"Not now Junior. Talk to one of my deputies."

"They can't help me. Sheriff, I saw your boy."

Ben froze. He heard Junior, but thought he must be mistaken. Junior had no way of knowing Tommy. And Tommy didn't know where Junior lived.

"What do you mean, you saw Tommy? When? How do you know it was Tommy?

"I saw him three hours ago."

"Where?"

"He was with that guy your fella," Junior pointed to Carson, "were askin' me about. He came back to put gas in that fancy silver car of his. He told me to tell you he were sorry he missed you at home. He also said you need to teach your boy manners."

"What?"

"Your boy had a bloody lip and holdin' a hand ta his cheek. That good lookin' lady and a baby were in the front seat. They didn't say anything. She looked scared. The whole thing scared me, too. I came here as soon as he left."

The mention of Laura and Carl instantly grabbed Carson's attention.

"Mr. Berry, did he say where he was going or what his plans were? Did he have anything else to say that might help us find them?"

"Nope. He said nottin bout where he were goin'. He said that were the last time he'd be by. He did say sumptin bout" Junior scratched his head, "good thing bout tomorrow being the 4th of July, cause it were also his independence day. That's all. After that, he drove off. I came as soon as he were out of sight."

The level of tension was palpable – compounded because no one knew what to say.

For Deputies Orlanger and Johnson, this was deja vue. When Ben's wife died, he seemed lost. Day after day he sat motionless in his office for hours; only able to address the most routine problems.

At the time, Libby made sure no one bothered the sheriff; no one except Tommy, Fred and Ruth. When they came to the station, Ben tried his best to act as normal as possible. But, he became obsessed with Tommy's whereabouts. Only recently he loosened the reins on the boy.

For Carson, Laura's and Carl's kidnapping left him with conflicting emotions. He'd lost her once before. He couldn't bear losing her again. After living with her and Carl, he knew he could never go back to his bachelor ways.

But, he enjoyed his job with the State Department, which was no job for a family man. At least Peter was out of the picture for good – or was he? Carl would forever be her physical link to Peter, unless Josef was the father.

Bess arrived at the station to drop off a written account of her time in DC. She instantly picked up on the edgy, grim, heavy mood from everyone within the station. Excessive questions would not be tolerated. Quietly, unobserved, she peeked at the note left behind in Ben's house and learned most of the story by listening. Finally, she was brave enough to speak out.

"What does he mean by '*go down with the others*'?"

"I think it means he's going to drive them out of their minds, somehow," said Deputy Johnson.

"I don't think so, Deputy Johnson," Carson corrected quietly.

Carson's comment squelched any further discussion for a few minutes until Deputy Orlanger spoke.

"Well, what do you know about this guy? How does he work, think, act and react?"

"He's smart and deadly. Peter Franke came to fear his brother, before being murdered by him. Josef has no scruples." Under his breath, Ben added, "He wouldn't blink twice before killing my son."

"Tommy, Laura and Carl are all safe – scared but safe," Carson insisted.

"How do you know that, Mr. Grey?" Deputy Johnson asked.

"Because, if he wanted to kill them, he could have done so at their homes. Why bother kidnapping and then leaving messages? He's after me."

Carson got up off his chair and began to pace around the room.

"From the very beginning I knew I was mixed up in this, but I didn't know why. I still don't know the answer. Because of me, all of you are now involved."

"Don't say that, Carson. Deputies Johnson and Orlanger and I are just doing our jobs."

"I asked to be involved, so there's no need to apologize to me either," Bess said. "Still, I wish I could be more help, damn it!"

As if a light bulb flashed in his mind, he finally understood.

"Dam. The dam! That's what he meant."

Carson, Bess and Deputy Johnson jumped up and headed for the front door. Deputy Johnson had his gun drawn.

"Stop!" Ben ordered.

The group stopped where they were. Carson ran his hand through his hair out of frustration.

"Why just sit here when we know where they are? Why not go there now?" Bess asked.

"Because we don't know for sure that's where they are, and we need a plan before we go rushing out there. Don't you think I want this over with, too? He has my son."

"So are we supposed to just sit around here and wait?" Deputy Johnson sounded wounded.

"We need to put our heads together and try to think like Josef, if it is Josef," said Ben.

"Dead or alive – it ends tonight," stated Carson.

"Do you think he's at the dam now?"

"Personally, Deputy Johnson, I don't know. He could be, said Carson. "He obviously wants a showdown, but he can't afford to be found out before tomorrow morning. He wants it to symbolize *his* independence in some way."

"Wow, that's good," said Deputy Johnson duly impressed with Carson's deductive reasoning.

"I agree," said Ben. "I agree he's using the day as some sort of symbolism for himself. He may be at the dam. I don't know, but I think he's close by. He's invested too much time and effort staying ahead of us this far. He wouldn't chance making a mistake this close to the end. He may be watching us now, for all I know."

After listening to their opinions, Carson's shoulders dropped and he walked back to his chair.

"I think Ben's on the right track. He likes having the upper hand and the element of surprise. He has to feel like he's in control."

"So, where does that leave us?" asked Deputy Johnson.

Ben sighed and sat back in his chair. "Unfortunately, right where we started."

Junior Berry seemed to have been forgotten. He sat alone in the corner of the office next to the window. A close crack of lightning lit up the station followed by a boom so loud it shook the building. Junior shrieked and jumped across the room.

The conversation in the police station momentarily stopped. All eyes shifted to Junior, who wiped his sweaty palms on his grimy bib overhauls.

"Say, Sheriff, looks like we're in fer another bad storm. My truck wipers don't work. You gotta place back there where I can stay – just until the storm passes?" Junior nodded toward the back room of the station.

He no sooner got the last sentence out of his mouth when the full wrath of wind and rain assaulted the building.

"Sure, Junior. There's a cot back there that'll do. Deputy Johnson will show you where it is."

The lights flickered off and on for a few seconds.

"Take some candles back there with you," Ben added.

As soon as Junior was out of sight, Carson continued where they'd left off.

"He's close by and probably has been all along. I'm sure he has them at his hiding spot– why change things now?"

"And that thought alone plagues me," Ben lamented. "For the life of me, I can't think where he's been. Where can he be hiding that I don't know about?"

"Ben, stop beating yourself up. You're forgetting all the people he's fooled so far and for so long," consoled Carson.

Defeated, Bess plopped down in a chair, "Let's face it, he's still in the driver's seat. All we can do is wait until the storm lets up, which probably won't be until tomorrow morning."

Ben heaved a tired, frustrated sigh. "On second thought, it wouldn't hurt having someone out there at the dam. Deputy Orlanger, grab a radio and go out to the dam. If you see or hear anything before five o'clock radio it in to me."

Deputy Johnson just re-entered the room when Ben ordered Deputy Orlanger to go to the dam. Carson saw the brief hurt look in Deputy Johnson's eyes, until Ben addressed him.

"Johnson, I want you to help Carson and me come up with a plan. And, in the morning, you're going out there with us to put an end to all of this madness."

Ben turned around to say something else to Deputy Orlanger, but he was already gone. No one saw or heard him leave the station.

Carson's anxiety heightened. "How do you catch a ghost? He's proven to be elusive, and we're only assuming he'll be at the dam. What if we're wrong?"

"A minute ago, you were convinced he was there, half way out the door. If we're wrong, my guess is that he will let us know. You said it yourself, he wants you."

The time between midnight and five o'clock felt like days. The wind and rain the only background noise until just before dawn.

At one point in the night, Deputy Orlanger radioed in to talk to Ben. Carson couldn't hear the conversation and Ben never shared any of the information.

Finally at 4:45 a.m. Ben started to pace around the office in nervous energy. The enormity of the situation, especially the possibility of failure and losing his son won over.

"We're leaving for the dam now. Anything you need to do, do it now. I want to be there in plenty of time, before Josef shows up. We'll have the upper hand this time."

There wasn't even a whisper of a breeze after the storm. It was like Mother Nature had exhausted herself in the night's wrath. Nothing stirred the whole way to the dam. It was eerily quiet, as if the town collectively held its breath, waiting for the outcome of the impending showdown. The only sound came from the gravel crunching under the weight of the tires and the quiet splashes as the car drove through puddles.

As they turned onto the long, winding driveway leading to the dam, Ben shared Deputy Orlanger's information. They saw Orlanger's car parked on a path, on the wooded side of the dam where it would be hidden from the dam.

"Orlanger assures me there is no way Josef will be able to get in or around the dam without being seen. I told him if he's able to get a clean shot, take it."

"No. What if he doesn't have Laura, Carl or Tommy? If Orlanger shoots him, and they are not with him, we may never find them." The anger mixed with panic in Carson's voice rung loud in the quiet car.

"He'll have 'em," said Deputy Johnson confidently.

"How can you be so sure?" Carson asked.

"If he is half as evil and dangerous as you say, he'll use them to try and make you do something stupid. You did say he's after you."

"Johnson, you surprise me. I've never seen you so calculating." Said Ben maneuvering the car around muddy ruts.

"Never been so motivated, Sir."

"Bess, as soon as Carson, Deputy Johnson and I get out of the car, I want you to drive back to the station and wait."

"This is the story of a lifetime..."

"This is extremely dangerous, and we don't need anyone who's not trained for these situations to add to the danger. We'll radio you if we need you to call for extra backup. Staying put at the station is the best way you can help."

She slumped back in her seat with a huff, annoyed being left out of the action.

"Something's not right!" Carson announced when they pulled up to the dam's guard house.

The place looked deserted. No sign of Deputy Orlanger.

"Johnson, go to the guard house and look for Orlanger. Carson and I will check around the dam."

Deputy Johnson sprinted in the pre-dawn toward the guardhouse. There he found Orlanger's unconscious body behind the door, half propped against the wall.

From the tail-water side of the dam, everything looked fine. The power house, the lock and spillway showed no signs of anyone being there. The only way to reach the large cement platform, behind the power house, was up a set of stairs adjacent to the barrier wall. Going through the power house would be a waste of time. Whatever Josef had in mind would happen outside: Carson felt sure of it.

Unhurried, they took each step with deliberate measure, until they reached the platform.

The platform at the back of the power house ran the length of the building and had a series of square openings in it. The openings were the depth of the cement platform.

The bottom of the openings revealed the river beneath. Each square opening was about six feet by six feet and surrounded by a railing.

At the far end of the line of openings, leaning on the railing, stood Josef – smiling. Tommy and Laura were blindfolded, gagged, and sitting on the platform with their legs dangling into one of the openings. Their hands were bound and tied to the railing.

"You're late. I was beginning to think you weren't going to show up or didn't care."

"Where's Carl?" Carson demanded.

"Calm down. He's where all boys his age should be." Josef nodded to the wall of the power house. Carl lay on the ground, next to the wall, completely still. Was he asleep or dead?

At the sound of Carson's voice, both Tommy and Laura started to squirm and cry out from their gags. Dried blood congealed around Tommy's mouth and nose, his face swollen.

"He's just a kid, you bastard," yelled Ben.

"Yes, just a kid, so what. I got tired of telling him to shut up."

Outside of the obvious cuts and scratches on his face that must have come from killing Jean, it was uncanny to Carson how much Josef looked and acted like Peter. Even his mannerisms and gestures and posture were indistinguishable from Peter's.

"For whatever reason, you want me. Let them go."

"Tut, tut, Mr. Grey. First things first. Both of you throw your guns into the water – now."

A sound like a scrap came from the stairs behind Ben and Carson, pulling Josef's focus away from them for a second. He whipped out the pistol from his coat pocket and fired it at the noise.

The gun shot startled Carl and he started to cry.

Ben and Carson turned to see what Josef shot at. Deputy Johnson lay sprawled on the top three steps of the platform. Blood quickly covered his uniform and chest. Ben turned around and took a step toward Johnson.

"Stop where you are, Sheriff, or you'll be joining him sooner than I planned."

Carson made a slight movement forward, and Josef placed the gun next to Laura's temple.

"Everyone calm down." Josef regained control.

"Josef, you want me," pleaded Carson. "Stop this senseless killing."

"Senseless. Everyone I killed had a purpose."

"And just how many people have you killed?" Ben asked.

Josef didn't say anything at first. It was if he was waiting for them to try and charge him. He seemed to dare them. When he realized they weren't going to move in on him, he answered Ben.

"To date, that would be about fifteen or so," he said smiling.

"Don't you know for sure?" Carson mocked.

"It's sixteen if my mother died from the poison I gave her. I don't know if she died from one her diseases or from my hands. So I'm not sure. Peter wouldn't tell me what she died of. That secret is the only one he took to his grave."

By now, Carl was wailing. The tension started to show on Josef's face.

"Shut the brat up, or I will," he screamed at Laura.

He ripped off her blindfold and quickly pulled a knife out of his other coat pocket and sliced through her bonds then he slid the knife back into the pocket.

Laura started to cry.

Josef yanked the gag away from her mouth.

"One scream from you and your son will pay. Do I make myself clear?"

She head jerked in agreement. Pointing the gun at Ben and Carson, Josef pulled Laura far enough away from the square opening that she could get up. She ran to Carl and tried to soothe him with quiet singing through her crying.

"He's hungry. Let me feed him his last bottle."

"Sure, why not? I'm sure your old lover has a few questions for me. Go ahead, Grey, ask away, but don't take too long. Halt!" Josef yelled suddenly.

He openly smiled an oily smile, enjoying being in control. He backed up and stepped to the side shifting the gun barrel back at Laura's head. "It seems we have one more guest arriving late to the party."

Ben and Carson turned their heads around, again, to where Josef was looking behind them.

Bess had tried to use Deputy Johnson's body as a shield, while she crept up the last few steps.

"Come join us. In fact, I'm going to put you to work right away. Since the brat is quiet now, you can assist Laura back to her place on the railing. When you are through with her, there is more rope next to the wall. Then tie up the good sheriff and agent Grey. They'll be filling the spots opposite of their loved ones. Cozy, don't you think. The family that drowns together stays together – forever."

Red faced and with eyes cast down, Bess timidly scooted across the platform to Laura, who propped up part of the blanket for the bottle so Carl could continue to eat.

"Since you're so eager and proud of yourself, humor me and list your accomplishments," Ben goaded Josef.

Laura looked back at Carl lying against the power house wall and started to sob. Bess wrapped her arm around Laura's shaking shoulder trying to console her as she led Laura back to the railing. Laura cried harder with every step she took away from Carl. Josef followed the women's movement with the gun pointed at them, until Bess retied Laura up.

"My bragging rights, oh yes. Keep your hands where I can see them, Sheriff. This won't take long. Now, go back to the wall for more rope," Josef instructed Bess. "Tie up the sheriff first." He turned back to the men.

"Where was I? Yes, yes, now I remember. My father was my first, I guess you would say. I got tired of his controlling me; telling me what to do and who I could and couldn't have for friends. I decided to put an end to his rants. Years went by, and I figured I was ready for my next step up in life."

"You mean the training camp," Ben said as Bess led him to the opening in the platform across from Tommy.

"Ah, so you're familiar with my life in Germany. They didn't think I was tough enough for the job - too soft."

He looked over at Bess as she wrapped the rope around Ben's wrist and the railing. "Make sure those knots are tight!" Then he returned his attention back to Carson. "They changed their minds once they realized it wasn't only a little drinking party. Of course they figured that out after the poison started to take effect. I had to make it look like an accident. I robbed them and then I started the place on fire. I had to leave Germany after that. I needed everyone thinking that I died in the fire. With no family around to identify me, I could become who ever I wanted. So, that brings the count up to twelve.

"Then, out of pure luck, I found my brother, good ol' Pete, in London. When he told me about his life, I decided it was my turn to have it all. I never had anything growing up. We couldn't afford it. I always had hand-me-downs. He never had anything but the best. Pete was generous, though. He offered me a future with his stepfather's business. I had a different plan." He motioned for Bess to stand by Carson as he inspected how tight she tied the ropes on Ben. Then he returned to where he previously stood. "Problem was Pete didn't understand the new rules. He just couldn't comprehend that I was now in charge – totally in charge - thirteen.

"What about Charlie Ballard?" demanded Ben.

"Charlie Ballard somehow discovered that I wasn't Peter. He was going to spill the beans. Fourteen.

Carl started to fuss again. This time Josef backup up to the wall, gun still aimed at Bess and Carson. He roughly popped the bottle back into Carl's mouth.

"Then came Jean. She was quite useful. I found her in Soho, selling herself in the back streets for a living. I saw Peter's pictures of Laura and I recognized a similarity between the two and I took her under my wing."

Again with the point of the gun, he motioned for Bess to the wall for the rope to tie up Carson. "I changed her hair color, helped her lose a few pounds, dress better and had her study Laura, until we were ready. But in the end, she started to think she was indispensable. She was wrong. Fifteen. "And as I said earlier, I don't know if I can claim my mother or not."

"And Owen Anderson? Aren't you forgetting him?" Carson hoped that if they kept him talking, he'd slip up somewhere, but hope and time was running out.

"What about him?" Sarcasm returned to Josef. Feigned innocence brushed his face. "Oh, I see. You think I killed Owen. Sorry, I can't claim him. He was Jean's kill. He discovered she stole the shipping records for me. Hurry up." Josef directed his last angry comment to Bess who tripped on the rope and scrapped her knee on the platform. Instead of scrambling to her feet she inspected her knee. This incensed Josef and he started to quickly walk to her.

As soon as Josef's attention turned to Bess, Carson lunged at Josef, but not quick enough. Josef stepped back.

"Halt." He screamed pointing the gun at Carson.

Carson slowly moved back and Bess cautiously stood up. Back in control Josef finished his explanation.

"Anderson was going to tell you and the sheriff about Jean. Jean panicked and made quite a mess of everything. I thought I trained her better than that. That's all of them. I hope I answered all of your questions."

"You forgot Allen Clarke," Carson reminded Josef.

"Who?"

"Allen Clarke. A young man in DC."

"Was that his name? Oh. He was Jean's. I told you she was good. Too bad she got greedy."

"Yeah, that was his name. Tell me something, why kill Allen? And what's my part in all this?"

"It's your boss's fault Jean killed him. If he'd sent you here right off, this Allen nobody would still be alive."

Tommy started to squirm then cry. This seemed to please Josef. He smiled wider and he continued.

"Peter's body wasn't supposed to ever be found. I was – I am, Peter Franke. That's why all of you here have to go. You're all liabilities – especially you, agent Grey. I knew I couldn't just kill Laura. According to Peter, you're like a dog with a bone when things don't look, sound or feel right. You would have sniffed around and asked a lot of questions that might make other people ask questions."

"Why tear up Peter's house?"

"Sixteen," Josef called out. "Correction. The answer to your earlier question is sixteen or seventeen deaths. I forgot about Hewes. Loyal, faithful, do-the-right-thing Hewes. I thought Peter would keep Carl's birth certificate close by. If not, he would hide it until he could give it to Hewes. That brat would inherit everything. I ripped that house up looking for it. He can't exist. I've come too close to lose it all to a little brat!"

"So you kill anyone in your way," Ben said with disgust, looking over at a still Tommy.

Josef shrugged his shoulders casually, "It's worked for me so far."

Bess finished tying Carson's hands by this time. She stood up and faced Josef hiding the very loose knots.

"Ah, the reporter. Are you getting all of this down?"

"Ye, yes," she sputtered, "If you don't mind, I've got a question for you."

Josef laughed. "Always ready to oblige the press. What's your question?"

"Jean.... Why did she take the shipping reports?"

"Why, for me of course, Miss Nosey. If you know about Hewes, then I'm sure you've found out about the changes at *my* company. We're going to be shifting our focus to exporting ammunition – to the Germans. I needed to know what was sent, when and where so we could intercept it."

"Just one more question. What are you going to do with Carl and me?" Bess asked a slight tremor in her voice.

"This square," Josef nodded at the space in front of him, "is looking a little crowded, but there are others. Just so you won't be alone, I'll throw in the baby."

Josef started to laugh at his own joke.

"Throw in the baby. The water looks harmless now, but that will change. In a very few minutes, the pressure and vacuum the turbine makes will suck you down under the water and easily keep you down, drowning all of you very quickly." He scanned the other square opening in the platform. "Which of the other openings do you want to share with the brat?"

As he said his last sentence, he swept his hand with the gun like a pointer, indicating the rest of the platform openings.

Bess charged Josef the second he turned around, taking him off guard. The gun fired as she slammed her small body into him, and she shrieked.

"You bastard. You shot me."

When both of their bodies hit the platform the waters beneath them started to churn. Josef's gun flew out of his hand and slid next to Ben. Bess tried to pull Josef's knife out of his coat pocket. He realized what she was doing and grabbed her hand. It was the wrong hand. She had the knife and used it to jab him in his side. He pulled back just long enough for her to scramble up and run to Carson.

For a split second he stared at Bess as if trying to decide to charge after her or not. He turned and ran away across the platform to the bridge above and over the lock. A bridge connected the narrow railroad tracks, which extended across the spillway area, to the opposite side of the river.

Quickly, Bess severed the rope on Carson's wrists. He pushed Bess aside, grabbed Josef's gun, and ran after him, quickly catching up to the injured man. By the time Josef got to the railroad tracks, Carson had closed the gap to only several yards behind him.

Carson aimed it at Josef and pulled the trigger. Josef's left shoulder jerked forward and then slumped. Halfway across the spillway, Josef lost his balance, slipped on the wet railroad tracks and lurched for the railing. In doing so, Carson caught up to him.

The turbines turned on and the forty-one tainter gates of the spillway opened. The rain from the previous night had raised the level of water. The spillway created a mini-Niagra Falls effect. Water mist filled the air.

Even injured, Josef's strength was amazing. Blood gushed out of his shoulder. He lashed out at Carson, each of his punches as powerful as a man at full strength. He managed to lock his arm in Carson's and swing Carson around. Then he slammed his head into Carson's back on the wound from the burning shingle.

The pain of the hit took Carson's breath away. Carson used his free arm to grab onto the rail. Then he used his body weight to swing Josef back around against the rail. When Josef's body slammed into the rail, it gave Carson a split second to pull his arm out of Josef's grasp.

The men continued to punch each other, equally matched in the fight. The water impeded their vision and fighting. Josef tried to dig his fingers into Carson's eyes, but Carson bent over the rail, making the reach too far for Josef. Then Josef tried to knock Carson off his feet, but he slipped, again, on the wet railroad ties. Both men teetered on the railing, trying to regain their own balance while struggling to throw the other over. Josef put his hands around Carson's neck and began to choke him. The weight of Josef on his chest and the rail pressing on his back had Carson reaching the breaking point. Then Josef loosened his grip for a second. Carson freed himself and turned the tables on Josef.

He quickly hoisted Josef's legs up over the railing in an attempt to throw him into the deadly water below.

But Josef grabbed Carson's arm pulling Carson off balance and over the railing with him. Both bodies slammed into the cement embankment. Carson latched on to the railing's base as he slid down the wet surface. Josef didn't react to the fall quickly enough. He tried to cling onto Carson's leg, but his strength rapidly diminished. He made one last attempt for a better grip on Carson's pant leg. His hands slipped off the drenched material, and he fell into the swirling mist. His body disappeared, instantly pulled under the crushing currents of Lake Wisconsin.

Carson tried to pull himself up to safely, but his hands kept slipping off the slim, wet railing base and his strength was quickly dwindling. Then a strong hand reached through the mist and clutched Carson's forearm.

Chapter Twenty-Three

Three days passed, and the small villages of Prairie du Sac and Sauk City were still abuzz with the early morning July 4th events.

Some of the townspeople claimed they heard loud pops early in the morning but assumed firecrackers or cherry bombs were set off by an early celebrant. Others swore they saw a man down stream pull himself out of the river later that morning.

Carson, Laura and Carl pulled up to the police station seeing Ben's car out front. The station felt empty, especially without Libby there. Ben sat at Libby's desk, trying to type something, while Tommy practiced casting with an old cane fishing pole.

"What's biting?" teased Carson.

Tommy smiled. He put down the fishing pole and gave Laura a hug. Ben stopped typing.

"He's waiting for me to finish. I promised we'd go fishing today, after I wrap up things here."

"How are Libby and Deputy Johnson doing?" asked Laura as she handed Carl to Tommy.

"Libby's stiff. Her face looks like a rainbow, but she'll be fine. I was over at the hospital this morning. Deputy Johnson has a long recovery in front of him. I hear that you'll be seeing a lot Bess in the future."

"Why is that?" said Carson.

"She's been offered a job by your boss, and she accepted."

"I'm happy for her," said Laura. "But we may not be seeing a lot of her."

Ben looked up, confusion written all over his face.

"We've been talking a lot in the past few days and have decided that State Department jobs aren't a good fit for family life. We're going to go back east and straighten out the Franke Import/Export mess, now that it's Carl's company. And after that, who knows. We'll just have to see one day at a time."

"How can Carl run a company?" asked Tommy. "He's just a baby."

"Well, Tommy, this is new for all of us. I suppose that's what lawyers and executive boards are for," said Carson.

"I was thinking," said Laura, "that the real hero in all of this is Stevie Maier. If he hadn't been on that property that day, Peter's body might never have been found, and Josef might have gotten away with everything."

"I know," said Ben. "I'm going to have a special award ceremony for him, once Harold is out of the hospital."

"I think that would be nice and fitting," said Carson.

"Dad." Tommy's impatience was starting to show. "Are you done? You promised!"

Carson saw a pained look wash over Ben's face.

"I'm sorry, Tommy. This has to be finished today."

"I have an idea," said Carson. "We were just going to go for a drive today. Why don't we take Tommy fishing, and you can join us when you're done? I haven't been fishing in years. I think we could all use a day to relax."

****

The little fishing pond in Leland was a bit out of the way, but worth the drive, surrounded by a tiny settlement of houses, a small business or two and farm fields; the perfect place to quietly sit and enjoy each other's company. If they found themselves thirsty, they could walk over to the local saloon for a root beer. But best of all, everyday worries could drift away as fast as the water ripples, made by the cane pole's gentle casting.

Off in the distance, a tractor puttered down the road. Birds chattered at the group for disturbing the silence.

Laura lay a blanket down under a tree and started to set out food from the picnic basket. Carson baited his pole with another worm as Tommy looked on. No one saw the car drive up and park next to Carson's.

"What's for lunch?" Ben said smiling as he walked to the group.

Tommy left Carson's side, running and laughing as he launched himself into Ben's arms.

Ben hoisted Tommy into the air and twirled him around before setting him back on the ground.

"Fresh cut hay. Isn't that the best smell in the whole wide world?"

ABOUT THE AUTHOR

Julie Short was born and raised in Wisconsin only forty miles from where the recently demolished Badger Ammunitions Plant stood. A graduate from the University of Wisconsin, Julie still lives in the Madison area. This is her first novel.